ABOUT THE AUTHOR

Christian Wharton is an artist who specialises in painting water in watercolour. You can see her work on her website – christianwharton.com

Brought up in the Scottish Borders and a graduate of St.Andrews, she has spent the longest periods of her life in London and Skelmersdale in Lancashire, with a four year interlude in Wales in between.

Her book "Painting Water in Watercolour" (David and Charles) was published in 2003.

She lives on the Berwickshire Coast in a house constructed according to the principles of ancient Indian Vastu Architecture.

TOMATO IN A
BLACK HOLE

CHRISTIAN WHARTON

PRESS

ISBN: 978-1-5272-7365-8

Editor: Sally Orson Jones
Book & Cover Design: Vicky Wharton
Artwork: Christian Wharton
Photography: Duncan Wherrett

Website: christianwharton.com

To all artists trying to make a living from painting according to their own vision.

Author's note

This story is set in 2002 – when Google and Texting were in their infancy, Amazon was a river in South America and there was a world shortage of red plastic tomatoes – now, fortunately remedied.

Chapter i

Encounter on A Train

"It's not difficult to find your way out of the labyrinth. The hard bit is to realise that you are in one."
"But Chlorinda, what happens if you feel that you are being sucked into a great dark hole and can't get out?"
"You mean a Black Hole?" Amarillys said.

Mark closed the book with a sigh. He was losing interest in the fortunes of Chlorinda and Amarillys. The book which he had bought on the spur of the moment in the station was beginning to bore him, or perhaps to touch on areas which he would rather not have touched. He turned his eyes to the sodden Hampshire scenery and reflected with a grimace that there was nothing in the book to distract him from the landscape and nothing in the landscape to distract him from the book.

While he was musing on these things, or perhaps for some time before he closed the book, the awareness grew that there was a pair of eyes fixed on him – eyes that were an intense shade of violet blue. The owner of the eyes was an old lady with a mop of curly grey hair framing her face.

Her expression was kindly and there was just the hint of a smile which suggested both sympathy and humour.

As he raised his eyes to meet hers, she spoke.

'It is a long journey to Paddington, is it not? But at least the train is on time today.'

'Indeed,' he agreed and then feeling that it would be impolite not to continue the conversation asked, 'Do you live in London?'

'Oh no. I live near Yeovil. I am going up to London to visit my nephew who mends wirelesses.'

'Wirelesses?' He had not heard that word for many years. Not in relation to radios anyway.

'Well not exactly. Not all the time. He prefers to build them. And not just wirelesses but gramophones.'

'Gramophones? You mean like His Master's Voice with the big horn coming out?'

'No, no. Much more modern than that. Those contraptions that help to increase the volume of an electric gramophone – I've forgotten the exact word, I'm no use at technicalities.'

'You mean loudspeakers?'

'No, it's more basic somehow.'

'Amplifiers?'

She beamed at him.

'Yes, that's right. You see, he has this system that he's invented for making the sound come out from inside you – not just from anything outside. Isn't that amazing?'

It sounded horrendous but he nodded.

'But no-one wants to buy it, so he mends wirelesses instead. In his spare time he writes poetry so he is really an artist like me.'

'Are you a poet too?'

'No – I am an artist – painter.'

He could just see it – apples, teapots and roses. 'What sort of things do you paint?'

'Oh, apples, teapots, roses. That sort of thing. And more recently, angels.'

'Angels?'

'Not very often. Only when I see them.'

He felt rather stunned by this reply so he was silent.

'Now you know all about me, tell me what you do.'

'Oh, I'm a gallerist.'

'A gallerist? What on earth is that?'

'Well... I suppose you could say that I'm an art dealer. I have two galleries and I promote a certain type of art.'

'What sort of art?'

'Modern art. We're on the cutting edge.'

'Do you sell pictures?'

'I do sell artworks but never pictures.'

'Why not?'

'Because no-one at the cutting edge produces pictures nowadays.'

Lucy removed a handkerchief from her bag and blew her nose.

'What do you mean?' she asked.

'You see it's like this. Art today has broken the boundaries of centuries-old constricting picture frames. It comes out at you. It relates to you.'

From somewhere at the back of her mind a memory came through. 'Oh yes.' She rubbed her hands together, 'I know what you mean. The Tate Gallery bought a pile of bricks and everyone said it was art although if you went to a builder's merchant you could have seen exactly the same thing.'

'Yes... it's all part of breaking the boundaries and reaching new territories.'

Lucy sat in stunned silence for a moment, then she said, 'You know that old fairy tale about the Emperor's New Clothes?'

He nodded.

She continued, 'Well isn't it all a bit like that? You know, the fraudster persuaded the Emperor to walk down the street naked because his new clothes were too fine for anyone to see!'

'Exactly!' he cried waving his hands. 'Right! Right! The Emperor's naked. He's the People's Emperor and the People should see him what he is. That's what we are doing with the

New Art – Exposing Reality!'

Lucy shuddered. Somehow she always thought of the Chinese Emperor as being fat, white and distinctly flaccid. She also had a feeling that the logic was missing somewhere but she couldn't put her finger on it. 'But who buys this stuff?'

'You'd be surprised by the numbers of our clients: public corporations, businesses, private individuals.' He winced slightly, 'We even have waiting lists from abroad.'

'Abroad? How very interesting. So you're really an art dealer then?'

'You could say so. But if I say I'm an art dealer all my mother's friends want me to sell their watercolours for them.'

'Don't worry – I'm not looking for an exhibition myself. I have a friend, Maud who sells as many as I need. And besides, I have, in addition, what Jane Austen would call "a modest competence".'

'And an equally competent modesty?'

She drew herself up. 'My modesty is quite competent enough to cope with the demands I make on it. What about yours?'

He laughed, 'Touché! But I have to confess that I've so little to be modest about.'

'Tell me the name of your gallery.'

'Oh, it's the Arniston Crocker Gallery. I'm not sure you'd really like our stuff.'

'Nevertheless, I should still like to visit it.'

'I'll give you my card.'

There didn't seem anything to add so she dozed off once more.

Just as they were reaching the outskirts of London, she woke up. She again fixed her sharp blue eyes on him and asked a question. 'But tell me... are you really happy with what you are doing?'

Just for a fraction of a second, he hesitated. It was as if he was hearing a distant rumble of thunder, barely audible over the noise of the train. 'Of course! Of course I am. It's been huge fun building this up, pleasing lots of people and getting lots of money for doing something that I enjoy. I'm in charge of a big outfit and I love driving it forward.'

As the train drew into Paddington, he gave her his card, with a mild sense of misgiving. Then he helped her with her baggage and escorted her to where her nephew was waiting.

And then he forgot all about Lucy Bleddoes.

A few days later, Lucy was in the greengrocers when she met Maud.

'How was your trip to London?'

'Oh, it went very well. I met a most extraordinary man on the train'.

'Really? What was he?'

'Oh some kind of an art dealer – a gallerist, I think he said.'

'Sounds dreadful – who was he?'

'His name is Mark Arniston Crocker,' she replied as she fingered some peaches.

'Oh, he's always in the news. Markets that dreadful stuff like giant toothbrushes and headless birds in formaldehyde – Installation Art, all that kind of thing. You didn't actually like him did you?'

'Well actually, I did.'

'No, not those peaches – far too hard. Why did you like him?'

'He was good looking, witty, charming, pleased with himself and...'

'The nectarines are all right. I had some last week.'

'I just had a feeling that, at some part of himself, deep

down inside, he was not entirely deceived by himself.'

But Maud had lost interest. 'The tomatoes are very good,' she said.

Lucy did not forget about Mark.

CHAPTER 2

Cold Cassoulet

Mark, who was not good looking in a conventional way but exuded charm through lively brown eyes, his tall figure and the long hank of hair which swept across his forehead, came into the room expecting to be able to fling himself down on his favourite armchair. But then he noticed his wife, Millicent, sitting in the chair opposite reading some large, typewritten tract. He crossed over and gave her a quick peck on the cheek. 'Hi Millicent, surprise, surprise!' he said as he sat down. 'Not often that we coincide in the late afternoon.'

'So what happened?'

'Gallery had to put off the party because they had a pipe burst.'

'You mean they had a flood?'

'Yes. They were in the most awful mess. Blood everywhere.'

'Blood? You mean the pipe was leaking blood?'

'Well – yes. It wasn't human blood though. Show was called "Life Support Systems" and it was just a mesh of transparent plastic piping with ox-blood being pumped all round it. One of the valves sprung a leak which they didn't notice until it was too late.'

'Good heavens!' Millicent pushed back a scrap of hair that had fallen across her forehead. 'What a weird world you inhabit.'

'Yes,' he said, feeling that he was being reprimanded. He gave himself a Brownie point for not saying Well it's more lively than your one. Instead he said, 'What are you reading?'

'Oh, this is just a dissertation from a trainee whom I'm

mentoring at the bank. It's about new developments in statistical procedures for assessing futures in the copper industry.'

He suppressed a yawn, 'And I thought it was a cover for the latest Harry Potter.'

Millicent shot him a look of contempt. They fell silent.

Then she looked up and said, 'By the way… Mark?'

'Yes?'

'You know that I'm going to that conference in Sweden next month?'

He had forgotten but he said, 'Yes.'

'Well it's been extended to four days and I've been asked to give a paper, so I won't be able to collect the children for half-term. Would you be able to go down to Hastings for them?'

'Course I can. No problem.'

'Good.' She began to pack away her papers in a large brief case.

'I'm going now. I've got a meeting. Library committee again. There's plenty of food in the fridge. You might like some of that cassoulet we had the other day.'

'Thank you. Have a nice meeting.'

As she was going out of the room she said, 'And by the way, Mark, when I come back from Sweden, I don't want to find any traces of that ghastly Wigwam game.' She gave him a brisk kiss on the cheek and left the room.

Wigwam? He had forgotten all about it but gradually it came back. Quite a long time ago when she had last inflicted the children on him on a wet Sunday, he had allowed them to play in the drawing room. They had turned most of the chairs and tables on their sides and draped them with rugs to make houses and tunnels. One of them at the end of the room was a "Wigwam" because it was larger than the rest. The game was that they had to crawl along the tunnels and get across the exposed bits while he counted up to ten with his eyes shut. If he caught them then he could tickle them, or bomb them with cushions. The game became wilder and wilder and they ended up all three of them lying on their backs on the floor, convulsed with laughter.

Then the door had opened and Millicent came in. Thunder, Lightning and Hailstorm. A long time later, with the room restored to its original, pristine dullness, three subdued individuals made their sombre way back to their respective quarters. But Mark made a point of going up and seeing them. They giggled, 'It was a fun thing, Daddy!'

He now listened for the front door to close and when he heard it, he fished out his mobile. 'Hi Honey! Got some good news... Got four days off next month. Got to be back to collect the children from Kent, but we could get away for two of them.'

There was whoop of joy at the other end of the line.

'Where would you like?... Malta?... Ibiza?... what's that?... I can't hear you very well... Granola? No that's a sort of Muesli... Oh, Granada! That's a good idea. Let's go and see the Alhambra... Yes... See you soon. Lots a love,' and he rang off.

And then, not feeling at all like cold cassoulet, he went out for an Indian meal.

CHAPTER 3

The Power Of Positive Thinking

Jane and Freddie sat facing each other across a table in a small gallery in Little Venice. Jane looked as though she had been crying; Freddie was comforting her. Even though her face was a little blotchy and her mouth turned down, she looked beautiful with her fine well-coloured cheek bones, green eyes and mass of black hair that fell to her shoulders where it ended in curls. He was good looking in the way that gays are, with thick, curly black hair and long eyelashes.

'Look,' he said, 'have you ever thought that it might be the other way round?'

'What do you mean?' Jane said.

'I mean that, well, you said you're depressed because the gallery's not making enough money…'

Jane interrupted. 'Well that's reasonable enough.'

'Yes, but sometimes reason isn't enough.'

She ran her hand through her hair. 'I don't know what you mean.'

'Just suppose for a minute that the gallery is not making money because you are depressed.'

'But that's not true!'

He sighed. 'You see – you're not the only one that gets miserable, I do too. And recently I found a book on a bookstall about dealing with depression and I did one of the exercises in it and I found it helped and I just wondered if it might help you.'

'Oh yes?' Her grin was saturated with disbelief. 'What's

the quick fix then?'

'No quick fix but if you can accept the idea that sometimes being depressed can cause negative events and if you find a way out of it, then things might happen more, er, favourably.'

'Ye-es.'

He went on, 'Would you like to do the exercise that helped me?'

She wouldn't, but she didn't have the heart to tell him. 'OK, I suppose it wouldn't do any harm.'

'So what you have to do is to write down in your own handwriting on a piece of paper or in in a notebook, three things that happened recently, that you feel pleased about. They can be things you did, or things that happened – it doesn't matter.'

Jane found a notebook and picked up a pencil. She closed her eyes and wrote in her mental diary:-

Three things that I hate about Freddie.

1   *He's a busybody*
2   *He wants to control me*
3   *He thinks he's right*

Then she opened her eyes and saw him looking at her with such a look of concern on his face that she became contrite. After chewing on her pencil for some time she came up with:-

1   *I found the tin-opener.*
2   *I unblocked the sink.*
3   - - -

She was stuck.

Freddie said, 'How are you getting on?'

So she told him and just as she got to the second item, she remembered something else.

'Yesterday, when I dropped a piece of buttered toast on the floor, it landed butter side up'

'Wow!' he said. 'That's really good. Highly auspicious in fact – the buttered toast trick. Feeling better?'

Oddly enough, although she didn't want to admit it, she did. Just a little.

He rubbed his hands together.

'You're looking a bit more cheerful! You see, it works.'

'Possibly,' she admitted grudgingly.

'And now you've to do the next step of the exercise.'

'Do you mean there's more to it?'

'Look, if you want to get out of being depressed, you have to work on it a bit. You know you're feeling a bit better. You want to get up the next step of the ladder.'

She sighed, 'Go on then, Mr Guru.'

'What you have to do now is write down three major things that you have to be thankful for.'

Jane sipped her tea, and thought for a moment, screwing her face up.

'It's so hard.'

Freddie also sipped his tea, 'I'll help you if you like.'

'Go on then.'

'Well… what about your home? Where do you live – Willesden or Neasden?'

'No. You know perfectly well I live in Primrose Hill.'

'Isn't that a bit good?'

She squirmed slightly. 'I suppose so.'

'And do you own your house completely?'

'Well – I own the bit I live in, the top two floors, to be exact. Ben's parents bought it for us when we got married.'

'So you own a property in Primrose Hill. I'd have thought that was something to be grateful for.'

'I suppose so.' She sniffed.

'And what about the gallery? Do you own this shop?'

'Well – yes.' She sniffed again.

'And the bit upstairs?'

'Yes. Ben's parents gave us a bit of a hand when we started the gallery and then when they died they left us enough to pay off the mortgage.'

Freddie drew in a deep breath. 'Phew...! Jane, you own two properties in prime parts of London. Have you any idea of what they might be worth? Prices have hiked recently. If the worst came to the worst, you'd get a fortune.'

'But where would I live?'

He opened his mouth to reply but he was cut short by a crash as the front door was flung open and an exuberantly dressed woman rushed in.

'I can't stay long. My husband's due home any minute and he's out without a key. I just wanted to ask if that painting of the window is still for sale?'

Jane told her it was.

'Good. I'd like to buy it. I've been thinking about it ever since the party and I can't get it out of my head. I've simply got to have it.'

Jane told her the price, £1000, and the lady wrote out a cheque, gave out some contact details and arranged a collection date. Then she swept out.

Jane and Freddie looked at each other in stunned silence and then they burst out laughing.

Jane said, 'OK, you win.'

'Well, it could have been a coincidence – we don't really have any proof. I've never known something like this to happen so rapidly.'

Freddie stood up, 'Jane I've got to go, I'm meeting a friend. It's been nice seeing you.'

'Just before you go... you said I had to find three things

and we've only got two so far? I've just thought of the third.'

'So what's that?'

'You,' she said. 'I'm sorry I was so grumpy earlier. You've really got me out of it.'

Freddie looked embarrassed, 'Aw Shucks! It was nothing. Thank you for the tea.'

He gave her a quick hug and was gone.

CHAPTER 4

A Life On Oiled Wheels

He was right about having so little use for his modesty, for Mark Arniston Crocker lived a life which ran on oiled wheels. It was smooth, successful and full of delights. Parties, travel, people and possessions seemed to come to him with an ease which others could only envy. Effortlessly he sank into a job he found rewarding, and over the years he easily rose to the top of the management ladder. His talent for promotion, presentation and public relations found him his niche and it was a comfortable one. He had everything he could wish for.

More than anything, he congratulated himself upon his ménage. For in his wife, Millicent, he had everything he could possibly want in a woman from the neck upwards, whilst his mistress, Louisa had everything that was desirable from the neck downwards, while the restrained elegance of his Canonbury house contrasted nicely with the riotous colours and cheerful shabbiness of Louisa's flat in Bayswater.

He liked to think that he was similar to an average Arab husband, a modest Sheik perhaps and that what worked for them worked for him. The thought never occurred that this was not Arabia and his two ladies might not be so happy with the arrangement, but he was careful to respect the unwritten code. Louisa never came to his home and never went away with him unless Millicent was away. He avoided telling Millicent direct lies. He was punctilious in observing all birthdays and other anniversaries, wonderful at giving flowers and presents at the right moment and despite a lot of temptation, was remarkably faithful to his two women.

There were, however, aspects of the situation which were not entirely similar to the conditions of Arab marriages and which represented flaws in his moral construct. One of these, he was shortly to discover.

Louisa liked to give him surprises and as he approached her flat that evening he had a slight shiver of apprehension. Her surprises, like her cooking, were unpredictable. They could be awful, for Louisa, although not what might be termed a 'seeker' in life, had many friends on the fringe of the New Age. On various occasions she had inflicted on him Astral Reprogramming, the Slink System for Inner Integration (he had rather liked that one) and the Cricklewood Spiritual Revivalists. On the whole, they amused him if they were not too boring, although this was slightly marred by the feeling that Louisa wanted to change him in some way. On the other hand, her surprises could be delightful. As he rang the bell, he hoped that it would be one of the latter tonight.

He was early – Louisa was never on time and he liked to catch her unprepared. Sex had always seemed to him to be the best preparation for an evening designated for personal improvement and at least he could lie in the warm post-coital glow watching her put on her clothes and her make-up.

Unfortunately, tonight he was not so lucky. She opened the door and kissed him.

'I've got a naked man on the floor, like.'

'So this was the surprise?'

'Nah… more of a surprise for me.'

She led him through the hall and into the living room. There on a rug in front of the radiator was a placid baby boy amiably gurgling and dribbling over a small plastic pig. Mark was torn between relief and horror.

'He's Woody,' Louisa explained. 'Elaine's gone out shopping like and her fella, Aron, is supposed to be picking him up but he's a bit late, like.'

'So you're running a crèche now, in your spare time?'

'No, of course not. Hey let me have that Woody!'

Woody had now inserted his fat little paw under the sofa and drawn out a pair of scissors. She deftly replaced them with a teddy.

'But that's your teddy.' Her collection of teddy bears was one of the things he liked least about her, but he respected her addiction. He found it puzzling that she would lend one to this little creature.

'You don't like babies, do you?' she asked brightly as she poured out some whisky for him. 'Have this; it'll make you feel better, like.'

'Well no. It's not exactly that I don't like them... but... I like them better when they've stopped dribbling and shitting and peeing and all that.'

She laughed. 'Cos you see so much of it in your work?'

'Possibly.' He grimaced.

Woody, who had not quite reached the stage of being able to crawl, now rolled over onto his stomach and began to beat the floor with his little hands, gurgling and cooing all the time.

'Ain't he sweet? How could'yer not like the little fella?'

'Don't you think he aught to have something on? Like a nappy, perhaps?'

'Oh. He's just done a big poo and I'm letting him have a bit of a kick. But I'll start dressing him now and then he'll be ready for Aron, like. Hey I've got to get his bottle ready – can you keep an eye on him just a mo?'

Mark watched the baby in abject horror as he now rolled onto his back. And then a strange thing happened. The baby fixed his eyes on Mark, stared at him intently for a moment and then exploded into a smile. His mouth opened wider and wider, the smile spreading through his whole body. He kicked and beat his arms up and down, all parts of him vibrating with delight. This was not the smile of ingratiation, mockery or patronage. Just the simple sign of a single human being recognising another on this strange planet and reacting with joy.

It touched Mark in a hidden region of his heart – a cave rarely visited. He felt disturbed. He could not remember either of his own children smiling at him like this as babies. But then in his efficiently run household, they were dried, dusted and whisked away from the earliest moment, to be cared for by nannies in another part of the house. Woody's smile made him feel as though he was forgiven for something that he had not repented of.

'He smiled at me,' he said as Louisa came back. It sounded almost like a complaint.

'Well,' she grinned, 'that's allowed in't it?'

'But... why?'

'Well... maybe he likes you.'

This was exactly what had puzzled him, so he was silent.

Louisa asked, 'But you've got kids like. Didn't your own babies smile at you – sometimes?'

'I can't remember if they did. You see they were looked after by nannies from the moment they were born and then they were sent to boarding school when they were five.'

Louisa was shocked. 'So young to leave home?'

'Well... it wasn't exactly my idea, but Millicent was studying and she said there was no other way.'

Louisa was silent. She now picked up the baby and he noticed an expression in her face that he had not seen very frequently.

'You really do like babies, don't you?'

'It's just that they don't come my way very often, like Oh, there's the bell. It must be 'im. Can you let 'im in?'

'Can you take us to Shepherd's Bush?' she said when they were in the car. *Oh, God*, he thought, *not a lady in a long grey cardigan talking about 'self actualisation' in a seedy basement.* After all that baby stuff, all he wanted was a stiff drink and some normality.

But Louisa's surprise was not what he had anticipated. She took him to a small night club run by some Cypriots. 'There's a Romanian singer coming who I think you'd like.'

In an ecstasy of relief, he flung his arm round her plump shoulder. 'You're amazing! This really is a surprise.' The evening was picking up.

The club, which was off Shepherd's Bush Road, was small and dark. It smelled of thyme, garlic and smoke from a wood oven. They settled down on plain chairs at a bare scrubbed pine table with candles on it and enjoyed an excellent meal of slowly cooked lamb with herbs.

When the singer came on, the room suddenly grew quiet. Her name was Maria Turnova and she had an electric personality. She was small and stout with a rather wizened face, a mass of dark hair no longer rich and soft but now wiry, although there were no streaks of grey. Her heavy figure was crammed into a dark purple satin dress and she wore masses of ethnic jewellery.

When she started to sing, he was carried away. Her voice was full of passionate intensity and she had a huge range. She could leap up several octaves in the middle of one syllable and her voice seemed to get stronger as she got higher. She glided down through quarter tones almost like an Indian vocalist, or even at times like a yodeller. There was anger in her songs but also occasionally an exquisite tenderness.

But what did it mean – these passionate words and soaring notes?

Her English was not good and when she explained what she was singing about, it was hard to hear. There was something about oppression and she seemed to be against lies and deception. More than that was impossible to know.

There was a song that hit him particularly. It was called "Pratiranya". It started very angrily indeed but ended on a note of beautiful peace. Her intonation of the word "Pratiranya" which came in the chorus, varied with each repetition. It was quite hypnotic. Her audience was struck silent when it finished; then there was a roar of applause and she had to sing it again. They had to let her go after that; she said she was tired and brusquely stamped off.

For the second time that evening he was disturbed in some unexpected way, but this time it went much further. She had held him in her eyes many times and he felt that she was singing especially for him.

He saw Louisa back into the car.

'You were right,' he said, 'I did like her. Especially that last song.'

'I thought you would, like.'

'But she had it in for the men. Why are so many songs of oppression always sung by women?'

'Are they? I never noticed,' Louisa said mildly.

'I thought you would rise to that one. What you should have said is that women are oppressed by men. Aren't you a feminist any more?'

'Oh yes. It goes without saying really. We get exploited all the time. Like.'

'Do I exploit you?'

'Nah… Course not.' She paused and then said, 'Well…

actually, yes you do.' She flushed with a little surge of spirit.

'But you like it?'

'Sometimes.' What she really meant was that she didn't.

Neither of them wanted to continue with this conversation – the topics were familiar.

She yawned. 'Jesus, I feel so tired. It takes it out of you, all that feelin' stuff don' it!' She laid her head against his shoulder.

When they stopped outside her house and he started to get out, she put her hand on his arm.

'Do you mind? I just feel I need to rest. I've been a little off colour recently.'

He did mind but he covered up his disappointment.

'No of course not. I'm also tired. It's been a long day.' And this was true. 'Honey – it was a great surprise. It really was! Thank you... Bye now.' He kissed her and she got out of the car.

CHAPTER 5

In The Gallery

The strains of "Pratiranya" continued to haunt him. Not just the memory but the tune itself would come back to him from unexpected places, like a distant radio station, or even a busker in the street. He couldn't understand why it so affected him – this strange combination of allure and menace. Perhaps the puzzle would be solved by getting the meaning of the words, but even then he was not sure that he would really understand because so much went on in that performance – there was such a lot of eye contact and body language.

Mark knew that his success depended on his ability to round up anything that was not conducive to his immediate benefit and put it in a safe and silent place. For there were other things – tiny dark clouds way out on the horizon but clouds all the same and these are what caused his slight hesitation when Lucy had asked him her question about enjoying his life.

Clients from Eastern Europe were one and a man called Henry Striffelguese was another. The former were a law unto themselves – changing their minds about purchases with a regularity that had nothing to do with their aesthetic needs. He had his suspicions about their financial dealings which made him uncomfortable – it was an area best left alone.

As for Henry Striffelguese, he was a mystery. A lunatic or a crook, or maybe even a blend of both, he not only claimed to be another gallerist intent on replacing Mark as the pack leader, but he indulged in weird practical jokes at private views with the aim of disrupting sales and undermining confidence. Maybe he was a serious threat, or maybe it was just nonsense but his presence added another element to the work of setting up a show – there had to be contingency planning.

With these thoughts quietly simmering at the back of his mind, Mark now entered the gallery.

'Morning Mark, Hi!' The two girls chorused.

'Morning Michelle, morning Sharon, Hi.' It was the daily ritual.

Michelle and Sharon manned the reception desk at the front of the gallery. Their duties were limited and mostly consisted of keeping out unwelcome intruders, particularly the press, which Mark had now become successful enough to regard as a pest. They also typed letters which his personal assistant, Hazel, dictated, and took all phone calls that were directed to Mark and not Hazel. Michelle and Sharon had been given the discretion to reveal the existence of Hazel if the new caller sounded like a promising buyer. Mostly they chatted as they alternated between painting their nails and working on the computers.

The topics of their conversation, dictated by visitors and passers-by, were restricted to sex and clothing, depending on gender. If it were male, it was something like '... ee's had a hard night, wonder who ee's shagging now he's dumped Pauline. Do you know what Kevin and I did last night?' If it were female, speculation consisted of the name of the designer and how much it cost. They were well informed about fashion.

Sharp and cheeky, they adored Mark and he returned this feeling in a parental fashion. Sometimes he wondered if they couldn't be used in an installation themselves. It would be easier to organise than most of the others, but then who would man the reception desk?

'Any messages?'

'Yeah… that German guy who looks like Leonardo di Caprio wants you to ring him.'

'Dieter Von Gropius?' It was his German agent. It was this big deal with Eastern Europe in the pipeline.

'Yeah… Deet the Grope… And Maxwell Bream and Karen Kettering.' These were two young artists in his stable who needed careful handling.

'Did they say what they want?'

'Nah… sounded a bit out of sorts though.' Sharon leaned back in her chair and extracted a nail file from a small drawer to the side of her desk.

'Anything else?'

'Clive Bradley's secretary rang to remind you about lunch today. Oh, and Millicent was on about some fingy bowls or something. I didn't catch it all as her mobile went funny – something to do with Liberty's and a dinner party.'

'Oh yes… finger bowls.' He feigned comprehension but this was the first he had heard of it.'

The collection of messages was fairly typical. Hazel would have received them and would be prioritising with an action list. Von Gropius obviously the first – the deal was worth half a million for a couple of Rum Tuggers known as "Doggydoes 1 and 2" whose precise nature was best left to the imagination. ("Rum Tugger" was the name adopted by the artist Felix Cove who picked it from the ether without any conscious awareness of T.S. Eliot, just because it had good, brazen resonance.)

Maxwell and Karen could probably be handled by Hazel who had a wonderfully soothing manner. The young artists, who like all the artists in his stable, were as sensitive as race-horses, had to be handled with a combination of iron and velvet. Both Mark and Hazel were adept at this.

'Morning Hazel.' He went through to his office at the back of the gallery. Hazel was a comforting woman in her mid-thirties. An ideal personal assistant, she was intelligent, sympathetic, discreet and very conscientious.

'Morning Mark, I've made a list for you and I've been on to Max and Karen.'

'So what's that all about?'

'It seems that they were upset at a party last night by a new gallerist who was claiming that you are on the way down and any artist whom you represent was as doomed as a passenger on the Titanic.'

'Oh really?' Mark suspected that he knew exactly who it was.

'Odd name – I'm not sure if they got it right – something like "Henry Steffelgauze." He's new to this country. Comes from Boston.'

'And has ideas about replacing me in my business?'

'That's about it.'

'Well, he's going to have to change his ideas. Did you manage to reassure them? Or am I going to have to cosy them up?'

'Well, I explained and warned them about the dangers of being taken in by appearances and they calmed down.' Hazel looked down at her notes.

'I think I'd better talk to them. Can you get me Maxwell?'

Maxwell sounded very frightened. 'It wasn't what he said – it was the way he said it.'

'What do you mean?'

'He just looked at us with a really mean, snide sort of smile and said he was sorry for us – if we went on with you we'd be like passengers on the Titanic. Big trouble. We're really doomed.'

'But did he offer you a contract?'

'Well... no, not exactly, but he implied that he could rescue us.'

'But without making any promises?... Look,' Mark said picking up a pen and starting to make a doodle on his pad, 'that man's a fraud. You've got to be very careful. If you break your contract to this gallery, you'll have to pay a fee. You wouldn't want to do that unless you had an offer in writing of something better. And if you did, you should ask your lawyer to look at it. This Gallery is NOT in financial straights – we're actually doing pretty well and we can keep all our commitments to our artists. And we're pleased to have you.'

'So that's OK then?' Maxwell sounded relieved and rang off.

Mark went on fuming for some minutes to Hazel. 'But what a cheek! I've never discouraged other gallerists. It's a wide field. I spend a lot of time in other galleries. I'm always passing on artists that might suit them. You don't succeed in this game by attacking your rivals. We're not warlords!'

'Yes I know. But it's OK now. You've calmed him down and given him a caution. Anyway here's the priority list. Would you like a coffee?'

'Thanks... I'd love one. Hazel you've done well. Can you get me Herr Gropius?'

Herr Gropius was almost always reached on his mobile as he was continuously on the move and Mark was used to shouting down a crackling line or pausing while the BMW went through a tunnel under a mountain. Today was no exception.

'... great to hear you Mark... (silence – crackle – crackle).'

'Are you there?'

'... just coming... Magdeburg. My client vants... zee Rum Tuggers... you are heving still?'

'I've still got them.'

'OK, OK. Price is still same? Ach Zoh... I'll be seeing him next...'

'Next when?... I didn't hear.'

'Oh... line not so good... I... next veek.'

The line then went flat, but it didn't matter; the deal was still on. Mark had feared that there was going to be some bargaining, which never happened in London. If there had been this would have been a sign that the London Market was on the decline; but it was all right.

He put the phone down and turned to his mail, although he didn't have much chance to read it. A whirlwind surged into his office leaving in its wake a gasping Michelle and Sharon... 'Wow! Prada – the coat. Shoes – Manola... Bloody 'ell' – Millicent'

He always loved Millicent in a fury. It was the nearest she ever got to animation. Millicent Militant. Her great grey eyes glittered and there was colour in her cheeks.

'What IS happening? I'd just like to know?' she demanded.

'About what? I'm sorry, my love, afraid I don't know.' He pleaded innocence. Obviously he was supposed to know. He must have been told and forgotten.

'Look Darling! I told you yesterday over breakfast. Where WERE you? I'd like to know. Liberty's sent the wrong finger bowls. They're dark blue glass and I wanted grey frosted. They said they'd send them over here and I could pick them up after the hairdresser. But those stupid girls seem to know nothing about them.'

'I don't think they can have come. We'd know if they had. Would you like to use my phone?' He patted his phone as though it was a kind of peace offering.

'I can use your phone, but I haven't time to wait. They promised they would be here by ten. What's happened? You know we want them for the party tonight.'

'Well, if you can sort it out with them, I'll bring them over when I come back this evening.'

She looked highly dubious about his capacity to fulfil this simple promise.

He said, 'Look… you sit down and ring them. I promise I won't forget and I'll get Hazel to remind me just in case.'

Still looking mistrustful, she allowed herself to be persuaded.

'But when do you think you'll be home?'

It was an acid question. The trouble was that he was not sure. There were serried ranks of parties in his life and he had promised to appear at at least one private view before his own dinner party tonight.

'I'll ask Hazel.' It was his stand-by when other ideas failed. He called through the open door to Hazel's office. 'Hazel, Millicent wants some finger bowls delivered to the house before the dinner tonight and…'

'Hazel!' Millicent interrupted…'the problem is that the house is empty until the caterers come just before the dinner and I want to have the finger bowls unpacked and all ready to be set out because there's always so much to do. It's so maddening of Liberty's to behave like this. I don't know what's got into them. And Mark could take them but he's got to go somewhere else first and doesn't really know when he'll be back.'

The diplomatic Hazel was just about to offer to deliver the bowls herself, or get one of the girls to, when Michelle burst in.

'Man from Liberty's 'ere wiv a big box for Mrs Arniston Crocker.'

The tornado subsided. Mark, Millicent and Hazel, breathed a large sigh of relief.

Chapter 6

Afternoons In Two Galleries

Jane wrote in her pad –

1 Clear run at the dentist
2 Aunt Griselda came to visit
3 Aunt Griselda left the next day

Three things. They came quite easily. Now for three big things. She looked up into the distance and sighed. It wasn't so easy.

At that moment the door of the gallery opened quietly and a young man came in. 'Aha!' she said to herself. 'It always works!'

But the young man, smiling shyly just went round the paintings and when he had finished he said, 'Lovely show!' He wrote something in the visitors' book and left.

Jane heaved another sigh and went back to her writing. Nothing came so she decided to make herself a cup of tea. She spilled some milk on the floor of the tiny pantry at the back of the gallery and wiped it up carefully before gingerly carrying her over-filled mug back to her table. 'I must be positive. I must be positive,' she kept repeating to herself – but what came up was an enormous bolt of misery which could no longer be contained. 'I'm SO DEPRESSED!' She said out loud.

'Why are you depressed?' a voice asked.

Jane, startled, looked up to see an old lady standing quite near. She must have got in while the milk was being mopped up. She had piercing blue eyes and a mop of grey hair.

Jane was stunned for a moment and then she said, 'I'm so lonely!'

'Why are you so lonely?'

'I've been running this gallery on my own for seven years ever since my husband died. I just wish there was a man in my life.'

'Haven't there been any since? I would have thought a lady as beautiful as you…'

'Oh yes… there have been a couple. The last one ended about a year ago and I'm still feeling the pain from getting dumped.'

'How sad,' said the old lady.

She had such a winning manner that Jane felt at ease with her. 'Would you like a cup of tea.?'

'I'd love one.'

She fetched the old lady a cup of tea and invited her to sit down.

'You know this is a very nice gallery. You have a good eye for paintings.' She sipped her tea.

Jane said, 'Well, Ben and I were both artists but when we left Art School we didn't feel like teaching, or struggling. We were helped to set this up and we enjoyed helping our friends to sell.'

'How long ago did you start it?'

'About fourteen years ago. It was easy to make it successful. We knew all the critics because they came to the degree shows. But now it's changed. They're all different. Critics seem to have a short shelf life.'

'Oh dear,' said the old lady. 'That must be very hard. By the way, my name is Lucy. What's yours?'

'Jane.' She picked up a pencil and began doodling on her pad. 'But there are nice things about it. Like meeting people like you. You never know who's going to come in.' She looked intently at Lucy. 'Tell me, are you an artist?'

'I am. But I'm not looking for an exhibition. I sell locally all the paintings I need to. But like you, I'm also a widow.'

The scenario of a comfortable widowhood – enough money, a place in the country, flipped through Jane's mind. There was something about Lucy which smelled of country; lavender and rosemary perhaps.

Lucy continued, 'My husband was killed in a rail crash thirty years ago... and... as well...' she began to falter 'our ten-year old son who was with him.'

'Oh My God – how awful! That's so terrible – it's beyond anything I can imagine.' Jane rubbed a hand over her eyes and they were both silent for a few minutes.

Jane straightened her back, 'How did you cope?' she asked.

'It wasn't easy. I couldn't speak at first. Then over the days and months and years I put the pieces of my life back together. I worked for a charity in India for a few years. That helped.'

Jane said, 'You were very brave.' The doodle on her pad was slowly turning into a tangle of flowers.

'I don't know. I just did what came next. Anyway, now I have come to accept what happened. I have a happy life.'

'Really?'

'I have the most lovely cottage. It has honey-coloured stone walls with pink and white roses on them.

Jane sighed, 'I'd love to see your cottage – it sounds so dreamy.'

'Well you must come then. It's in Somerset.'

'Perhaps Freddie could bring me some day.'

'Freddie? I thought you said you were alone' There was a hint of sharpness in the voice.

Jane laughed, 'Oh Freddie. He's not my lover. He's gay and he's one of the most successful artists I show in this gallery. He's a very sweet man – like a brother to me. We go away together sometimes when he is looking for subject matter.'

'Oh that's all right then,' the old lady laughed. 'He would be welcome as well. If you have some paper I can write down the address for you.'

Jane found her address book and Lucy wrote down the details, then said it was time to go. Jane escorted her to the door but before she reached it she turned and said 'I really have enjoyed seeing these paintings.'

'I just wish I could sell more of them. The gallery is losing money. It used to be quite successful but since the rise of this awful Young British Art, all the publicity has gone away. It's this nonsensical Installation stuff.'

'Oh dear. I'm sorry to hear that. I met an Installation Art dealer on the train the other day. He seemed quite nice to me.'

'Who was it?'

'I can't remember... Oh... something like Emerson Crockup...'

'Not... Mark Arniston Crocker by any chance?'

'Yes that sounds about right.'

'He's one of the pack leaders. I'd like to shoot him.'

'Oh... don't do that! There are all sorts of things going on which can affect sales of paintings and anyway there may be something that we have to learn from this modern stuff.' She paused as she pulled her coat firmly round her shoulders and then she continued, 'He struck me as having something on his mind – somewhere on a deeper level – that meant he was not quite as cocksure as he pretended to be... but perhaps I am wrong.'

'Well, thank you for coming into my gallery. You've done a lot to help me today. It's been a pleasure talking to you.' Jane held open the door.

Lucy stopped in the doorway. 'Oh... just one thing more.

It's really so important to have flowers around you. Particularly if you are feeling low.'

'I'll go and get some straight away,' Jane promised.

After she had closed the door she leaned against it and drew in a deep breath, and said out loud, 'Phew...what a remarkable lady!'

It was now almost time to close the gallery and she decided that she would close it early as it was not likely that she would have any more visitors. She started going into the closing-down routine and was just about to lock the door when a hand appeared and pushed it open, gently and firmly.

'Oh... Edwin!' She forced herself to look pleased. 'I was just about to close – can I help you?'

The man who now entered the gallery was one of her clients. She did not know him very well, but he had bought a couple of small paintings and had also taken her out a couple of times to dinner at a small vegetarian restaurant. He was tall, thin and shabby with that slight air of distinction almost redolent of an impoverished aristocrat. With his stoop, his thinning sandy hair and his shambling gait he seemed older than his 27 years. His friends described him as having all of one foot firmly rooted to the ground and also as having been dragged kicking and screaming into the nineteenth century. He did not have a job and seemed to be living on air. When cross-questioned he admitted to writing poetry. He had a slight impediment in his speech which meant that he talked with many pauses, but there was an air of sweetness bout him.

Only slightly boring, Jane thought, but it was late in the day and she wanted to go home.

'I hoped to find you alone... and thought this was my best... er... chance. I have come to say... something important for both us.'

'Oh really?' She noticed that he was carrying a large bunch

of red roses.

'Jane, dearest Jane… I… would like to ask you… to marry me!' and without more ado he knelt down on one knee and proffered the roses.

Jane was torn between abject horror and a desire to giggle. She pulled out a tissue, blew her nose firmly and took in a deep breath. 'I'm sorry Edwin – but no. Not. It's something that's not on. I can't possibly.'

'Oh dear,' he sighed. 'Might I have an explanation? Might you change your mind and… '

Jane said firmly, 'We are not in love and we have almost nothing in common.'

'Well – er – we're both lonely – and intelligent… And love art.'

'Not good enough reasons. And there's no way it could ever be different.' He looked so crestfallen, she was sorry for him. 'Look Edwin – it's like this. I like you a lot, as a friend. I've enjoyed your company. And I hope you'll go on being my friend. But I just couldn't go any further. The basis just isn't there. Marriage is hard enough even when you are in love, but without it, it must be terrible.'

'Oh – that's so sad!'

'No it isn't. It's not sad at all, it's realistic. You sound like a refugee from the 19th century. You don't want to saddle yourself with something that would only bring misery.'

'Yes… but… '

'Edwin, there are no 'buts'. I hope you don't mind my saying this but I want to close the gallery now and go home.'

'Oh yes of course.' He rose to his feet, looking embarrassed. 'I'll go now. But you might as well… have these!'

'Thank you very much. They're lovely. They'll really cheer the gallery up.' She smelled them.

'Good-bye,' he said.

At least I've got the flowers, she thought as the door closed.

And then she burst out laughing.

Before she left she had a look at the visitor's book just to see what the young man had written.

I was feeling low cos' my girlfriend just left – the pics here are so good they made me feel much better. What a lovely show!

Being an art dealer has its compensations, she reflected.

Mark was talking to his two junior directors, Anthony and William, two young men whose overweening characteristic was smoothness, about the threat posed by Henry Streffelgueze. It wasn't often that they were all three in the gallery together as they all spent time with clients, artists, and corporate backers as well as making trips to the second gallery in Hackney. There was a lot of reporting to do.

'It's appalling,' William said.

'Bloody cheek,' added Anthony. 'Do you think we should do anything?'

'Well, I don't think he's a serious threat, but I have a feeling that we ought to find out a bit more about him.'

'If he's given to saying things like that he could be sued.'

'But only if he puts it in print,' Mark said. 'What I think you could do, is keep your eyes and ears open. Don't repeat what he said to anyone, but just make discreet enquiries and we'll see what's what.'

'I have heard someone mention him,' Nigel said. 'It was someone at a party. It'll come back to me. It could have been Henrietta... or Charlene... maybe. Talking of Charlene, is everything going all right with her new show?'

'It's fine. I saw her this week and she was in great shape.'

'So that's OK.'

They fell to discussing other matters.

There were a few other phone calls to make and then it was time to go to a Private View at Canopy. Canopy was a gallery in Covent Garden which compensated for its lack of space by specialising in Performance Art. The shows changed almost every week and there was always something stimulating happening. On one side of the gallery there was a coffee bar and you could just hang out and meet friends – the art did not intrude on you. The private views were crowded out. Mark liked the director; a wiry, sandy haired man called Edward De Boze, who was known to everyone as "Bozie".

The usual crowd was there. Also – Henrietta Bisquet. Ah – Henrietta, perhaps she could enlighten him about Streffelgueze.

Henrietta was an interesting person. As an only child, born rather late in her parents' life, she was given the name "Henrietta" to compensate for not being a much longed-for son. Unfortunately, her French Canadian parents didn't realise that the commonality in Britain did not understand their surname was pronounced "Biscay" as in the famous Bay, or that "biscuit" was English for "cookie". The result was that when their darling daughter was in junior school she was horribly teased and given a range of offensive nicknames, such as "Choccybick" and "Digestive" and even "Bickypeg".

When Mr and Mrs Bisquet found out about this, they removed Henrietta from the school, bought her a horse and engaged a private tutor for the rest of her formal education.

Henrietta hated the horse, but thrived on what was to become a succession of tutors with the result that she got into Cambridge at the age of eighteen, where she read social anthropology. She made several expeditions to the Congo basin and wrote a book on childcare based entirely on her observation of primitive tribes, coupled with her own experience of raising an orphan chimpanzee. For a brief span of time, it was all the rage, but then was soon forgotten.

By this time, having been left a substantial legacy, Henrietta, in her late forties, discovered that her real passion was avant-garde art. Her age hardly showed. She was tall and commanding with somewhat untidy hair which varied in colour. Tonight it was a rather smart deep chestnut.

She wasn't exactly a gallerist since her collections were not open to the public but she was a dealer, for she was quite happy to part with exhibits and invest in more. She had a large flat in Chelsea and held a party there every month or so, which usually paid for itself quite comfortably in sales.

She had a good eye and her speciality was penders. The term "pender" was the name given by Mark and colleagues to pictures hung on walls that had hardly any image and no paint. Images were not completely banned but they should always be blurred, outrageous, funny or shocking. Henrietta understood these things exactly and picked up all sorts of interesting pieces in her constant journeys between San Francisco, New York, Paris and Tokyo. Perhaps her taste was a little too dictated by her love of monkeys, but this did not stop her clients from buying.

She came towards Mark and kissed him. She was always outrageously dressed – so much so that he wondered what she would wear if she went to a fancy dress party. Sometimes he had to stop himself asking what she had come as today.

Today it was not "The Corsican Pirate," or "Principal Boy" or "Boudicca's off duty". Today's outfit was, for Henrietta, comparatively restrained. It was a floor length caftan in a black substance that had a purplish luminous glow. It was slit at the sides from the floor to the underarms but held together at the thighs with a pair of large gold chains. The front was similarly slit from the neck almost to the waist. The outfit revealed little of her figure, (perhaps because there wasn't much to reveal,) only her lack of underwear.

'Mark, darling. It's been absolutely ages…'

'Not my fault. You've been on your travels again.'

'Only Venice.'

'Did you enjoy it?'

'Fabulous. And what are you up to?'

It was just as well that Henrietta travelled so much, Mark reflected. She had a sort of devouring quality. She was utterly wonderful of course, but best in small doses.

'Henrietta, I've been wanting to ask you. Have you heard anything about someone called Henry Streffelgueze?'

'Henry who?'

Mark frowned, 'Henry Streffelgueze. If I've got the surname correct.'

'Oh, you mean Henry Striffelperse. Yes, I do know him. He comes from Boston. Very clever and dynamic. Full of ideas.' She sipped her wine thoughtfully.

'Is he starting up as a gallerist or something?'

'Yes, as far as I know he's bought a old sugar mill in Deptford and is converting it.'

'Has he any money?'

'I don't know, really. He's rumoured to have a flat in Kensington so he may, but that could mean a bed-sit in Earls Court. Why do you want to know?'

'He's a bit sinister and seems to have it in for me. I wonder if you could find out something about him.'

'I'll have a go.' Henrietta was always willing to help. 'But what do you want to know?'

'I'd just like to know what he's really up to.'

At this point, Bozie climbed onto a chair and told them all to be quiet, the performance was about to begin.

Everyone shuffled to the sides, the lucky ones finding chairs and the less lucky squatting on the floor. Mark found himself trapped beside Henrietta, on the side of the gallery that was furtherest from the front entrance. He cursed under his breath. It was going to be hard to make a discreet exit.

The performance struck him as utterly mediocre. Its climax was a man sitting with a tape-recorder strapped to his chest miming to the sound of a telephone directory being read. Mark looked at his watch. Hell, it really was time to go. He could feel Millicent's militancy gradually accumulating. Fortunately Bozie was slipping past. He touched his shoulder and whispered. 'I've got to go. Is there any way I can get out without disturbing everyone?'

'I'll let out through the back,' said the agreeable Bozie and took him through the office and out to the back door. 'What do you think of the show?'

'Oh, fantastic! Very unsettling. Just what you want.'

'Yes... I'm really pleased.'

'By the way.' Bozie dropped his voice to a near whisper, 'Have you heard anything about this guy Henry Streffelgueze?'

'Well, just a little. Actually I was going to ask you.'

'Well, I do know a little, because one of my artists met him'

'Oh yes?'

'He seems to be converting this sugar mill, but he keeps his cards very close to his chest. He says that what he is about to do will blow the current notions of contemporary art sky high. There's something very strange about him.'

Mark said, 'Actually he got hold of two of mine as well and made vague and unspecified promises.'

'Interesting,' Bozie said as he reached for a handkerchief.

Mark started buttoning up his raincoat. He really had to go.

Bozie continued, 'Yes, that seems to be his game. He likes to tease young artists into thinking that he's trying to seduce them away from their stables, but actually he hasn't much intention of using them, as far as I have been able to find out. It's as if he's grooming them'

'Oh yes?' Mark swallowed. 'That's exactly what he did with mine, only he went a bit further and told them that if they stayed with me it would be like going down in the Titanic.'

Bozie blew his nose and sniffed, 'He seems hell-bent on destroying you and every other gallerist in the trade. It seems odd, in a large field like ours. You don't become successful by destroying your rivals.'

'He's a warlord!'

'Yes. I think that's what he is. But why? He seems very driven but not by enthusiasm – more like hatred. But at the same time, he's careful not to do anything obviously illegal. Also he stages pranks at private views.'

'I see.' Mark knew that he could not continue this conversation, it was getting late, 'Well thanks Bozie – that's very helpful. I'm going to try and find out some more. See you and thanks again,' and he left the gallery.

It was raining. Knowing that it would be impossible to get a taxi, he walked to the Tube. The busker he had heard the other day was playing inside the station. It was not "his" tune but something similar. But he smiled to himself. The day's activity had not been entirely wasted – his lunch with Clive had produced a contact to someone who would know the words. He was stages closer to finding the meaning of "Pratiranya".

CHAPTER 7

Frosted Glass

He opened the drawing room door and went in. A modest surge of enthusiasm came from the throng in the room. Everyone was pleased to see him with the exception of Millicent who flashed him a glance of pure ice. Indeed frosted glass could have been the title for the whole ensemble – both the guests and the room, for she was wearing a closely fitted grey silk chiffon dress which together with the moonstones at her neck and ears, set off both the grey of her eyes and the restrained decor of the room. Her natural pallor was discreetly camouflaged with make-up, her hair newly done, her neck and head superb both frontal and in profile. The guests were mostly in restrained greys browns and blacks – the only exceptions being a Japanese lady photographer in cyclamen silk and a small, fat lady in bright green whose name he could not remember.

Mark felt as though Millicent, himself, the house and all their guests were a unit, a single entity vibrating harmoniously together in the fumes of alcohol and the gentle sound of subdued jazz.

The guests were a fine selection from their lists of party fillers. Drawn mostly from the ranks of the rich and successful, the role call of their names would have been music to the gossip columnists. Company directors, barristers, surgeons and socialites. To add piquancy to this group of about twenty, there were a few of the young and aspiring – there were a couple of nephews of Millicent's and a very lovely young blonde, whose name he did not know.

They were about to eat. He hurriedly downed the cocktail that had been put in his hand and strolled over to the stair-well which gave onto the wide, spiral glass stairway that led down to the dining room. It was a splendid sight – the finger bowls now in place on the opaque glass table set up with white napery; gleaming, silver candlesticks and cutlery with, at intervals, Etruscan glass bottles each of which held a tiny spray of miniature orchids. There were also bowls containing minute tomatoes placed there just for the colour.

The meal was announced and they made their way down-stairs. He found himself sitting between the short fat lady whose name he couldn't remember and an elderly female brain surgeon whose name was Rosemary.

He was lucky that in the first part of the meal – the oysters – they were so occupied that not much conversation was necessary, for he was beginning to feel that he had done enough talking for one day. And then both his neighbours engaged the people sitting next to them on the further side.

He listened to the stout lady talking to the young man on the far side of her.

'Ethel Grulk,' she said. 'And you?

'Hubert Wargrave. What do you do Ethel?'

'Oh, I make Urr…' She spoke with a strong American accent and her speech was loaded with glottal stops.

'Urr?' Hubert was trying to conceal his apprehension about what sounded thoroughly disgusting.

'Yeah, I'm an Urtist'

'Oh,' he said with relief. 'What kind of art?'

'Oh – Edible urt.'

'Edible art?' It sounded frightening. He didn't think it could be to do with cupcakes or cookies somehow.

'Yeah… wull right now um vurry into labsters.' It

sounded even more frightening but Ethel rescued him, 'an' tull me whajya do?'

'I'm an astrophysicist. Millicent is my aunt. I'm just working on my dissertation for my Ph D.'

'Oh...' Ethel was entranced. 'That's just so in'erestin'. Tull me d'ya know anothin' about Black Holes?'

'Black Holes?' Mark now interjected. 'We've got this show coming up after the next one, called "Black Holes – White Spaces". It will turn the observer into the observed – influenced by measurement theory you know.'

'Oh – yes, measurement theory. Isn't that something to do with Quantum Mechanics?' A voice chimed in from the other side of the table. 'I've had it explained to me many times but I never really quite understand and I couldn't begin to explain it to anyone else.'

Hubert said, 'It's really quite simple. When you start trying to measure the movements of sub-atomic particles, the act of measuring actually interferes with what you are looking at... so it becomes impossible to separate the observer from the observed. Your exhibition, Mark, must be doing something pretty extraordinary!'

'But hang on,' said a new voice, from his other neighbour, the brain surgeon. You're talking about Black Holes one minute and then sub-atomic particles the next?'

'Well there is a theory that the micro is reflected in the macro level.'

'Interesting,' said the lady.

'But tell me...' someone else cut in, 'what do Black Holes actually look like?'

Hubert dipped his fingers in the finger bowl and dried them on the napkin, 'I'm sorry to disappoint you, but I don't think anyone knows what they look like. The thing is that they suck you in so fast you get stretched to an impossible degree.'

Ethel said, 'Like… wall, if a sushi piece would turn into a string of spaghetti?'

'Much worse than that. If you were astral travelling, my advice would be to keep well away from Black Holes. They'd suck you in before you had time to throw in a tomato. If you went near enough to do that you'd become a long string yourself.'

'Awesome,' Ethel said. 'But what'ud happen after that?'

'Nobody knows.' Hubert did not want to get drawn into the theories of dark matter and parallel universes. Fortunately they were distracted by the arrival of the next course and thankfully the subject was changed and conversations became more individualised. Ethel told him about her lobsters and he just put his attention on what he was eating, which was delicious.

A long time later, they all basked in the warm afterglow of a fine meal. After the oysters, there had been venison en croute followed by an elaborate variation of creme brulée with caramelised oranges, as well as many side dishes and garnishes. Coffee and brandy was served upstairs in the drawing room; the music a little louder now and dancing started – always the sign of a successful dinner party.

Mark danced with the Japanese lady. She asked him, in her excellent English, (for she had been brought up in Britain), 'How is it that every thing about you can be so perfect? This house – your wife, your career, this meal – all so beautiful? You must be so happy!'

'It is rather amazing isn't it? Sometimes I find myself wondering how I got here!' He laughed. But it wasn't quite true that everything was so beautiful. Complaints were reaching him from a certain region of the intestines that they were being asked to do more than they were designed for.

However, the pain was not yet intense and he was able to cover up. 'Anyway, you're an excellent photographer and I'm sure you have wonderful parties in Japan.'

The pain became a little worse and he had to leave the room in order to alleviate it. When he returned, it was clear that the party was dying down. People were beginning to go and fetch their coats. He felt greatly relieved.

It was two thirty when the last guests left. Millicent and Mark stood on the doorstep, framed by light, the very epitome of a happy and successful couple enjoying an evening of exemplary hospitality and pleasure.

As soon as the door closed, Millicent rounded on him. 'Why did you do it darling? You knew I wanted you to be there at the start. It spoils everything if I have to welcome the guests myself, as though I'm a widow or something. Where the hell did you get to?'

He groaned inwardly. He just wanted to go to bed. 'I told you I had to go to Canopy. It was a performance show and I couldn't leave early without disrupting everything. Fortunately Bozie came along and let me out of a side door or I'd have been much later.'

'Huh...' which sounded very much as though she did not believe him.

'Look,' he said gently, 'Milly, it's been a fabulous party. One of the best I'd say. Everything looked so good. Finger bowls and all. Candles, flowers, food and that lovely touch of the little bowls with tomatoes in them. And you looked superb. You really shone, my dear.'

'It's no use,' she said. 'You've played that card just too often. Flattery gets devalued after a bit. I'd have preferred it if you'd been here at the start.'

'All the same, I was telling the truth you know.' He could tell that she was slightly mollified. 'It was a lovely party, wasn't it?'

'I think…' She drew in a big sigh.

'What d'you think?'

'Oh…' she expelled the air. 'It's time for bed.'

But it was not the end of the evening as far as Mark was concerned. His digestion as well as the excitement and the talking would not let him sink into the deep oblivion that he craved. He dozed off fitfully with dreams of being pursued down a long tunnel by Ethel Grulk waving a huge lobster.

In the end he decided to fight it no longer and went down to the kitchen to make a cup of ginger tea – his tried and tested remedy for this condition.

As he sat at the table, the cat rubbing her back against his legs, he reached out for the radio and started twiddling the random knob. He knew what he wanted to hear, but he also knew it was unlikely that he would. He tuned in to a variety of stations offering strange and interesting fare, but "Pratiranya" eluded him. It didn't matter he told himself, he couldn't expect always just what he wanted. But then, suddenly, to his surprise, he did hear it – coming from a great distance on a crackling line. The same tune and the same singer.

He smiled – but his smile soon faded. There was something that he had not noticed before about this piece – something just the least bit menacing. Perhaps it was just the way the singer had glared at him, or perhaps he was just imagining it. He was too fuddled to work his brain – tomorrow he would ring Clive's friend and then he would find out.

CHAPTER 8

A Day Of Dry Wheels

Some days he felt like singing when he woke, but the following morning was not one of them. He wanted to groan as he peeled open his eyes and reconciled his bleary mind to the waking state. He decided that he no longer liked the Lichtenstein on the wall opposite the bed. But on reflection it did not seem a good moment to mention this to his wife, who was up and dressed and making up her eyes in the mirror – showing very little sign of the night before.

He remembered that the German agent had not phoned him back yesterday.

Splashing cold water over his face did not help. It was the sort of day when you avoided your reflection in the mirror. At his age, just turned forty, you did see the odd grey hair. There seemed to be a few more today. Clumsily he made his way downstairs to the kitchen where everything was white, black or stainless steel. Sometimes, just occasionally when he had a hangover and it was raining and there was a slight problem with a German agent, it reminded him of a hospital. There were white marble work tops and white quarry tiles on the floor, mosaic whites and off-whites backing the work tops, black cooking areas with stainless steel handles and rails and stainless steel chairs in clever curvy shapes with black linen cushions, around a small white, frosted glass table.

The flavour of the morning did not improve over breakfast. There were no warm croissants nestling cosily in a napkin on a basket and with Millicent deep in The Financial

Times he reached out and inserted a piece of bread in the toaster. Almost immediately it burst into flames and emitted a loud bang. He fanned out the flames with his newspaper, disconnected the toaster and went to the fuse box to reset the trip switch.

Now the smoke detector belatedly leaped into action with a crescendo of a howl. The switch was awkwardly situated at the back of one of the high cupboards. He pulled over a chair to the cupboard but just as he was about to reach it he realised that the phone was ringing. It was Dieter, his East German agent, calling from somewhere in Eastern Europe on a very bad line.

'Is no good time for you? I call back?'

'No, no… it's good.'

Millicent was climbing on the chair and reaching for the switch.

'OK, so you see… about this deal for the Rum Tugger the price be coming down just a few K…? you know just to getting him right mood.'

Millicent reached the smoke detector switch and flicked it, but now their cat Sushi, (reputed to have Japanese blood which might account for her extreme sensitivity), intent on calming her shattered nerves leaped onto the table and began to lick the butter.

'Get off!' Mark let out a roar and the line went dead. The cat jumped off the table taking with her a jar of marmalade and a jug of milk.

'Damn. That was an important call.'

'Well… perhaps he'll ring back.'

He did not ring back, nor was it possible to trace the number he was ringing from. In stony silence, they set about restoring order to their embattled kitchen.

'But I don't understand,' Mark said eventually, 'why it is

that a toaster which cost over a hundred pounds, should burst into flames just because I put an innocent piece of bread in it.'

'Oh… it was probably an oatcake.'

'An oatcake?'

'Sometimes they get stuck behind the carrier and little bits get onto the element.' Millicent sounded quite complacent.

'But why toast an oatcake?'

'You know Dr Beresford said I was not to eat flour, and oatcakes are so much nicer when you toast them.'

'Well that oatcake has probably cost me a deal worth half a million. It must be the most expensive oatcake in the history of the universe.'

'You wouldn't care if I had cancer.' Millicent stormed out.

Of course she didn't have cancer – that was just a bit of female histrionics, probably PMT. But then Millicent didn't go in for histrionics and didn't noticeably have PMT because she was continuously tense. It was quite likely that she had been put on some faddish diet by one of these fashionable alternative medical practitioners she was always consulting, although it was unlike Millicent to say something unless she meant it; her quiet statements were often unnervingly near the truth. For example, if Millicent said she was thinking of buying Hoxton Square, that meant she had had an offer accepted and the completion date was in sight and when Millicent said she felt sick that meant you had to fetch a bucket or even a mop. On balance it was quite likely that she did have, at least, a suspicion of a cancer awaiting further tests.

He sighed, then firmly put the thought out of his head and donned his morning mind-pattern, together with his raincoat. There were good things in his day. He was not going to Cork Street this morning but the AC2E in Hackney. Then lunch in St John's Wood with a client, followed by a visit to Louisa who had the afternoon off so that they could go shopping. The day could only get better, he reflected.

It soothed his nerves to drive. What a joy his car was. She seemed to anticipate his every whim. He called her "Princess Seraphina" and thought of Mozart when he drove her. She insulated him from the journey through the degenerating prosperity of the areas they passed until they arrived at the little street off Hackney Road where AC2E was situated.

It was now raining quite heavily and he raced down the little alleyway into the back entrance of the gallery where the curator, Susan, was waiting for him, anticipating his needs with a cafetière of freshly made coffee.

The building had originally been a large and severe chapel but many years ago had lapsed into secular life as a warehouse. Mark had gutted it, blocked out most of the windows, given it large roof lights and set up a small coffee bar on the upper gallery floor. The walls were stark white and there was an excellent lighting system mounted on gantries. It was used for the very large installations, and works which needed to be shown over a longer time than in the Cork street gallery.

The exhibition was impressive, but Susan was worried because there had been hardly any viewers in the last week.

They took a look outside the gallery and noticed that the end of the cul-de-sac had been blocked off by some road works. Also there was a large wrecked car sitting in the middle just by the bollards. If you were used to entering the gallery, none of this caused any problems – you could get by quite easily, but from the junction of the cul-de-sac with the main road, it looked as though there was a blockage. Visitors were obviously being discouraged by this.

A frustrating time phoning local authorities and the police did little to remedy the situation although they were assured that it would be put right as soon as possible. Mark wondered whether the fell hand of Henry Streffelgueze had managed to get a finger in this pot of bureaucratic mismanagement.

Eventually he got free of the gallery and drove to St John's Wood for lunch with his client, a wealthy invalid who owned two luxury flats overlooking Regent's Park – one for living in; the other for storing his large collection of avant-garde art.

His cook, frustrated by his master's restricted regime of beef tea and melba toast, had prepared an enticing dish of pork, cream and mushrooms for Mark, who lacked the nerve to say that he would have preferred the beef tea.

It was not a satisfactory occasion – his client revealed that he had been buying art in Paris and invited him to see his new purchases.

Paris! For Goodness Sake! How could anyone not know that London is the centre of the art world now that the days of Impressionism are over?

However, once he had managed to leave his client he found he could spend a few minutes in his car in privacy. He dialled the number that Clive had given him for a man who worked in a Romanian Cultural Institute.

He explained the problem and was told that yes a translation of the song would be emailed to him.

Mark said, 'I'm just so pleased. I've wanted to know since I heard it. Can't quite understand why it's got such a grip on me.'

'Would you like me to tell you a little about the background.' He had a thick Romanian accent but his English was very good.

'Oh, yes please.'

'Very well. "Pratiranya" is a song of the Romanian gypsies. These are a people who have had a very long tradition of oppression and suffering in almost every country they have lived in. They are very strong and passionate – very much in touch with their emotions, like American Blues singers. And they have a huge anger. "Pratiranya" is a song about anger, deception and lies – but it also ends on a more positive note than many of the others.'

'Thank you for all that.'

'Not at all, it's a pleasure. Myself, I think this song takes a hold on people because the lies it is objecting to might be the lies people are telling themselves – but that's just my own feeling.'

'I see.' Mark didn't, but he rang off with a sense of gratitude. He was stages nearer to understanding it.

CHAPTER 9

In Little Venice

Things could only get better, Mark reflected as he started the engine. Now for Louisa.

But Princess Seraphina, his beautiful vehicle, his very own space capsule, his chariot, his cradle, his comforter, the friend who seemed to know his every whim, now glided quietly to a halt and he drew into the side and pulled on the handbrake before realising that he had not exactly instructed her to stop. With a small quiver of irritation he instructed her to start again. She gave a discreet little cough and went silent; further attempts to revive her were equally futile. She was not out of petrol and her battery was fully charged. With a larger quiver of irritation he rang his garage. Normally helpful and subservient they told him they were short of staff due to sickness but would pass the matter on to an associated garage which called him shortly and told him to wait with the car – they might be an hour. An hour? But he was a busy man. This would not do at all.

He rang the gallery – someone should be able to come out and sit with the car, then he could continue by taxi. Unfortunately his secretary was having her day off, his assistant was out visiting a studio, and of the two receptionists, Sharon had had a dental emergency and that left Michelle holding the fort. Hell. There was nothing for it but to tough it out.

Well, at least Seraphina had a phone and an excellent sound system. There was some business he could do and when that was done he could surround himself with music.

He rang Louisa and told her he would be late. She sounded tired and lackadaisical. Then he was left, stranded in Little Venice, watching the rain pour down his windscreen, twiddling his thumbs and trying not to think about whether or not Millicent really did have cancer.

He could only find Vivaldi on the excellent sound system and it did not plug the gaps of his boredom. He scrolled through the various other stations but there was nothing except the brutish bumps and squeals of heavy rock and rap or the hackneyed cadences of cheap slush.

He looked around him at the dreary little street. There were some shops in it and there was a brightly lit window opposite the car. It was an art gallery with a seascape in the window.

Mark and his colleagues at the cutting edge of the modern art trade had a word to describe this sort of gallery. It was "retro". Retros were a quaint survival that was totally out of place in this day and age but somehow they refused to acknowledge this fact and die a quiet death. They were a bit like the Amish in America; not only knew they were out of place, they positively rejoiced in it. Everything, but everything, that was done in two dimensions, figurative or not, and sat inside a frame, was Retro. Retro was everything from Van Gogh to Hockney. Everything that did not fill the canon of a modern "pender" was retro. Retro work was all right in the context of its time, but that time was over. You dealt with Retros quietly and respectfully; you didn't have to force them to face up to reality. Sooner or later they would realise what an anachronism they were and die quietly.

The rain continued to pour down relentlessly. He drummed his fingers on the walnut dashboard. The channels of water on the windscreen went through an interminable variety of routes. Was it more or less interesting than watching paint dry?

He looked again at the window of the gallery.

You couldn't do it could you? Go into a rotten old Retro gallery just for the sake of diversion when you were stuck in the rain in a broken-down car? He was nothing if not a dedicated modernist. Suddenly, he found himself opening the car door and walking across the road.

Jane had managed to find at least two things to be pleased about that day. The bank manager has sent her a kind letter in response to her request to increase the overdraft and the young man who had come into the gallery and found comfort for the loss of his girl friend, had come back and spent more time just looking at the paintings.

She was celebrating by playing one of her favourite songs – "Oh You nasty man". She loved this song because it combined the best feminist principles with the worst female dilemma which was, simply, that bad or nasty men are very often both attractive and fun.

For some moments now, she had been aware that an expensive car was sitting opposite the gallery. The driver was talking on a phone and then doing nothing. The idea that this was a wealthy client flashed briefly through her mind, but he would have got out at once if he had been. More likely that he was just suffering from a breakdown – unusual though this was for an Aston Martin. She could see that he was good looking but tired, so she invented a scenario in which he was a Mafia Boss waiting for some rich haul.

He was now getting out of the car and crossing the road. Dark hair streaked with grey and a strange look of guilty innocence, like a furtive school boy caught with the peach in his hand trying to protest that it had just fallen naturally into it.

To her surprise, he now entered the gallery. Hastily she turned off the record player. There was something familiar about him. She wondered where she had seen him before. He was smartly dressed in a pale mackintosh which opened to reveal a pale green tie over a dark green shirt and navy blue jacket and trousers.

'What was that you were playing?' Mark asked. He wanted to tell her that she was beautiful with her long dark hair tied back and her simple grey tunic over a pair of brilliant pink velvet trousers.

'Oh – that's just an old song from the 30's. It's so funny. It cheers me up on rainy days when no-one comes into the gallery except strangers whose car has broken down.'

He looked embarrassed. 'Well... I was so bored sitting there by myself.'

'Would you like to look round?'

'What I'd like more than anything is a cup of coffee.'

'Do you make a habit of strolling into art galleries and asking for cups of coffee?'

'Please... don't want to tell you the story of my life but I'm not having such a good day.' The trouble was that this first statement was not true. He suddenly felt a desperate urge to tell her everything.

Jane took pity on him. 'All right – I'll get you one... Sugar? Milk?'

'Neither. But will you play that tune again?'

So she put it on. He listened in silence while she made the coffee. It was the antidote to "Pratiranya". It made him laugh.

She brought in the coffee and he sat down opposite her. 'Thank you – that's so welcome. What's your name?'

She told him.

'I'm pleased to meet you, Jane. I'm Mark Arniston Crocker.'

Now she knew where she had seen him before – it must

have been on some TV programme about New Young British Art. 'Oh no! You're the leader of the pack. I'd never have made you a coffee if I'd known!' Her eyes blazed.

He thought she was even more attractive when angry. 'I'm sorry – I didn't mean to upset you.'

'It's just that you and some others like you are undermining my business by promoting a type of art that isn't art. It's associated with corruption.'

He didn't want to get drawn into a discussion of art – that happened too often. Instead he said gently, 'These are heavy accusations. Is there anything else?'

'It's just that I've heard enough about the new art breaking the boundaries. It's nonsense. What you are doing is rubbish! There's art and there's non-art. I'm not against modernism but in the present day art scene hundreds of good artists go un-noticed, while a select few sell their work for millions. When there's money like that involved, there's corruption.'

She is clever, he thought. She had hit him where it hurt.

He shut his eyes for a second. 'There's also such a thing as closed minds and a lack of ability to move with the times.'

'You can put me in that bracket if you like. I don't mind. I've got the satisfaction of doing something that I believe in. There's not much money in it and I get depressed sometimes, but then people come in here and say that my show has comforted them, or even, sometimes, that it's inspired them.' She waved her hands round the gallery. 'I expect you're going to tell me about the great service you are doing the British Public by broadening their minds, with things like piles of bricks or men peeing over each other! It's rubbish. What you're really doing is making lots and lots of money for yourself and your backers.'

He opened his mouth to speak – but she forestalled him as she had just noticed something outside. 'I say – there's a breakdown van outside your car.'

'Not a minute too early,' he said a little grimly. But he wanted to part on good terms. 'Do please give me your card – I'd like to keep in touch.'

She gave him her card and he thanked her politely for her hospitality.

'I hope you don't think I'm a nasty man,' he added as he left – a bit ruefully.

'Well… actually I do,' but she was laughing now.

Jane thought; *A nasty man came into the gallery and I trounced him. Something to put in my book of blessings? Must tell Freddie, he'll be most impressed. But why the hell did I give him my card?*

Chapter 10

Louisa

Princess Seraphina refused to give the rescue mechanic any immediate clues as to her ailment – it was the privilege of expensive cars to have highly strung nervous systems, which went by the names of "electronics", "phasing" and "timing" and which were extremely difficult to diagnose. She was soon put on the transporter and driven to Mark's garage, which was in the opposite direction from his destination. Mark rang Louisa who sounded, not surprisingly, despondent. Eventually, he arrived in Bayswater in a courtesy car after a long drive in the heavy traffic.

Louisa let him in without saying a word. She looked as though she had been crying. His heart sank.

'Darling – I'm so sorry.' He embraced her but she stiffened. He was always letting her down in some way or another, usually by being unpardonably late. Being used to her stormy moods, he was well practiced in the art of turning them round. You gave her lots and lots of strokes; you told her what a lovely creature she was; you praised her patience and her forbearance and so on; you arrived with bouquets of lilies and bottles of malt whisky, but this time nothing seemed to be working. Eventually he cried out, 'Just what is the matter Louisa? It can't be just that I'm late. There must be something else. What is it?'

'I'm fed up.' Sniff. 'What with being at the tail end of your list, like,' sniff 'and having to fit in with everything else in your life,' sniff, 'I just feel like I give more than I get.'

'Oh yes?' It was familiar territory. A storm that blew up at intervals and he knew how to calm it.

'I just feel that I'd like to count a bit more for you – that's all.'

'Do you mean that you'd like me to divorce Millicent and marry you?'

Of course she would, but she couldn't admit it when it was thrown in her face like this. So she sobbed again and again.

'Louisa,' he began reproachfully, putting his arm round her shoulder again – it had been thrown off the first time. 'My darling Louisa. You know we've been through all this before. I'm not the sort of man who could make you happy. You know that. When we go away for a weekend, I get increasingly vile as time goes on. D'you really want to spend your life with someone like that?'

She nodded. He was right. Prolonged exposure to Louisa meant a rising streak of irritability due to the boredom of her conversation. Louisa was for one thing only. It was hard for him to understand that Louisa wanted, hoped and believed, in the innocence of her affection, that he might possibly change and become a reformed character.

'You see it works very well for both of us, just to have a sort of partial thing and then you can have other boyfriends.'

'Don't give me that line,' she said with sudden sharpness. 'You know I don't have other boyfriends, like and you know bloody well why.'

'Have we had this conversation before? Remind me.'

'I'm… I,' she faltered, 'I'd just like to do something like… a bit more creative with my life.'

'Oh yes.' He'd also heard that one before. Louisa was not entirely fulfilled in her job and had vague aspirations to paint or sculpt. She wasn't an artist in the modernist sense – far too gentle and unassertive. As far as retro art went, she had no talent at all for drawing but had a natural sense of colour.

He discouraged all talk of leaving the shop and going to art school, being unable to see that it would do her any good at all. Evening classes in patchwork, etching, hat-making or, at most, textiles – that would be much more her scene.

'Like what?' he asked, nastily.

'Like… having a a baby.'

'My God!' he shouted. 'You can't be…' It was the last straw in a difficult day. He closed his eyes in disbelief, 'You can't be.'

She sobbed noisily for a few minutes.

He got up and paced round the room. 'Can't believe this. It's just too much. Today's been bad enough as it is.' He sat down again and buried his face in his hands. Louisa sobbing beside him. *I just want to get out of this,* he thought, *just to be on my own and in peace. I'd like to rescript all this. I'd like it to be not happening. Why can't we change these things?*

After a long silence he said, 'Are you quite sure?'

She nodded, sniffing.

'But you told me you had a coil?'

'Like… these things can come out.'

'I see what you mean about being more creative. It's just come as a bit of a shock. Something I never expected, that's all.'

She went on crying.

He put his arm round her. 'There, there, don't cry. I suppose I should have known when I saw you with Woody the other day. I can see that it's something that you might want. But I don't. Just don't. It's a quagmire.'

She said nothing but went on sobbing and sniffing. He found himself hoping that the lovely silk cushions would not be damaged by the salt tears. Then, at last, some genuine compassion overtook him. 'There, there… don't cry my love. My darling Louisa. It's what you want isn't it?'

She nodded tearfully.

The tears began to subside and she allowed him to cuddle

her. A baby. What a nightmare. 'Tell me,' he said with the greatest restraint, 'when we talked about it before, we had sort of reached an agreement that it was better for babies to be born into a situation where daddy and mummy are married, and you know… er… it was a mutual decision.'

'Yeah. You conned me into agreeing with all that. But I didn't know then what I know now.' The tears were over but now anger was overtaking her.

'What do you know now?'

'That I've wanted a kid for ages and ages and I'm not getting any younger or into any marriage situation when I'm hanging around waiting for you. Living for you really.'

'What else?' he asked very gently.

'Don't try to kid me. You're just covering up. You're really mad at me but you're just sitting there being polite. I hate you! You just don't care a fig about me do you? You think it's fine to just come and see me when it suits you and fits in with your wife's plans. You think it's all fine for me because that's what works for you. Do you never think that I want a bit more for my life? I've been in love with you for five years. I put up with this because I know it's all I'm ever going to get out of you. You wouldn't leave her for me, but do you never think that I might want a fellah who could put me, like, first in his life? Does it never occur to you that you're just using me. If you weren't around I'd have probably found a husband by now.'

'Hang on a moment.' But she was unstoppable.

'And do you really think that I could give up on the idea of having a family, just because it's inconvenient for you?'

'So you did this deliberately?'

'Not a bit. I'm not that sort. But since it's happened, I've found out just how welcome it is.'

'Yes, well it is nice for you…'

'And I can see that it's not quite so nice for you, but I don't bloody well care any more.'

'You feeling all right?' Suddenly there was a note of real concern in his voice.

'Yes,' she said angrily. 'Well no. I mean I'm delighted about the kid, but I feel sick all the time and tired and a bit miserable as well.'

He jumped up with alacrity. 'Shall I get a bucket?'

'No, it's OK – I don't throw up very often. I just feel nauseous all the time.'

'Poor Louisa,' and he started to stroke her hair.

'Get off.' She was suddenly angry again.

'Louisa… I'm going to have to go. This has been a bit of a shock for me and I've got to get used to it. It's been quite an eventful day what with one thing and another.'

'Go then.' She lay back on the cushions and closed her eyes. Telling him had been less awful than she had anticipated – he'd been quite good really, although the whole scene had exhausted her.

He rose to go.

'Louisa… Louisa… if it's really what you want, it's good news. I'll see you very soon. Sorry to have upset you and sorry our afternoon was spoilt.' He bent down, kissed her and departed, feeling abject and ashamed.

The courtesy car was boring, and seemed a yappy, snarly thing after the Aston Martin but perhaps it was the right vehicle for his emotions. The surface layer of compassion now broke up and a deep fount of anger broke through. How could she be so ungrateful, so selfish as to get pregnant after all that he done for her and spent on her? The selfishness was the worse aspect of it. She knew his feelings very well about babies – he had made them clear on a number of occasions – babies should be conceived as the result of a joint decision not by unilateral action. Accidents should be removed by surgery. That was the only fair thing in this overpopulated planet at this time. He wondered whether he could bribe her to have an abortion, but he knew instantly that this avenue was not open to him.

At the private view, he felt withdrawn and so detached that he could hardly engage in any conversation. He walked round the room pretending to be engrossed by the exhibits – penders with light bulbs projecting from a very blurred background. It was a slight comfort to have something to engage his mind, but in spite of this, it kept on coming back to Louisa.

He began speculating about whether it was an accident or design – but he would never know, because she would not admit to anything so fell as deliberately having her coil removed. He wondered about Louisa and realised that he knew very little about her. Those teddy bears marked the parameters beyond which he did not want to pass. Their interaction possessed enough quality for him not to be interested in its quantity. It had never occurred to him that it might be otherwise for her. Hell.

The private view was a very different affair from the one of the previous night. It was in the heart of Mayfair at a very large gallery. There were crowds of minor celebrities, journalists and press photographers. Tonight, he was not at his best among the flashlights and the jostling of the would-be successful against the successful. He seemed to be painfully aware of a grabbing sort of quality among the guests. Perhaps he had been subliminally affected by Ethel Grulk and her lobsters, but everyone seemed to have claws and feelers tonight. The lights made him blink and he had a growing and entirely novel feeling of wanting to go home.

He was quickly engaged by a young man who kept on asking him questions. Mark could not remember meeting him but his face was vaguely familiar. He answered in a routine sort of way, feeling that his sermon about breaking boundaries was getting a little past its sell-by date. But his mind was elsewhere – full of Louisa.

He began to contemplate the bleak possibility of life without her. For an instant, the pleasures of tumbling about on her cushions in a candlelit room flashed before his eyes. It would be an impossible pain to give up seeing her, he needed her, but this possibility was now on the cards. Marriage was out of the question – at least she saw that – but neither did he want a mistress with his bastard. Perhaps this was due to a streak of retrogression in his moral code that was positively self-destructive, but there it was.

Louisa was for him a piece of private indulgence; another comfort station like his car; something he thought he could rely on if he provided the correct attention, but today both of them had let him down. He felt doubly betrayed.

'Ah here's Mark!' someone called Nigel, whom he did not know very well, greeted him. 'He knows all about this sort of thing. Hey Mark, can you explain about this light thing to my friend Gwen here? Gwen thinks all this is nonsense – well rubbish, really.'

Mark suddenly found himself in a circle of enquiring faces.

'Well,' he mumbled. 'You see everything is art really. When you look at unusual things in a gallery it helps you to have a better relationship with ordinary things like – er... piles of rubbish on street corners. That sort of thing anyway... but if you'll excuse me, I've to go, I've got another appointment.' There was another flash from a photographer and he thought he saw a microphone. Hurriedly he made his escape.

At the dinner party, which was, fortunately, quieter and more discreet, he was distinctly preoccupied. But at least, since it took place in a restaurant, he has some control over what he was eating, for he was still affected by the previous night, and lunch had been heavy. He remembered that he had planned a trip to Granada – would that still happen? Or would she be too busy being sick, as his experiences with pregnant Millicent had taught him.

'I wonder what's happened to our Mark,' his hostess remarked after he left. 'He seemed to be a bit off colour'

'I expect he's just done too much socialising – you know what he's like. There must be limit somewhere,' her husband replied.

Meanwhile Mark returned to his speculations on the journey home. The bombshell that Louisa had unloaded on him now obliterated the success story of his day – his progress towards understanding the meaning of "Pratiranya".

It was late when he finally slipped into bed beside the recumbent Millicent. He slid a hand onto a thigh whose boniness was mitigated by her thick, silk-satin pyjamas. In these hard pressed times you had to find comfort where you could.

He whispered, 'You awake?'

'Of course not. Are you sober?'

'Not terribly. You?'

'Desperately sober.'

His hand was gently removed from her thigh.

'Night night.'

'Night'.

Chapter 11

Nasty Man

Oh you Nasty Man
Taking your love on the easy plan
here and there and where you can
Oh you Nasty Man!

You ain't foolin' me
You're just as bad as bad can be
But you're darn good company
Oh you big Bad Man!

Jane hummed this song as she chopped vegetables at her kitchen sink. She felt happy – Freddie was coming to supper and she was making risotto. Her kitchen, on the first floor of the terrace house where she occupied the upper two floors, looked out onto the gardens and back additions of the row behind. Some of the gardens were a mass of semi-tropical growth – palm trees and large ferns – a little like a Duanier Rousseau jungle. She felt a desire to paint them. Perhaps one day she would. Although she had given up painting, she still occasionally felt a desire to do it. Perhaps it was due to the season – early Spring.

The doorbell rang. She put the garlic bread in the oven, turned down the burner to keep the risotto warm and put on a pan to cook the asparagus before running downstairs to greet Freddie. He was carrying a bunch of daffodils and a bottle of wine in a bag. He was wearing a smart dark blue raincoat with brass buttons.

He hugged her.

'What a lovely coat!' They went upstairs.

'You look happier – what happened?' he said as they reached the top and he took off his coat. 'And what a nice smell. Can I help?'

'It's just about ready – the asparagus has to cook. But you can help me put out some of the dishes.'

He carried plates through to the dining area of her living room. 'I love asparagus,' he said as he opened the bottle of wine.

'Well – it's only risotto to follow. I'm not in your class when it comes to cooking.'

'Oh nonsense! Now – tell me. What's happened. Why are you looking so cheerful?'

She told him briefly, about the visits of the young man and the old lady, adding 'And then what happened? Today I actually had the leader of the pack – Mark Arniston Crocker himself in my gallery!'

'No… Really? What on earth was he doing there?'

'Oh, his car had broken down and he was waiting for the repair man. I gave him a trouncing.'

And what was he like?'

'Well – very smooth and charming. Very well dressed. I told him he was a crook. The asparagus is ready now – let's eat.'

'And did he like being told that?'

'Not exactly – but he didn't have time to say much as the garage turned up. Actually, I felt a bit sorry for him. He looked rather beaten up. He had a sheepish look on his face.'

'Do you think he really believes in what he's doing?'

'Oh yes. The bags under his eyes were probably just a sign of eating and drinking too much.'

'But you felt sorry for him?'

'Well – yes.'

'Maybe you shouldn't have attacked him so hard.'

'Maybe – but it was fun.' And she told him about telling Mark that he was a nasty man.

Freddie was silent as he pondered this.

Jane said, 'And the old lady I was telling you about – she had also met him on a train and said she liked him. But I didn't. And Freddie – the old lady has invited us to stay with her in Somerset!'

'Tell me more about her,' Freddy said as he helped himself to the salad.

So Jane told him about the old lady.

'She sounds nice. A bit like the granny we'd all like to have.' He smiled but now his eyes had strayed to something over her shoulder. He said, 'Tell me – is that painting of a lemon on the wall behind you, one of yours?'

'It is.'

'It's awfully good, you know. Every time I see it I like it better. Do you ever regret not going on with your art?'

'No... not the least. Ben and I just didn't have the drive – the confidence to brazen ourselves into the art world. I think we both kept on feeling that we could do it better all the time. We just decided that we would like to promote other artists. More risotto?'

'Yes, please. It's delicious.' He helped himself to some more, then he said, 'That's so interesting about confidence. I've been reading about an artist in the sixties who went into one of the top galleries with a few paintings before he even went to art school. When they asked what he had been doing he said he had been working in Paris – this was on the strength of a holiday in France. The gallery took two paintings and sold one.'

'And what happened then?'

'While he was at art school he fortified his position by grooming two leading critics, one with sex and the other with Left Wing Political discussion with the result that the year after he graduated, he catapulted right to the top.'

'But what was his name? Have I heard of him?'

'Harrison Winfield.'

Jane sipped her wine, thoughtfully. 'I have heard of him but I can't bring to mind any of his paintings.'

'Nobody can. It was very sad. He became an alcoholic and insulted the wrong people as he was drunk most of the time and then he got relegated. The drink killed him in the end.'

'What a sad story!'

'Yeah.' He helped himself to some more salad.

'But would that happen today? I mean the catapulting, not the drinking?'

'Well – it's now much more organised. There's a group of publicists, gallerists, museum curators and critics who get together and select front runners from a short list of candidates whom their scouts have chosen from the degree shows. They take just one or two a year and promote them as hard as they can. Because the finances are just that more rewarding if the artists get into the million pound bracket. And if they are fairly well behaved, that's where they stay.'

Jane had vaguely suspected something like this but had not given it much thought. She asked, 'And is Mark one of this group?'

'He is.'

Jane took a another sip of wine. 'I've always known there must be something like this, because when I go to the degree shows I'm always struck by the consistent quality of the work whether it's figurative or abstract or installationist. I'm always puzzled by the fact that just a few of them will make it to the top and the rest will be forgotten.'

'They're not looking for quality. They want strong personalities.'

'Oh…' she sighed. 'Freddie…let's not talk about this any more. We can't change it can we?'

'No, but it's worth remembering that when someone buys a painting to hang on their wall, both the artist and the client get something. If art's being bought just to go into bank vaults then no-one sees it! It gets sort of messy. I think of this when I feel that I'd like a bit more money!'

'Right.'

CHAPTER 12

Henrietta's Mission

The morning that brought trouble to Mark in the form of toasters, troublesome cars and mistresses, rained with equal intensity upon Henrietta Bisquet, but brought her fewer misfortunes.

If she strode out that morning with a little more purposefulness than usual this was because she was on a mission and there was nothing that Henrietta liked more than a set goal. Mark had asked her to find out about Henry Striffelguese and this is what she intended to do. As she had business in the city centre, she took a taxi from her home in Chelsea to North Islington to the house of Mona and Marcus Morebattle, two young artists whose work she liked.

Mona and Marcus were slightly out of the mainstream of avant-garde artists, which means that they had not managed to get their act of togetherness accepted by enough promoters and sponsors as a piece of Performance Art. Their act, called simply "The Act" consisted of sitting on a bed facing each other and shouting obscenities. It was a performance that required a lot of practice and they put in many hours a day perfecting it. Nor were their differences of opinion entirely simulated. Marcus had found fairly early on that he was bored with conventional swearwords and loved creating his own. Mona, however, was more conservative and stuck to the original repertoire. As a result she seemed to have forgotten that there were any other words in the English language. It was too bad that Canopy had turned them down. Their two megalomaniac egos had been badly buffeted by this experience, (as well as other rejections) but, resourceful to the hilt, they had also developed a minimalist form of pender, which Henrietta was finding that she could market.

She descended from the taxi and rang the doorbell. Instead of ringing, it made a very rude noise followed by a loud hollow laugh. Henrietta stood back patiently and waited.

Eventually someone opened a window and shouted an expletive at her.

'Hi. It's me,' said Henrietta.

'Oh yeah. It's ******you. Well you ******* better come up.'

This was the standard reception. They were obviously in a good mood today. Sometimes they threw things, like for example, rotting fish, or decaying plastic sponges. As she could not come up until the door opened, Henrietta waited until it was opened by a tousle headed Mona. '****?'

'I'm fine thanks. How are you?'

'**** **** **** **** **** **** **** **** ****'

Mona gave her a self-pitying look.

'I'm sorry to hear that – but I'm sure you'll feel better soon.'

'**** **** ****'

'Really?'

'**** **** **** **** ****'

'No? – are you sure?'

While this somewhat contrived conversation took place they were ascending a dilapidated staircase until they reached a large room on the top floor. Here Marcus was sitting, stark naked on a large leather pouffe in front of an electric fire.

'Hi Marcus, what are you doing?' asked the imperturbable Henrietta. If you had seen and heard what she has experienced in the Congo Basin you would not be thrown by anything.

What a wretched skinny little thing he was though.

'Firk, Girk and Hoooey. Fibblebottoms. I've found a new one. "Rat-tailed maggots' pee." How about that?'

'★★★★★?', said Mona.

'Yes I'd love a coffee,' said Henrietta. And Mona obligingly went off to put on the kettle. 'Milk but no sugar,'

Henrietta called out.

'★★★★★★★', said Mona.

'Maggots' peebottom,' said Marcus. 'What do you think?'

'If you ask me, I think it's childish,' said Henrietta, firmly. 'I've come to see your new penders.'

'Oh penders. Not interested. Forby Dunstable thinks he could get us into Arniston Crocker.'

'Who is Forby Dunstable?'

'He's a PR. Friend of someone we know. Got good contacts!'

The interesting thing about the Morebattles was that they were eternally optimistic.

'And we met a whole load of people at the party the other night. Real contacts. Just couldn't get over what we are doing. It's so original.''

Mona came back with the tray of coffees. '★★★★.'Thanks.'

'And there's this new gallerist. He's a rave. He's great.'

'★★★★ ★★★★ ★★★★,' agreed Mona.

'He's going to be The Absolute, when Crocker falls,' said Marcus.

'Is that what he told you?'

'Yeah – well he's fantastic. We've got it made.'

'Did he make any offers?'

'Well – not exactly. But he hasn't seen The Act. When he has, he can't fail to.'

'And he has a gallery up and running?'

'Well – not exactly. But he's just bought a sugar mill in

Deptford and he's going to spend a good few grand on converting it.'

'And what is his name?' Although she knew it already.

'Henry Striffelperse.'

'★★★★ ★★★★ ★★★★★★★★ ★★★★'

'And the great thing is, if we get in with someone while they're on the up and up, we're really in and we'll be there for life because of the bonding.'

'Sure,' said Henrietta sipping her coffee thoughtfully. Then she stood up. 'Well if you've really found your man, then there's no point in selling penders. I might as well be on my way.'

'★★★★ ★★★★,' said Mona helpfully.

'Hey wait a minute,' Marcus said hurriedly. 'There are a few things we could show you.' He got up and went to a pile of canvasses stacked against a wall. He turned them round to display surfaces that were mostly all black emulsion paint, but had a few delicate pressed leaves stuck to them. In their spare time Mona and Marcus bought up old green vegetables and put the leaves in a press. When they had flattened and dried, they stuck them down on the canvasses. They were not unpleasing to look at and were a little like the dried flower collages that used to feature so strongly in village flower shows about fifty years ago – except that the ratio of empty space to contents was somewhat higher and they were much, much darker. Sometimes the leaves collapsed, so just a few small fragments remained scattered on the canvasses.

Henrietta chose six, which she would have framed and sell on a sale-or-return basis, the frames being paid for out of the sales. They did not like the fact that her commission was 60% and Mona came out with her first polysyllable of the day, 'Fuckinell'.

Henrietta beamed sympathetically and said they could

take it or leave it. They took it and Mona showed her out, asterisking her way down the stairs. As she strode down the stairs, Henrietta heard an almighty shout.

'Ayeeoooooooooooh...'

Marcus had dropped the bread-board on his foot. Vainly he struggled to find an expletive violent enough express the intensity of his pain. It was useless. '.....BLAGH..... UGH.......SAUSSAGE.........BOTHER!' was all that emerged from the debris of some previous stage in his development.

Just as Henrietta reached the front door, the taxi she had summoned from her mobile, drew up and she grabbed the door, thankfully.

'★★★★ ★★★★ ★★★★.' Mona waved goodbye grinning manically.

'Finsbury Park,' said Henrietta. 'Goodbye Mona, you need to wash your mouth out.' Mona had already turned and was running upstairs. She let out an enormous string of expletives to Marcus who replied calmly. 'Yeah. I know. But we gotter live. Let's try this one! I'll say "Maggots' pee bottom" and you'll say...'

'★★★★!' said Mona.

Henrietta's framer was in Finsbury Park. She left the penders in his competent hands and took the rather uncharacteristic step of taking the underground to Piccadilly. She did this because the rain was now coming on thickly and it was harder, even with a mobile, to get a taxi. On the journey, her thoughts turned to Henry Streffelgueze. There was something rather puzzling about him. He flirted with young artists and prophesied dire fates for established gallerists, but everything seemed to be up in the air and futurist. It didn't seem to have quite the correct ring of professionalism about it. There was just nothing on the ground.

By the time she arrived at Piccadilly, she had forgotten about Henry in the pleasure of marching up Regent Street in the rain in her fashionable and powerful raincoat. It was black and shiny with massive sleeves and a cape over her shoulders. If you are rich and powerful it's important to be seen as such and Henrietta felt, that day, extremely rich and powerful. She strode comfortably along, knowing that heads were turned. It was probably her hat, which was large, black and wide rimmed and threw off the rain in an admirable fashion. She knew that in her mid-forties her figure was as trim as an eighteen year old and her energy had not diminished.

She turned into Carnaby Street and then into a little cul-de-sac off it, where her corsetière had a workshop on the first floor.

'Madame Bisquet how nice to see you.' Madame Bonberg was frail, ingratiating and very slightly sinister. 'If you would like to wait here, I will get your piece for you.' She waved Henrietta into a velour-covered settee.

It may seem unlikely that Henrietta, who had a spare figure both above and below the waist should be consulting a corsetière, but in fact, it was for this very reason. Corsetières are sometimes employed to build up a figure rather than reduce it. Henrietta loved dressing up and dearly wanted to have more frontage than she possessed but lacked both the nerve and the effrontery to have silicone implants. Madame Bonberg worked for many theatrical costumiers and had the experience to produce the outfit that Henrietta wanted. This was for a very grand party at a large gallery in Bond Street. Henrietta had conceived the notion that she would like to wear a pair of gold breast-plates under a black fishnet body stocking. Below the breast plates, on her lower half she would have some gold lamé bikini bottoms and on her legs, gold thigh boots. The gold breast plates had already been made for her, and now Madame Bonberg was concocting something to go underneath, which would give her a bit more shape and even suggest something of a cleavage. It was quite a feat of brassière engineering but Madame Bonberg was completely up to it. Henrietta let out a yelp of satisfaction when she saw herself in the mirror. It would do. It was perfect.

She strode down Regent Street feeling even more happy and confident. She hesitated about turning right for Cork Street and Bond Street for there were many galleries she wanted to catch up with but she knew that the new show at the ICA was her priority so she continued on down to the Mall.

As she poured down Waterloo steps, a man's voice hailed her. 'Hi!' It was Henry Streffelgueze.

If you were hovering twenty feet above those steps, the encounter between Henrietta and Henry would have appeared to you to resemble the meeting between a battle-ship and a submarine. Henry, moving rapidly upwards now slowed and turned to accompany the battleship, which slowed down very gradually until at the bottom of the steps it allowed itself to turn and start ascending again. Henry had deflected the battleship from its attack on the ICA by persuading it to have lunch with him at a nearby restaurant.

Henry Streffelgueze could not be described as attractive by any manipulation in the meaning of the term. The most you could say of him was that he was jolie-laide, and that was only if the proportion of laide to jolie was about four to one. He was tall and thin with a sallow complexion, sunken cheekbones, hooded, reptilian eyes and a large mouth whose corners drooped downwards even when he smiled. He looked fishy – so like a criminal that you couldn't really believe he was one. No longer in the first flush of youth – probably in his mid-fifties, Henrietta decided.

He was, however, like most people, considerably

improved when he did smile and when he laughed it was even better – you could see the flash of his gold teeth. There was something about him that reminded Henrietta of her days in the Congo – something wild and unpredictable. Henry was a dark adventure and Henrietta was an adventuress.

Over lunch she began to grill him for the information she wanted to pass on to Mark.

'You've been telling lots of young artists that you can bring them more hope than the established gallerists?'

'Yeah. Sure. Why not?' His Bostonian accent was lightly tinged with something clipped and European; Germanic? Italian? Slavic? it was hard to say.

'But isn't that a little premature if you don't even have a gallery yourself?'

'I'm in the process of setting one up just as fast as I can.'

'Oh, whereabouts is that?' She knew already but asked for sake of form.

'I'm converting a sugar mill in Deptford – it's going to cost megabucks.'

'And you think it will be the place for Performance Artists? This large space?'

'Sure.'

'And you've had some experience of running galleries?'

'M'am, let me tell you. I've had experience of everything.'

He laughed, showing his gold teeth. 'And what I'm doing here is just going to be the greatest thing ever.'

'Well – isn't that great.' Henrietta sipped her wine thoughtfully. 'You're from Boston?'

He nodded.

'One of my favourite cities. You had a gallery there?'

'I had an art business. I bought and sold wall hangers.'

Penders. It was pretty solid. 'So why come here?'

'Lady, you're asking a lot of questions! Isn't it obvious why anyone in the art world would want to go to London. It's top at the moment as you know very well. It's at the summit of the volcano and I am going to blow its top.'

Henrietta was reduced to silence as she cut up a piece of steak and put it in her mouth.

'And what do you do — apart from going to parties?' Henry asked.

'Oh nothing much. I travel a bit. And write books and things. And I have a business myself in penders.'

'You have a gallery?'

'No. I sell them from my home.'

'Where's that?'

'Chelsea.'

'I'd like to see it.'

'This afternoon?'

'Yeah. Why not.'

And that was how Henry and Henrietta became an item.

CHAPTER 13

The Fartoo

The next morning, Mark awoke with a splitting headache and a deep realisation that he did not merely dislike the Lichtenstein, he hated it. His car was in the garage and Louisa was pregnant. He had also lost an important contract because of a stupid cat and a burnt oatcake.

Millicent, by contrast, was bright and cheerful this morning and hummed to herself as she did her make-up.

In the kitchen on the table by the jug of fresh orange juice, the oatcakes and the cafetière, there was a basket with fresh croissants nestling in a pure white damask napkin. He felt a pang of contrition and said, 'Milly, I'm sorry about... yesterday.'

'Oh that's all right. You've got your croissants anyway.'

'Thank you... I noticed. What you said yesterday worried me. I do care a bit about you, you know. You have cancer?'

'There was a test. I told you I was going for one.'

'I'm sorry... I must have forgotten – I'm just so busy these days. Was it OK?'

'Well – actually no. But then I had another and it was.'

'I'm so glad.' He touched her arm and then reached out for a croissant. The dream that was once their marriage had faded and he spent most of the time disliking her, but there was a level on which he loved her still. Sometimes he thought that he would like to get to know her again, but there was always some barrier. He looked at her now and saw that she was unhappy. He said, 'Milly, why're you looking so sad?

Have I done something to upset you?'

She was silent for some time and he could see that tears were forming.

'Please tell me what's the matter?'

She sniffed. 'Oh, I was just thinking…' But she couldn't begin to tell him.

Their dialogue was interrupted by the phone.

'Oh, Hi Mark.' It was his PRO, 'Sorry to disturb you so early, but I thought I'd get it in quick. Congratulations!'

'What for?'

'Oh, you haven't seen the gutter press this morning? You are all over the inside of The Cosmos. Listen to this, "Headline – Modern Art – The Big Hoax". Large Capitals. "THE MAN WHO OUGHT TO KNOW DUMPS NEW ART." Main Text – "At the opening of the new show at the Elnet Gallery in Dover Street last night, our reporter Max Shower asked leading gallerist and expert on Modern Art, Mark Arniston Crocker, what was the meaning of the New Art. He replied that it was rubbish. There you have it at last! The truth from the horse's mouth! It's what we've been telling you all along folks. Modern art is rubbish. Like the Emperor's new clothes in the fairy story. It just doesn't exist. But what we'd like to ask Mark, who must have stashed away a fair old lump by selling this rubbish, is just what does he think he is doing? Is it really fun to swindle the public like this?" '

Mark grappled with his memory and tried to steer it to the night before.

'Cripes, I didn't say that at all.'

'No, of course not. It doesn't matter what you've said. It's a brilliant piece of publicity you see, just when I thought they might be getting saturated with you! Listen, I've set up a press conference at the gallery for 11 o'clock, and you can explain all… see you there.'

'What's up?' Millicent asked as he put the phone down. The mask of brightness had now been replaced on her face.

'I said something at that party last night and some bloody reporter got hold of it and distorted it so that it sounds like I was denouncing Modern Art.'

'And were you?'

'Of course not, but the trouble is I can't quite remember what it was I said. I think it was something about rubbish... and it got taken up that I said modern art was rubbish.' In a flash it came back to him what he had said, which was the result of what he had thought of saying to Jane Gresham that afternoon That now seemed about a year ago. Jane Gresham! The woman who had told him he was a nasty man. And yet it had been, in a day of unmitigated disaster, one of the better episodes.

'I'll have to go now – a bit to sort out before the press comes.' He kissed her and went out.

At the press conference he pulled out his mental trumpet and blasted out the familiar message. It was his:-

Fanfare for the New Art

Puppa puppah puppahahaaaaaa!

Down with the old, bring in the New!...Move with the times... Progress getting faster... Change in the air. Shock of the new... Don't fight it – welcome it... Chuck-out time for:- the boundaries, old definitions, old prejudices... young British Artists on Top of the World!

Puppa puppah puppahahaaaaa!

New dimensions for the New Age... New shapes... New sounds... New smells... Wake up calls... Thrill of the New... Dynamism... Beauty in things you never thought of... No more sleeping puppies... No more bowls of daffs... See the sweet pearly teeth of the rotting dog carcass... See it in rubbish... The Naked Emperor's here for all to enjoy... Move with the times!... FUN!... Get Real!

Puppa puppah puppahahaaaa!

It went down very well. He spoke with huge enthusiasm and his audience clapped. He was aware of himself as he spoke. It was almost as if he was detached from himself and the slight dissonance caused by the memory of Jane's words 'What you are doing is rubbish' acted to give piquancy to the mix. It was like a sort of counterpoint to the trumpeting – or, as it were, salt in the stew.

He rang Jane just as soon as he could. 'I… I enjoyed meeting you yesterday.'

She was surprised to hear him, 'Oh yes?'

'I… er… just wondered whether we might be able to meet for lunch some time and talk some more?' he was rather hesitant.

'That's very kind of you,' she said. 'Very kind… But… no, I don't think we could.'

'No?'

'I don't have to explain myself do I?'

'But it sounds so rude…'

'About as rude as going into a gallery and asking for a coffee when you have no intention of buying, or even looking at the paintings.'

'Well… perhaps not rude – just a bit… crushing.'

Jane laughed. 'I'm at the blunt end of modern art. I don't like what you're doing and what you stand for. We're just on different sides of the fence. I don't want to land myself in long arguments about art. I know where I stand. I just couldn't possibly come out with you.'

'I'm sorry to hear that.' He rang off, confounded.

Mark was used to having his way with women. He was attracted to them in the same proportion as they were attracted to him, but he had learned after his phase of youthful promiscuity that women meant trouble and if you want to keep your sanity you have to ration them. Just two were enough – the cosy domesticity of his double stable. He had been faithful to them (apart from the occasional fling, justifiable in the circumstances of his life) in the many years they had been together; but now the pregnancy of Louisa had changed everything. Not that she was leaving his life exactly. He would probably pay for the baby, buy her a house in Palmer's Green and be acknowledged by the new sprog as some friendly "uncle". What was almost worse was the change in the whole status quo. His pleasures with Louisa would now be inhibited by restraint, as this new being, this tadpole, gradually prized them apart.

In the circumstances, there seemed nothing at all inappropriate in his desire to take Jane out to lunch. All he needed at the moment was her calm, gentle company, but just as he had extended this friendly hand and offered the prospect of a delightful and entertaining lunch, she had thrown it in his face. It was more than hurtful, it was disgusting. What a stupid woman – not worth bothering about. Nasty woman, in fact!

He turned to his computer to check the emails. He was startled to see the heading "Pratiranya" jump towards him. "Pratiranya" had been forgotten in the dramas of the last day and a half. He was surprised to find that his Romanian contact had been true to his promise to find the words.

Pratiranya

Who is it who binds
me to this wheel
this treadmill?
Who told the lies
That lured me in?
OH PRATIRANYA SET ME FREE
Who is it who?

Chained me to this wall
Who was it who?
gave me false promises
OH PRATIRANYA SET ME FREE

Who is it dragging me
down this deep dark hole?
Who is it cheating me?
Tell me the truth
OH PRATIRANYA SET ME FREE

Oh Pratiranya you will come to my rescue
You will set me free
Release me from myself
Take me to the hills
PRATIRANYA!
PRATIRANYA!

He stared at this for a few minutes but found it hard to understand. He was grateful to the Romanian who had told him a little about the Gypsy background. He supposed that it must have been the combination of the singer, the anger and the directness of the emotion, that had so gripped him but that didn't really explain it either.

The internal phone rang and Hazel told him that there was an artist come to see him. 'He told me that he has an appointment with you'

'Well then, send him through.'

The young man, was tall and thin and wearing a white shirt and tie, with a blue pullover, a tweed sports jacket and dark grey flannel trousers. He had a shock of light brown hair and intense blue eyes which were accentuated by the blue of his jersey. He looked like something straight out of the thirties. Mark knew at once what he was – he was a Fartoo.

In the world of retro penders, there was a subset, which was familiar to every gallery in the Bond Street area. These were the Fartoos – the hopefuls who trudged their way down Cork Street every day of the year with samples of their art, in the vain hope that the dealers would take them on. It was useless to explain that this was not the way galleries recruited these days. They came and still they came, the band of the Far Too Many Unrecognised Retro artists. They came in every size, shape, colour and sex. They brought their work in portfolios and plastic Selfridges bags, sheaves of slides and, recently, compact discs. Their courage and their optimism were commendable, but they could not realise that their enterprise was futile.

His gallery had a tradition, which he had never broken, of never turning an artist away without looking first at his work. Old Mr Booker had explained to him when he was a new recruit, 'Artists are all the same – good, bad and indifferent. We are making money out of them and the least we can do for the less fortunate ones is to look at their work. They don't really paint just for money. They like to show their work. If we look at it before rejecting them, it makes them feel better. We are a compassionate gallery.' Mark liked to keep the compassionate image. He turned to the young man and said, 'What can I do for you?'

'I made an appointment to see you. My name's Andrew Silverstone. I'd like to show you some work, if I may.'

'Yes, of course. I'm afraid I'm a little busy at the moment but if you'd like to leave it I'll have a look. And perhaps you could come back tomorrow.'

'Well… no. I've come from Derbyshire and I've got just one disc and I need to show it some other people.'

'All right I'll have a quick look at it. Tell me about yourself.

Where did you study and what sort of things do you do?'

'Oh, I came to art rather late. Did a law degree to please the family but wasn't happy with it. I trained in Lancashire and then the Academy Schools. My work is mostly landscape – in the tradition of Turner. Some say that I'm a romantic modernist.'

What one might call a classic Fartoo – Virtuous and Plodding.

The images now came up on the screen. As Retro art went, Mark could see that they were really rather good. Composition influenced by Cézanne perhaps, but style and technique completely his own. Landscapes with texture and a variety of different brush strokes both illuminating the form and suggesting great energy. Dark, strong and passionate colours. You could say it was a bit like Van Gogh out of Cezanne, but a Van Gogh of the North, tinged with the music of Neilson and Sibellius.

He said, 'Andrew I like these a lot… but they are not quite the sort of things we could show here, as you can see.'

'Yes,' he agreed amiably. 'I can see that, but I don't know how you can do it… this stuff – it's rubbish.'

Not more rubbish. He had had enough rubbish today. He smiled ingratiatingly. He was not to be drawn on this one.

'I'm sorry… but it's just not our style, I really can't help you. We show contemporary art here.'

'What you show is contemporary, but it isn't art.'

'Well, that's a matter of opinion. Styles change you know. It's the twenty-first century now.'

'You wear clothes don't you?' The young man became quite intense. 'Your trousers have two legs and your jacket has two arms. Clothes still fit. The style might be different, but you don't use things which aren't clothes and call them clothes, do you?'

Mark laughed at this. He had not heard it before.

'Look,' he said, 'I really haven't got all afternoon to argue with you about this. I think your work is very good for what it is. In fact, I know there is a gallery which might be able to help you.' He had had a brainwave and gave Andrew the address of Jane's gallery.

Andrew thanked him and got up to go. He waved his hand round the gallery as Mark showed him to the door. 'All this…' he said, 'It will pass. Art goes on and will survive.'

'Classic Fartoo,' Mark muttered to himself. 'Olympic class, Classic Fartoo.'

That night he dreamed that the Fartoos had formed an army and were marching against him. There they were, old ladies in hats swinging Sainsbury's and Marks and Spencer's carrier bags full of canvasses and rolled up paper; and young men and girls and Africans and Indians and Chinese, marching relentlessly down upon him. They were shouting 'Rubbish, Rubbish, Rubbish!'. Louisa was there pushing a pram, Millicent was a mounted police officer and Jane was armed with a Sten gun made of rolled up arts pages. There was a banner which he couldn't read, but which was getting larger by the minute. Then he saw that the banner was the Lichtenstein and was almost on top of him. Quickly he grabbed a red plastic tomato and squirted red ketchup all over the painting which now collapsed and lunged towards him. The neck of the tomato grew into a snake and the ketchup formed the word "labyrinth". He woke up sweating and shaking.

He was so shaken, he could not go back to sleep. He went down to the kitchen to make some tea. Sushi rubbed against him hopefully. He bent down to caress her. As he fumbled for the tea he found himself reflecting that the kitchen could really do with one single vulgar object like a bright red plastic tomato.

It was odd how the plastic tomato had returned in his dream. It was something he had seen as a child in his grandmother's kitchen in Hendon. Later on at a teenage party he had seen another and was fumbling with it, admiring its voluptuous curves when he was carried away by the urge to squeeze. The resultant parabola of crimson sauce surged over the table and onto the frontage of the only attractive girl at the party. It was the abrupt ending of any potential relationship.

Yet he still had a hankering for just one red, plastic tomato. If only an expensive one could be found in a gallery, he would be able to justify its acquisition. If only one of the bright new hopes for British Art could mount an installation based on nostalgic items from the '50s. But otherwise it would not be possible. There were disadvantages to living on the frontiers of art.

CHAPTER 14

Expanding Widthways

Mark was still in the papers, the serious ones this time, as well as The Cosmos, which gave him a cursory apology in the form of, *"Mark said he didn't say art was rubbish. Instead he explained why he thinks rubbish is art. That is when it appears in art galleries, it's to make you feel better about rubbish… Not very kind to art is it?"* The serious press said things like, *"Leading gallerist denies he said modern art was rubbish,"* and went on to give a fairly accurate summary of what he had actually said.

There was also more fallout. Some joker had managed to dump a pile of rotten mattresses outside the gallery with a note *"Best wishes from the Garbage Appreciation Society"*. It was irritating to have to organise its removal but his PRO was delighted. It was good publicity for the gallery and highly auspicious for Charlene's show.

He found that he was still angry with Louisa and decided that he would leave her in the cold for a bit. The trouble was that he missed her. She was his final refuge – his comforter. When he was with her he had a sense of being at home, a feeling that was completely absent from the impeccable house in Canonbury.

He did not feel at all guilty towards Louisa, and yet there was an uncomfortable twinge when she had accused him of having used her for five years. It was a bit like the "I've given you the best years of my life" line of so much cheap drama. Had he really monopolised her? He had always made it clear that he did not mind if she had other lovers. His advanced modern standpoint became a bit fuzzy at this point, because there was a discrepancy between theory and practice and he was jealous if he detected the slightest sign of a rival for her affection.

He was also angry with Jane. So angry indeed that he felt like jumping into his car and driving over to tell her just what a stupid, prejudiced and backward looking female she was. She was obviously used to having her own way in arguments and it was time she learnt something; something that only he could teach her. How dare she be so rude as to refuse his invitation on the strength of what she would no doubt refer to as her 'principles'? It was time she woke up, discarded her prejudices and learned to flow with the stream. It was such a novelty for him to be rejected and doubly frustrating when that rejection came from a well-educated and good-looking woman with whom he had enjoyed arguing. In the past, particularly in his undergraduate days, beautiful and intelligent women seemed to be queuing up to be seen on his arm. The problems usually came later, like when the reigning mistress resented her successor; but for someone to reject him out of hand on something so puny as a lunch invitation, just because of some sort of belief system, was totally outside his experience.

It was a neat idea to send her Andrew – a latter day Van Gogh – with failure written all over him.

At least his work offered distraction. The business of running two galleries, placating clients and sponsors, networking with important contacts, publicity and the constant swirl of social life, kept him increasingly busy. The whirlwind he was caught up in seemed to be revolving with increasing speed.

Millicent was, as usual, busy, tense and distracted. Sometimes she was in a good mood, but mostly she was rather cross and she was always in a hurry. There was never time to talk. The thought occurred to him many times that he ought to make a bigger effort to get her attention. He ought to ask her out to lunch, for example. Somehow, however, every time this thought came, it was replaced by another pressing matter and he never did anything about it. Millicent and Mark were mutually neglectful of each other.

When he thought about it, which was not often, he reflected that a slow change had happened since their early days together. In those days, although she had always been rather self-contained, she was more biddable, more interested in his work and less tense, but as the years went by, she had become increasingly driven. Her ambitions grew with every year and she organised her household with meticulous precision in order to achieve them. Mark felt continually pushed into the background of her life. When, occasionally, they passed some time together, a drink perhaps or waiting for the children, they made polite conversation and enquired about each other's lives with no real sign of interest. Nowadays her face, so beautiful in her youth, was slightly scarred with a sort of hardness.

But he thought again about the little scene in the kitchen that morning. Why did that look of utter dejection sweep over her face, when she had seemed so chirpy earlier on? Perhaps it really was time to ring her and make an appointment for lunch and then they could talk in peace.

Unfortunately, once again the momentum of his life swept him along. He was caught up in the business of setting up the new show which was to occupy him totally for the next few days.

This was Charlene Winterbutton's first one-man show. It was not, however, her first contact with the public, for Charlene rose to fame with her exhibit "Bloo Loo" which won the prestigious Charles Henry Darwin prize two years ago. Since then her work had been included in every group show of the work of the Young British Artists and she had become a television personality in her own right. Last year she exhibited the amazing "Map of my Love Life". This consisted of a wall-size map of England that included everywhere between Liverpool and London, (with a small insert for Belgium) with every place where she had had sex marked in yellow marker pen. It was a sensation. Like Mark, she now had to ration the journalists.

Mark was always happy when a new exhibition was being set up. There was a highly charged atmosphere in the gallery and a feeling of excitement and creativity. There were mishaps, quarrels, hurt feelings to be soothed and even occasionally blood to be wiped up but it was always fun, and spirits were high.

The work was done by a small company that he had set up himself. It was a group of talented and versatile craftspeople whose skills ranged from theatrical set design to metal and concrete construction and included sourcing for those things which they themselves could not provide, like, for example, formaldehyde. He was lucky to have found a considerable fund of talent, very often from the same source as the artists themselves, for art schools contained large numbers of people who were not going to make it into the headlines with the originality of their creativity and were only too happy to be employed in the materialisation of their colleagues' ideas.

"Expanding Widthways" took a week to set up in the Cork Street Gallery and this was just the small, condensed version. All day the team hammered and heaved and set into place a collection of cardboard tubes of varying sizes and immense quantities of a sort of rough white cotton wool, because the theme of the show was tampons. Not a new idea by any means – almost every art school degree show included tampons or condoms these days, but it was Charlene's supreme originality to have taken the concept a stage further and conceived of tampons of widely varying sizes, ranging from the minuscule to the mega. There were tiny little things, delicately embroidered and suspended in glass containers, larger ones ejecting from poster tubes, collections of which stood on end looking rather like organ pipes, which of course, in a sense, they were. The climax of the show was a vast explosion of white cotton wool the size of a double bed bursting out of a tube the size of a small rocket launcher.

It wasn't really cotton wool of course. On that scale it has to be a clever combination of foam with a covering of combed shaggy cotton, replicating cotton wool. On the opening night they would hire a scantily-dressed model to recline on this. In the meantime, the exhibits had to be assembled and fixed securely, numbered and titled, the whole gallery lined in red linen, and various little squabbles resolved, such as the relative sizes of the lineage for the sponsor, a well-known maker of sanitary towels, and Charlene. It was the sponsor's idea to have its name in a set of gold plastic letters two feet high under one of the red linen walls. This had to be fixed so that it did not fall and could not be kicked or even removed by unscrupulous visitors.

Mark surveyed the activity and felt a surge of excitement. It was going to be outrageous – something that was becoming increasingly difficult these days.

Charlene was a genius – of this he had no doubt. Ever since she had first been spotted by his scout in the second year of her degree course, he had known that she was outstanding. She exuded confidence, bursting with vitality. Of course she had changed a bit in the last few years. She no longer sported a short ruffianesque hair-do in dyed crimson, a nose ring and an obscenely short leather mini skirt. She still chewed gum on occasions but had learned to direct her spit a little more discretely, at the general public rather than the media and the clients. Like many of her successful colleagues she had shown her creativity in a variety of projects, singing in a rock band, starting her own restaurant, opening a boutique and staging her own group show with her friends in a disused chapel in Bethnal Green. To be taken on by Arniston Crocker meant that you had to prove that you had entrepreneurial skills as well as the personality of a successful pop singer.

She now burst into his office wearing a cashmere jersey over her designer jeans and an outrageous necklace made of miniature mobile phones and skulls.

'F★★★ing bloody 'ell, Mark. What's this about the lineage? I don't want these bloody great letters all over the place. It's not their thing is it? They've done bloody nothing.'

'Well they have paid for the installation.'

'F★★★ing 'ell.' She walked in fury up and down the office.

'And they're buying the largest exhibit for their New York Office.'

'Bloody Hell.' She picked up a chunk of cotton wool and started fiddling about with it.

'And they're paying for your flight to New York later on this year. Do you really want to cancel all these things?' Mark gave her a big smile.

'Bloody Hell. They're bloody commercial creeps.' She began to calm down. 'OK… ok… I suppose I'll have to go along with it. What time's the press showing?' The cotton wool was now being spun into long snake-like strands.

'Ten o'clock. I like your necklace by the way.'

She grinned. 'Yeah. It's good isn't it? My friend Mick made it for the shop. It's called "Call Centre". I've gotter to go. There's a lunch at Tate Modern for prize winners.'

'Do you think it looks good — apart from the lineage?' He flicked a small piece of cotton wool off his jacket.

She threw the white, newly-spun snakes into his waste basket.

'Mark… it's greeate,' she accentuated her Liverpool accent.
She leaned over the desk and gave him a light kiss.
'Seeya…' and breezed out.

What he loved about Charlene was that she was so natural.
He felt that she was right to object to the lineage but there
was nothing he could do about it. The sponsors were going
to get a huge amount of publicity from her show. In fact
what she had done was to provide them with the material
for much of their advertising and promotion in the next few
years. They would make millions out of it, but then it was so
good that industry was now subsidising art. They were like
Renaissance princes in the days of Florence.

His secretary poked her head round the door. 'Call for
you.' He picked up the phone.

'Oh, hullo Mark, it's Andrew Silverstone.'

Who in the wide world was Andrew Silverstone? A waste
of time probably. 'Yes?'

'I just wanted to thank you for recommending me to Jane
Gresham. She's going to give me a show – and quite soon
because she's had a cancellation. I'm absolutely thrilled. I
can't thank you enough.' It all came back to him, the Retro
Fartoo of last Wednesday, while the mention of Jane touched
a sore place.

'Well… that's excellent. Congratulations.'

'Yes well… I'll send you an invitation for the private
view.'

'Yes do. Now I'm afraid I'll have to go, we're in the middle
of hanging a show here.'

'Oh, I'm sorry to have bothered you.' Andrew rang off,
politely.

He felt glad that Jane was giving him a show. He could see
it all. They would have cheap wine, not even Prosecco, orange
juice (from concentrate) crisps and oily peanuts at the private

view. A few members of his family and about twelve of his friends would come and three would buy paintings for three figures at the most. The rest of the framed work would have to be transported back to Yorkshire or wherever he lived. He would be unlikely to cover his costs and the show would be a disaster. Good for both of them. He smiled in grim satisfaction.

At the party for Charlene they would have champagne, quails' eggs and little pieces of lobster on cocktail sticks with a ginger sweet and sour dip. All the gang would be there – the gossip columnist dream list, loud voiced, extravagantly dressed – the people whose perception was so refined that they not only saw but loved, the Emperor's New Clothes. There would be music and the flashing of press cameras. In the background there would be a discreet signing of cheques for poster prints of the work. 'Art would survive' as Andrew had said.

He needed to leave the gallery early because he had to meet the Men in Grey – the backers for his East End Gallery, AC2E, which had been expensive to convert. Millicent had been helpful with her contacts and the little group met every quarter, 'just a courtesy meeting' to confirm that everything was all right, which it always was. And this meeting, at the offices of a City merchant banker, was no exception – the programme for the next nine months was approved unanimously.

At last he was free. Perhaps tonight, he might manage to have a few quiet words with Millicent? And soon perhaps, like tomorrow maybe, he might do something about the Lichtenstein?

CHATER 15

Two Couples

The news that Henrietta had a new lover was not met with any great excitement by her circle. It was too regular an occurrence to have any novelty value and speculation devolved as to whether it would last one, two or three weeks.

He bought her a crimson cape lined with emerald faux fur and she gave him a small jade elephant she had bought in India; but this rosy splurge of giving did not last. In the circumstances, it was indeed rather surprising that the whole affaire lasted more than a week for Henry and Henrietta were adept at devising new ways of winding each other up. They missed appointments, kept each other waiting, continuously disturbed and interrupted each other and complained loudly about how ill treated they were.

Henry found that Henrietta expected his attendance as a courtier while she held court with other admirers who, when they were around, took precedence.

Henrietta found that Henry was prone to making appointments he did not keep. Furthermore he was impossibly secretive. He wouldn't even tell her his address or phone number. Instead he gave her a little green mobile which had his number programmed into it. While she could turn hers off at any time, it was noticeable that he was unavailable for much longer periods than she was. He seemed to have several different mobiles – there was a yellow one that rang a lot and he would talk very fast in another language that she could not recognise. When she asked him, he just said it was a downtown Boston dialect.

She puzzled greatly why she could not be told his address. He said he lived in a penthouse in South Kensington. That could mean anything – a beat-up bedsitter off the Fulham Road, or something grand in Onslow Square. But which? He did not appear to be short of funds – they had some extravagant meals together and he bought her that fur-lined velvet cape, which she adored, but he could not and would not let her visit his home. She decided that he probably didn't live anywhere near South Kensington, but took the tube to his humble dwelling in Hounslow or Perivale.

Neither Henry nor Henrietta had much real attraction for each other. They were not in the least in love and what sex there was, was fast and furious. Novelty and curiosity brought and held them together and when the first had worn off and the second had been fulfilled (as much as was possible) then the affair was doomed.

They talked of art. Henrietta asked for his opinions about all the Young British Artists and he said they were great. Was he going to show them in his gallery? No.

Henrietta was suspicious. She steered the conversation round to his opinions of American artists. He liked all the well known ones.

'But what about Lonny Donsdorf in Boston – what do think about him?'

'Oh… I just love his work…it's so abrasive,' he said.

Aha, Henrietta told herself. *Just as I expected – This man is a fraud.* For "Lonny Donsdorf" was a name she had just invented.

'So if you're not going to show Young Brits what are you going to show?'

'What I'm gonna do is beyond present level of art. It's new generation – new level. It comes from art itself.'

'What do you mean exactly?'

He would laugh and tickle her under the chin.

'My sweet little thing. Don't you go asking too many questions. Your head may drop off.'

'But Henry, you've been putting up the hopes of the young hopefuls. Isn't that a bit unkind?'

'Who told you that?' he said sharply.

'The artists themselves – Mona and Murdoch.'

'They gat the wrong end of the stick.'

'Are you really going to destroy Arniston Crocker?'

'Sure. That's not an issue. When my gallery opens it will be a major detonation. It'll make Krakatoa as trivial as a bag of chips bustin'. I'm tellin' you, no-one, but no-one will go near Cork Street again.'

'I don't believe you!'

'Lady, you don't have to. This is for real. It's gonna happen.'

'I can't wait,' Henrietta said. It was not that she wanted anything detrimental to happen to her friend Mark, it was just that she wanted to see exactly what Henry could produce that was going to be so explosive.

Henrietta couldn't bear not being told Henry's address. One evening, when they had been to a show at the Tate Modern together, she took advantage of a sudden downpour of rain to offer Henry a lift. She had offered him lifts before but he had never accepted. But this time, the rain and the difficulty of finding a taxi made him give in.

When they reached Old Brompton Road, he said, 'Stop here – will walk the rest – it'll save you a journey.'

She stopped and let him off. To her surprise he did not walk further along the road but turned back the way they had come. She watched in her car mirror for a moment but then put her hand on the gear lever to start to move off. But just as she did so she noticed something on the passenger seat. She picked it up. It was a small metal box, like a cigarette case only not quite the same shape. It had a catch in the side but she couldn't open it. She looked in her mirror again and could still see Henry walking rapidly along the road. On an impulse she leaped out of the car and pelted after him not minding about the rain. She was just in time to see him turn up a side street and into a large terrace house with steps up to the front door. She went up to it and noticed that it had been turned into five flats. Four of them had names on the bell plates, but the fifth just said "Penthouse". *Aha* she said to herself, *now I know*. She reached out her hand to ring the bell, but before she could touch it a soft voice spoke from behind her, 'Hey? You lookin' for someone?'

It was a small, swarthy looking man in jeans and anorak. He was very close to her and a bit frightening.

'Yes,' she said, turning to face him, 'Henry Streffelguese.'

'Oh… I work for him. You wanna me take you up?'

'No… all I want is to give him something he left in my car.'

'OK… I take.'

She handed over the box and he nodded, let himself into the house and disappeared without more ado.

Henry did not speak of the incident. But nor did he ask about the box so she decided that he must have got it.

Shortly after that one Sunday morning, when they were in bed together, Henrietta found that she had a mysterious pain in her chest. She rang the doctor who promised to come right away. Henry got up and hastily dressed so that he could let the doctor in when he arrived. On the doctor's arrival, Henry was despatched to the sitting room next door while Henrietta, stark naked under the lace-bordered sheets on her king-sized bed, received him. The doctor, who was an old friend, could not find very much wrong with her and fell back on advising her to rest. It just happened that he was also very interested in anthropology and they had an intense and absorbing discussion about the Congo Basin, which lasted for about an hour.

When he left, Henrietta remembered that Henry was waiting next door – but Henry was not waiting. He had let himself out by the front door and left. That was The End! She walked down to Chelsea Bridge, anger having revived her strength, threw the green telephone into the Thames and watched it sink with glee. But she kept the cape.

'I'm coming to London soon,' Andrew had said on the phone. 'One of my new paintings has got stuck. I need to look at some Art.'

Jane enquired about his painting and he told her in great detail about the walk he had been on and the extraordinary and dramatic weather effects which he was trying to capture. He got so carried away that he forgot his main purpose. He rang again.

'Forgot to say. Would you like to come with me?'

'Whose work?' asked Jane.

'Turner and Constable. There's something I have to find out about skies. Something not quite right in what I'm doing just now and I know I've just got to look at a master. I'll be coming on Wednesday.'

'I'd love to, but I can't. I'm tied to the gallery on Wednesdays. My assistant only comes in two days a week and Wednesday is not one of them.'

'Oh.' He sounded so disappointed. 'But why don't you close the gallery. Does it have to be open on Wednesday? You told me hardly anyone comes.'

He was right. The idea was unthinkable but the more she thought about it, the more attractive it became.

'All right. I'll close the gallery and have an unscheduled day off.'

'Will you meet my train at Euston?'

'If it's not coming in at too unsociable an hour.'

The decision was taken. Jane felt a bit as though she was truanting from school, but this was absurd. She was in charge of her own business; she was entitled to take a day off now and then.

The train came into Euston on time and Jane waited at the gate. She spotted him long before he saw her. Tall, shaggy and wild-eyed with his bright blue sweater and tweed sports jacket. She wondered what he had worn when he was a solicitor. She couldn't imagine his ever having had a suit. She had a wild and romantic surge of excitement. Perhaps he would carry her off and they would dance and sing, naked upon a mountain top.

The day was like a blast of fresh air. Not so much a blast, more like a hurricane. They did so much. They went and saw Turner watercolours at the British Museum, where Andrew had a friend who allowed them to see the collection. They went to the National Gallery, the Victoria and Albert and the Tate Britain, to look at more Turners and Constables. He talked about skies and dynamism and infrastructure and subtle shapes and showed her things in paintings she had never noticed. It was like a condensed lesson in nineteenth century painting. They had sandwiches in coffee bars and he talked about his painting. It was exhilarating, but as the day worn on, she began to feel increasingly weary. There was so much to see and so much pushing about in crowds on tubes and buses.

At the end of the afternoon he said, 'I think we've had enough now of the Romantics. Shall we go to the Courtauld and look at the Cézannes?'

'Don't let me put you off,' she said with a sweet if wan

smile. 'I have seen enough art now – I feel rather tired and I'd like to put my feet up.'

'Oh,' he was suddenly all solicitude. 'I've dragged you round too much. I get so carried away – I'm not in London that often and I try and pack in as much as possible. But I really don't need to see Cézannes today. Let's go and have a drink.'

This seemed a much better idea and they went to a comfortable and not too crowded pub. He bought two beers and when he returned with them said, 'What are you doing this evening? I thought of going to the Coliseum and seeing if I could get in to the new Lohengrin everyone is raving about. Would you like to come too?'

'That sounds like a good idea. But I really do feel quite tired after everything we've seen today and I'm sorry but I think I'd like to go home and have a rest. It's been a marvellous day for me. I have felt very inspired by seeing those paintings with you. You have opened my eyes to so many things and I feel confirmed in my feelings about art.'

'Lohengrin is a very restful opera.'

'Yes, I'm sure. But I really do prefer Mozart.' She was beginning to feel pains in her feet.

'I love Mozart too.'

'Perhaps we'll go to one some other time.'

'I'd love that.'

She got up to go. 'I've got to thank you for a wonderful day.' She did not want him to try and persuade her to change her mind, much though she hated disappointing him.

'I'm so pleased that you are my friend,' he said very simply.

'Yes,' she said hastily. 'We are good friends.' She could not quite bring herself to add the corollary that good friends knew when to let each other go, but then he did not seem to be too disappointed at her refusal to accompany him to Lohengrin.

'I'll see you when you come to Buxton.' She had told him that she would come to his studio to choose the paintings for his exhibition, take them to London and supervise the framing with a framer she knew.

'I'm looking forward to that.'

They made their farewells cheerfully.

Jane could not stop yawning in the bus on the way home. Was she in love with Andrew? He occupied her mind a lot at the moment. He was so genuine, such a strong person, so enthusiastic and so energetic.

She had loved visiting the galleries and museums with him. He had such vision and such commitment. It was exciting being with him because you never knew what he was going to come out with next. What she also liked about him was the fact that he was very restrained, made no insinuations and no passes at her, although he also made it clear that he liked her very much. On the other hand, there was this voice at the back of her head – this voice which said 'and yet'. It was as if she had two personalities inside her – the passionate romantic self, "Appassionata" and the sensible, restraining "Prudence". At the end of the day, footsore from the pavements, it was "Prudence" who won out over the "Appassionata" who had stood that morning at the gate at Euston Station.

CHAPTER 16

Sushi Bars

The Sushi Bar was situated on the seventh floor of a building that overlooked the Thames. There was a view of barges calmly gliding up and down the cappuccino-coloured river – a colour which almost exactly matched her superbly cut suit.

Sushi was Millicent's favourite food. The ritual of preparation and service as much as the appearance and taste of the beautiful pieces. She loved watching the procession of delicate, bite-sized morsels on saucers, each one a work of art in itself, as they flowed round on the silent conveyor belt, while in the middle a team of Japanese men, as immaculately white-coated as surgeons, chopped, slashed and spread with gleaming razor-sharp blades, slaving to create more exquisite packages as fast as they were consumed.

There was always the slight frisson, which added to the excitement, that the person next to you might lift off the saucer you had your eye on, but it wasn't really a problem because it was always instantly replaced. It was so delightful to have small helpings, to be able to have more of anything you wanted and to have such variety.

Millicent and her companion were talking rather intently about investments, futures and business prospects generally, the sort of conversation that is utterly boring unless you happen to be interested in that sort of thing. It was Mark's great failing that he wasn't.

They were talking with great intensity, but there was a sort of nervousness about them, which an onlooker might have taken for the fact that neither of them was entirely committed to the conversation. They would draw to a stop and then start rather hurriedly as if the pause might be an excuse for discussing something they were afraid of. This conversation was a prelude for other matters.

Her companion was a benign looking middle-aged man with large craggy eyebrows and running to overweight. He was Sir Charles Ruislip, the chairman of a small merchant bank, Riverside Securities.

Presently, after another glass of Chablis, the conversation became even more desultory. He seized his opportunity during a pause and regarding her with great affection said, 'Millicent, you're keeping me in suspense, you know. There are two things I need to know… you know what they are.'

She looked down for a moment and then turned towards him, 'The second test was OK. It's only a cyst. I've had it seen to.'

'Thank goodness for that! I'm so pleased, my dear. And… er… the other thing… now that you've thought about it?'

'Yes.' She was silent for a minute.

'You mean 'yes' you've thought about it. Or 'yes' you will?' There was a prolonged pause.

'Yes … I will.' She was trembling and spoke very quietly.

'Oh my darling…' He was so overcome he couldn't speak for a moment. There were tears in his eyes. Then he reached into his breast pocket and took out a small package. In the package there was a dark red satin bag and in the bag a little leather-tooled box. He opened the box and tipped something out. 'I want you to have this. I know you can't wear it straight away. There's a lot to go through.' It was a very large diamond.

She gasped. 'But Charles… this is a bit premature! I've got to tell Mark and make arrangements, tell the children… and everything.'

'I know. I know there are things which are not so easy.

That's why I thought you'd like to have a big shiny thing just to prove it all the time. Something you can touch and hold when I'm not around.'

'It's finding time to see Mark. He's so busy. Sometimes I think I'll have to ring his secretary and make an appointment to see him.'

'He has neglected you for years.'

'No. Not really. It's just that he is so caught up with what he's doing. As long as he has clean shirts and warm croissants for breakfast, he's fine.'

'And you have to be the one who provides this as well as doing a full-time job!' said Charles, one of whose plans for Millicent was to release her from full-time work so that she could do these things for him. There was nothing like a nice warm croissant to round off a good breakfast of ham and eggs. He asked, 'Have you ever thought you might like to move on from investment management and take up directorship?'

'Well of course. I'd love to become a director.'

'I could probably find you some non-executive director-ships if you liked. But I can't have you over-working, my darling. We have waited so long to be together. I must have a little time with you.' His views of women in business were thoroughly modern and liberal. He felt fine about their being directors, but the really beautiful ones belonged in beautiful homes rather than City offices.

She beamed at him.

'As long as I'm in finance, I'll be happy. I'll microwave the croissants for you.'

Charles had been divorced for ten years.

'I can do a lot of things for myself. I'm really grown up, but I'm thinking about Galveston Place.' This was a large house he had recently bought in Buckinghamshire. 'It's going to take a lot of organising. I can't wait to show it to you.'

'I can't wait to see it. But Charles...' Millicent suddenly had a vision of herself in Wellington boots and a green quilted jacket. 'Much though I love the country, there is one thing I can never do.'

'What's that?'

'I could never vote Tory.'

He laughed comfortably. 'That's not a problem. We're all the same these days. You'll be saved from the boredom of the Conservative fête, that's all.' Quietly and methodically he put the diamond away. And then a thought struck him.

'And what about the children, will they be alright?'

'Yes... I think so. Mark and I don't have any issues about things like that. I'll probably have custody and he will have as much access as he likes. It's so much easier to arrange these things if they're at boarding school. In the holidays they tend to spend a lot of time with their grandparents. I worry about telling them, though. But as I'm going on that conference in Sweden quite soon and Mark is fetching them for half term, I think he will have to do it.'

'That's all right then.' Charles reached over and picked up her hand. 'Let's have some champagne to celebrate. And there's no reason why we shouldn't take the stone to a jeweller and decide how it's going to be made up, is there?'

She was silent. It was not a sudden decision, she had been thinking about it for weeks – he had given her plenty of time. Also she had felt like leaving Mark for a long time before that, though not continuously. She liked the externals of their marriage; the house, their style. She knew she would miss these. Also she felt a little apprehensive about what she was letting herself in for. But she knew inside that the marriage was over and had been for many years. It was time for something new.

He looked at her with great compassion and said, 'It's hard

isn't it? I know what it's like from the other side when Nancy left me. But I respected her for the way she told me. You have to be completely honest and avoid face-saving lies. Mark will be upset of course. You can't avoid that, but he'll get over it more quickly if you are straight with him.'

She fidgeted with her glass.

'Mark will be upset, but he's pretty resilient, and he does have other interests to distract him.'

'You mean he has a mistress?'

She nodded.

'It must have been hurtful for you.'

'Yes, but there were lots of things I enjoyed, although for a long time now I've had the feeling that we were somehow, both of us, complete and total strangers to each other. It was all outside.'

Charles gave her hand an affectionate squeeze, 'You might like to move out quite soon… into neutral territory, as it were, while you are sorting things out. I have a flat in Holborn you might like. I bought it for my son when he was at SOAS.'

Millicent closed her eyes.

'That would be very nice.' She sighed, though whether this was from happiness or the concerns of the moment was hard to tell.

The champagne came. Charles said, 'To another future – ours!' as they clinked glasses.

The thought of telling Mark hung over Millicent like the prospect of a root canal filling at the dentist. Their marriage might have dwindled to an elegant façade, but it was still there – a large part of her life. They were mutually neglectful of each other but there wasn't anything else until now; and now she was having to dismantle an edifice that had been created over a long period with a lot of care.

She pondered the enormity of what she was undertaking – a huge change in lifestyle. The surrender of left-wing radical chic to country and Conservative values. Even if she were allowed to vote Labour, avant-garde glitz would be replaced with fine art and antiques, Canonbury for Kensington and a whole new scene in Buckinghamshire. But, at least, it would not be too hard on the children. They would enjoy a large garden and the possibility of pets. Also, Charles, who had three grown-up sons, seemed to like children and had told her that he would enjoy their company.

She would like the blow to fall cleanly and painlessly. If only there as an agency that would carry out this sort of surgery for you, you could go away on holiday for a fortnight and when you returned everything would be sorted out neatly and efficiently.

She was helped by the knowledge that Mark was not faithful to her. This had not bothered her too much after the pain of her initial discovery. The intense business of both their lives meant that she was satisfied with what he was able to do for her. But now, as she felt the attraction of someone who could really place her first in his life, she was beginning to realise that Mark's infidelity had concerned her more than she had allowed herself to think.

So she would have to live through the dreaded, dramatic scene; there was no other way. She decided that she would take the bull by the horns and tell him that night. Then she remembered – it was the party for Charlene. He would be late home and rather drunk. It would have to wait until morning.

It was a brilliant stroke on Charles' part to provide her with an interim home where she could sort things out and gradually become acclimatised. Somewhere where she could have peace and the privacy of her own space.

She thought about Charles. She also had an agenda for him. It had to do with his waistline.

The phone rang and Jane picked it up.

'Jane?'

'Oh, hello Edwin.'

'I wondered if you would like to help me… celebrate. An aunt has left me some money. It's almost enough to reroof Lostock Hall so I might… as well spend some of it.'

'That's very kind of you. But…' She clawed around for excuses.

'Look … I promise I won't propose. It's not too difficult.'

She laughed.

Edwin continued, 'Have you ever eaten Sushi?'

'No.'

'Neither have I, but I just thought it would be nice to try.'

'That sounds lovely.'

'Next Wednesday perhaps? By the way, I heard that that dreadful… Arniston Crocker has been visiting you.'

'Well… yes. But he only came in because his car had broken down nearby. He wasn't the least interested in the paintings. I told him a few things. It was good fun. He rang me the next day and asked me out to lunch and I refused. I don't think he'll bother me again.'

'Oh good.' Edwin sounded relieved. 'I don't want to have to… mount an armed guard on your gallery.'

'I was quite blunt with him so I really don't think there was any risk.'

'I've been following the publicity in the papers recently – he sounds dreadful.'

'Yes I know. But Edwin, I don't think he's that bad. He looked so miserable and exhausted I felt quite sorry for him.

It's not entirely his fault that I'm doing so badly; it's no use making him a scapegoat.'

'What do you mean exactly?'

'I got the feeling that he was not as much in control as he would like to be.' Jane was feeling just the slightest twinge of regret that she had stuck to her principles and passed over the chance to continue the argument with someone who was clever. But she did not feel like further discussion with Edwin about this so she changed the subject. 'Anyway he has given me a present – in a rather strange form. He recommended me to a brilliant artist, Andrew Silverstone. I think he's a genius... a real romantic. You'd love him.'

'And are you... in love with him?'

'Oh Edwin! You don't understand anything, do you? I couldn't fall in love with anyone so instantly.'

'So perhaps... there's some hope for me?'

'Edwin if you go on like this I won't see you again.'

'I was only teasing.'

'I was telling you about Andrew because his painting is quite remarkable and his exhibition is going to be something to look forward to.'

'I'm looking forward to the Sushis... And Jane?'

'Yes?'

'Perhaps when we meet... you can advise me... how I'm to find a wife.'

CHAPTER 17

The Party For Charlene

While Millicent was having her momentous lunch with Charles Ruislip, Mark was lunching with Henrietta.

'I've got to see you,' she had said on the phone sounding rather dramatic. 'It won't be possible to talk privately tonight. I've found something out!' They met at a small, Italian restaurant round the corner from the gallery.

'I've got to know Henry Streffelgueze a bit,' Henrietta began importantly.

'So I've heard,' Mark replied with a grin.

'And he stinks.'

'Yes, I've heard that too. But in what way does he stink?'

'He's an absolute bounder. Horrible man. Manipulative, secretive and patently up to no good.'

'Anything else?'

'The trouble is that it's very hard to find out anything. He wouldn't even tell me where he lives – the only way I had of contacting him was on a mobile which he supplied with his number programmed into it in such a way as you couldn't even find that out. He's sinister.'

They ordered lasagne, spinach and mineral water.

'Did you find out what he's up to?'

'He seems to be converting this sugar mill, but he keeps his cards very close to his chest. He says that what he's about to do will blow the current notions of contemporary art sky high. He doesn't exactly say what this will be, but I have found out three things which are a little strange.'

'Yes?'

'One is that he likes to tease young artists into thinking that he's trying to take them away from their present dealers – but actually he hasn't much intention of using them, as far as I've been able to find out.'

'And the other?'

'Well, he says he has some experience as an art dealer in Boston. He didn't have a gallery there, but dealt in penders like me from his home – only he gave me to understand that it was a rather bigger operation than mine. I've got lots of friends in the Boston art world so I rang them and asked them about him. Not one of them had heard anything at all about him.'

The waiter now brought them antipasta in the form of olives, mozzarella and anchovies. Mark helped himself to a large slice of mozzarella, 'Of course it could be possible that he just dealt in a few works to big clients. You can hand over large sums of money in the art world these days without any attention.'

'Yes, it could be.' Henrietta attacked the anchovies. 'Or it could be that he had another name. But it is a bit puzzling all the same and he seems hell-bent on destroying you and every other gallerist in the trade. But why? He seems very driven by something, but it's not enthusiasm – it sounds more like hatred.'

'He doesn't give any reasons for his hatred?'

'Not a crumb. He just ticked me off in a patronising way for asking too many questions.' She played with a piece of ciabatta.

'You said there were three things – what was the third?'

'Oh yes. I tested him by asking him about an artist who didn't exist – a name I just made up and he said he loved his work! So he really is a fraud.'

'Henrietta, you are admirable. You've found out a lot. He

sounds really rather crazy.'

'That's what I think. Crazy and a bit dangerous. Will he be coming tonight?' She swallowed another anchovy.

'He hasn't been asked.'

'Do you have good bouncers?'

'The usual,' Mark grinned. The cutting edge of modern art was not without its hazards. There had been some private views for which the term 'lively' was a complete under-statement. Angry, frustrated artists, jealous ex-lovers, all sorts of situations would have ended in violence had it not been for his small team of tough but not too threatening men. There were four of them in all. They did not look like bouncers but they had all learned Japanese martial arts. They were known as "the friendlies". Mark was prepared for anything.

The lasagne now arrived and put further conversation at an end for the time being.

In the event, there were three incidents at the party that evening.

It started peacefully enough with a brief press conference before the public was admitted. Charlene arrived in a magnificent shimmering gown of puce ciré satin, that clung like wet seaweed to her fragile figure. There was an atmosphere of excitement.

'Charlene,' George Butternut of the Herald began, 'this is a great show. Can you tell us why you had to do it?'

'I wanted to do something that was just me.'

'But you always do something that's just you.'

'No. You see in "love map" it was about my lovers. I wanted to do something that just came out of me. No others. No men. You could say like crap. But everyone craps. I wanted something that was female. Tampons are it.'

'Would you say that you were making a statement for

femininity?' Elisabeth Jacob, of the Observer.

'Exactly. More like a celebration really.'

'But aren't tampons a shade déjà vu? Degree shows have had them for years.'

'Not six-foot long ones.'

There was a round of applause at this.

'It's an amazing show. I'm really thrilled with it. It puts feminism into a new dimension,' said Nigel Detchant.

'Yeah. Well I wanted to break out. Like blow out some boundaries. Get rid of the shit, like.'

'What are you going to do next Charlene?'

'I'm writing a book. I'm selling it page by page. They're going to be auctioned with my signature. Got as far as page 10 right now.'

'Do you like writing?'

'I love it. It's so much easier than art.' This caused laughter.

It was time for the public to come in. Charlene moved to the end of the gallery to receive, like royalty, the important guests who were presented to her by Mark and his assistants. The model, wearing a pink satin bikini top and pants, took up her position on the bed-sized giant tampon. Waiters began to take round trays of champagne and a group of quietly dressed men took up position round the entrance of the gallery.

As the guests started to arrive, Mark watched the critics talking amongst themselves. They were moving about excitedly, opening and closing up, almost as though they were in a dance. He heard fragments of what they were saying:

'Outrageously witty!'

'Challenges the last of our taboos!'

'Concept stretching!'

'Juxtapositional audacity!'

'Mind bogglingly brilliant!'
'Bloody cheek!'
'It's the red walls that do it for me!'
'So profound!'
'Terrifying!'
'No… just terrible!'
'Forces us to face up to the physical reality of our bodies!'
'Only if you are a woman, that is.'

The model lay back on the faked-up white fur and sipped her champagne. Mark felt very happy. He had chalked up another fantastic success.

The Arbuthnots arrived and Brünnhilde Strathpeffer with Albert in tow. Yvonne Miggins and stout old Stan Brontesfield. The Perenures the Dunwhatstabies and the Princess Oriana Fitzgibbon who was Russian; and there was dear Henrietta in her new outfit, gleaming breast-plates, cleavage and all under a sequin spangled fishnet body stocking, legs in gold thigh high boots.

More and more people came and the champagne began to flow freely as the waiters and waitresses brought round delicious canapés – the quails' eggs and the entrancing pieces of lobster and the delicate sauces to dip them in. Conversation flowed and the noise level rose.

Then there came a moment when it was apparent that a sense of strain was affecting some of the guests. People were disappearing off to the cloakrooms and returning with a look of slight frustration on their faces. Conversations were constricted by the need to watch the door and there was general sense of increasing discomfort. The toilets were reached by a lobby that gave out to a Ladies and a Gents. It was becoming clear that no-one had entered that door for some time.

It was the ever-responsible Hazel who realised what the problem was. She rushed up to Mark, gave him a gentle tug of the sleeve and whispered discreetly, 'Either someone has passed out in the toilets or the door has become blocked.'

'Oh my God!'

He started to move across the crowded room, but the situation was rescued by an unexpected intervention. Ethel Grulk, who said afterwards that not for nothing had she been trained as a sculptor, having had rather a lot to drink and poured out her heart to a very young gossip columnist, now saw her moment of glory and rose to it. She hurled herself at the door like a great battering ram and on the second attempt it cracked and gave way with a great splintering of the wood round the door handle. There was a cheer from the crowd and a wild surge of laughter. No-one appeared to be on the inside and the loos were now available again. A rather discreet queue began to form up and the sense of relief was palpable.

The next thing that happened was a man jumping on the model on the tampon bed. The bouncers pulled him off quickly before any harm was done, but she was very upset and had to be comforted in the office with a large whisky. Mark and Hazel decided that she had done her stint and could go home.

The party was now dying down but there were still many guests remaining. Now the crowd at the door felt a new sense of constriction – more people were suddenly arriving and pushing them further in. There were several young men in blue suits who rushed for the light switches, and four pretty girls in white drum majorettes' uniforms. They elbowed their way into the middle of the gallery and then all the lights suddenly went off. There was a loud bang and Henry Streffelgueze appeared in the entrance in a white suit.

The girls pranced round him chanting, 'Henry Streffelgueze, greatest of the great, prophet of the new art of the future, NOW, NOW, NOW!' and ended up cheering and kneeling in front of him.

Mark nodded at his team, who were recovering from the disarray of the previous incident and had been caught off guard. Henry and his maidens were escorted out gently and firmly. But the damage had been done; Henry had become the talking point of the exhibition.

Fortunately however, there were not so many journalists left at this point. The critics had all left and the gossip columnist had slunk off to write up the door-smashing incident for his deadline. The buzz of laughter and chatter started again. People were speculating as to whether the incidents had been staged by the same person. The waiters were now bringing round little pieces of deep-fried camembert and calm had returned to the gallery.

Mark suddenly felt very tired. 'Would you like a cup of tea?' Hazel suggested. He brightened. 'That's exactly what I'd love. And shall we have a spot of whisky in it?' He made it a rule never to drink at private views, but this one had been a bit more lively than usual.

Henrietta now joined the group in the office which contained, as well as a large desk, a round table for board meetings. 'I feel kind of responsible because Henry had the run of my drawing room recently. He must have looked at all my private view invites.' ·

'Oh – I'm sure someone like him would find out the private views in any case. Don't worry about it. But I'm really glad you warned me he might turn up. I had extra men on duty.'

'Do you think he was responsible for all three of the incidents?' Henrietta leaned back on her comfortable office chair.

'Who is this bummer?' Charlene asked.

'Should we call the police?' asked Anthony who was

fidgeting with a piece of paper to overcome his desperation for a cigarette. Fortunately, the office had a soothing atmosphere – it was lit by desk and standard lamps, not spotlights.

'He's the one who told Max and Karen that they were doomed if they stayed with me, but without making any promises to rescue them if I do sink like the Titanic.' Mark laughed hollowly and swung round to address those who hadn't managed to find a seat at the table. He continued, 'As far as we know, he's about to set up a gallery of his own in Deptford. He's got some crazy idea that in order to succeed he has to destroy every other gallerist in the field; and he hasn't even opened his gallery yet.'

'We ought to warn the others,' Hazel said.

'I think you should call the police,' said Nigel.

'I'd like to smash his face in,' was Charlene's contribution.

The whisky began to make a circuit of the table. Everyone had plenty of constructive ideas as well as quite a few destructive ones.

Mark said, 'I think we may have to call the police. There may be more to this than a mere publicity stunt. But I hate the idea, especially when it may result in giving him the sort of publicity he wants. So I think we might start with a debriefing session with "the friendlies". We'll ask them what they know; if we hadn't been so preoccupied we should have stopped them at the door.'

'Yes,' Hazel was discreetly gathering up glasses. 'And it might be an idea to alter the position of the light switches. They are a bit too accessible in that corner.'

They talked like this for some time as their nerves, aided by the whisky, cooled down. The party in the gallery was dying. The Arbuthnots and the Strathpeffers, neither of whom could ever leave a party without an elaborate play for the maximum amount of attention, came and said fond farewells and congratulated everyone.

Mark, feeling slightly sick, went home without any supper. He felt beyond eating, which was not typical at all.

CHAPTER 18

Telling Mark

He woke up with a half a yawn and half a groan as he remembered the events of the previous night.

'What's this?' He was a little surprised to be brought a cup of tea. It was something Millicent never did and there was something about the fact that she was fully dressed and made up that was ominous.

'I've brought you some tea,' she said.

She had drawn up a chair on his side of the bed and was looking horribly professional – like a consultant.

He propped himself on his elbows and took a sip of tea. There was a storm in the offing.

Millicent began, 'Mark, I have to tell you something.' Her tone was businesslike and quiet. 'It's something you won't like very much and I'm sorry if it's a shock. I'm going to leave you.'

'You are WHAT?' He took a gulp of tea.'

'I'm going to leave you. I want a divorce.'

He couldn't take it in, it was too early for his brain to cope.

'WHAT?' he repeated in a dazed tone.

She told him again.

He sat bolt upright in the bed and began to shout. 'RUBBISH!. You can't possibly… It's just not right…Not convenient at all. It's a piece of nonsense. YOU NEED THERAPY!'

'Mark I've been in and out of therapy for years. I've come to a conclusion and you are going to have to accept it. I am going to leave you and I want a divorce.'

'You have no idea what you want, Millicent. You're happy here. It suits you to be in this house.'

'You mean it suits you to have me in this house.'

He had blundered. Millicent always had a very clear idea of what she wanted.

He took another gulp of tea, closed his eyes for a moment and told himself to keep calm. It did not help. A wave of anger surged through him. He shouted, 'F… you. F… you Millicent. I don't want this at all! Do you know what you're doing. What about the children, for God's sake?'

Millicent pushed back a stray hair that had fallen across her forehead.

'I'm glad to hear you mention the children. It's such a long time since you spoke of Jonathan and Kate that I've been wondering if you still remembered that you had them. I'll have custody, of course, and you can see them just as much as you ever do, or more, if you want. They won't mind too much. It might be good for you to spend a bit more time with them.'

'That, coming from you, is rich! Whose idea was it to send them to boarding school when they were only five?'

Millicent did not rise to this. 'I don't think they need to suffer too much as long as we don't quarrel over them. Or in front of them. I've always believed you're reasonable and fair minded.'

Suddenly he thought about the anguish of being a single father and felt pathetic. You got landed with your little darlings for a whole weekend at a time. It was like having a ball and chain round your foot. Your scope for improvisation and adventure was totally restricted. You couldn't go out at night and they expected to be amused, restrained from quarrelling and fed all day. He knew all about this because it had happened to his friend Roger only a year ago. Trailing about with your kids to junk-food restaurants and going to see rotten films.

He sank back on the pillows and took another swig of tea. 'I don't want this Millicent. Particularly not now. I've got enough on my plate right now. You've chosen the very worst moment.'

'I am sorry not to have found a better time,' she replied tartly, 'but quite honestly, is there such a thing as the right moment for telling your husband that you are leaving?'

'All I would like to know is why? WHY?' He felt hysteria rising. 'We're so happy together. Everything works so well for us. We've got this lovely house and we've both got jobs we enjoy. I know we've been very busy recently and haven't had much time together.'

'We haven't spent any time together for years. And do you know why? It's because we don't enjoy being together. You have absolutely no interest in me whatsoever, as long as I manage your house and give good parties. Our marriage is a complete façade.'

She was right. Being right was one of her most irritating habits. But even so, he did not want it to end. He started racking his brains to think of ways of stopping her: holidays together, second honeymoon in Belize or Bali, counselling, another baby? What would she settle for? Could they enter negotiations? He winced.

'Could make it better... I mean, we could try... talking like now.'

She looked at him and shook her head slowly. 'It's too late,' she said and again he knew she was right.

Cogs began to whir at the back of his brain, 'Don't tell me you've found someone else?' He glared at her and noticed that she could not meet his eyes. 'You have, haven't you? You filthy bitch!'

Millicent went into the attack. 'That sounds very good coming from you of all people!' Anger had now overtaken compassion.

'What do mean?'

'You know perfectly well. Do I have to spell it out for you? I've been faithful to you, but you've been unfaithful to me for years and years. Now you've got a chance to marry your floosie'

'How dare you!' He was choked with fury. 'And might I know who the lucky man is? Presumably you're not going through all this in order to live on your f... ing tod?'

'Charles Ruislip.'

'That old fart!... Milly how can you?'

'I wouldn't expect you to think otherwise in the circumstances.' Millicent's prose would have qualified her for the civil service 'Charles and I have things in common which you and I don't.'

They glared at each other in silence for a few minutes. He was too stunned to speak and she was deadly calm and controlled.

'How did you know?' he asked suddenly, 'about... my other, my friend?'

'Your mistress,' Millicent helped him out, primly. 'I found an ear-ring in your underwear.'

'And you never said?'

'Well, how could I?'

There was a long pause and then Millicent said, 'I didn't think I minded much at the time, when I had got over the first shock, that is, but now I know that I'll have someone who puts me first – it's going to be quite different.'

'But I always put you first'

'Yes, as long as I took the children away for the weekend, so that you could have a little break with what's-her-name.'

'What did you do with the ear-ring?'

'Didn't you notice? I put it in your trinket box on your chest of drawers in the dressing room.'

He supposed he had noticed, but not given it a moment's thought. 'You were, you are very special to me. I gave you priority over my time. I respect and admire you.'

'But love me?… I think not'.

Right again, said the voice in his head.

'Just now I hate you…but…' he trailed off. His brain was becoming jammed with too many strands of thought. It was complicated. Love didn't seem to be a simple matter like an off/ on switch.

She sighed.

'Mark… I've got to go. We can continue this conversation later on. You need some time to get used to the idea. Bye now!'

And with that she rose and left the room, shutting the door gently.

He sank back on pillows and then as grief overtook him, he burst into tears.

But this would not do. He had the day to get on with. He washed, shaved and dressed and went down the kitchen.

On the table he found a note from Millicent.

OK Mark – this has come as a shock. I'm sorry about this. I really don't want to upset you. The point is that we both love each other in some part of ourselves – we would never have lasted so long if we didn't. But what we have isn't the basis for a happy marriage. Not now, although it could be the basis for a good friendship – and this is what I am hoping.

You have to let go of the old and accept the new. You can't hang on to the past. Time goes on and people change.

love

Milly

Could he hear the distant sound of a trumpet?

And there were no croissants. Gloomily he reached for the packet of muesli.

CHAPTER 19

The Battered Bigamist

Mark was not really a bigamist, but he had lived with this fantasy for so many years that he was deeply assaulted by the reality that his two women had now forced him to confront. This was that cultures that allow bigamy take care of the wives, who have complete security and babies are welcome (but other wives are not free to go off and find new husbands!). His cosy little mind-set had been shattered. He felt a bit like a peeled onion. He now had to become acclimatised.

His moods shifted violently between anger and self-pity. He was never quite sure which of his women he hated more. But occasionally, like the rays of sunshine which pierce a dark and stormy sky, little shafts of light appeared. There were small consolations, like knowing that Millicent would take the Lichtenstein, and he also now had the CD of "Pratiranya". He now played it. It depressed him. He could not understand the meaning and it churned up memories of the softness and sweetness of the woman who was carrying his baby and whom he did not want to marry.

Suddenly though, a thought struck him and he said out loud, 'My God what a fool I am.' He picked up his phone and rang Louisa.

A voice answered, sounding dull with suppressed grief.

He said, 'It's me. Look Louisa… are you feeling all right?'

'Nope.'

'What's the matter?'

'I'm just feeling sick all the time, like. And throwing up as well… and…'

'I'm sorry. I can't help with the sickness, but I don't want you to worry. It's my baby and I'm going to take care of you. Both.'

'Oh… that's good.' She still sounded choked off. 'I can't come to Granada with you. I just feel too sick, like. I'd like to go, but I wouldn't be up to much… I can't face the thought of Spanish food, right now. All I want is cornflakes and ice cream.'

He silently blessed her for letting him off the hook. He had already cancelled the Granada trip. 'Perhaps we'll go some other time,' he said lamely. But they both knew they wouldn't. 'Louisa' he said gently, 'I'd like to see you quite soon but I can't right now. Something's come up with my family and I've got to sort things out.'

Louisa sniffed.

'Please don't be miserable… I really will take care of you,' he said.

'I've got to go… I'm going to be sick…' She rang off.

Mark felt like crying because all he wanted was to cuddle her and tell her about Millicent's bombshell. But how could he expect her to comfort him about that?

A few days later, Millicent rang Charles. 'You know you said I could move into your flat in Bloomsbury.'

'Yes…'

'Life here is unbearable. I thought I could help Mark by staying on for a bit while he gets used to the idea, but it's just not working out like that. He's miserable and irritable and horribly silent and it's getting me down.'

'Of course my darling. You can move in whenever you like. Today if you want. I can get the keys to you within the next hour.'

'Oh… Yes that would be heaven.'

'The pleasure's mine! See you soon, my love.'

When Mark returned to the house that night he noticed as soon as he opened the door that the atmosphere had changed. It was as if there was a completely different smell in the place. He knew at once when he saw Millicent's letter on the table.

Dear Mark

There didn't seem to be much point in my remaining here. Charles has lent me a flat where I can be on my own while we get things sorted out.

I've taken just a few of my things but will be returning in the next few days to collect the rest.

As you know, I'm off to Sweden on Friday and you're going to collect the children for half term. So you will have to tell them. Please give them all my love and reassure them that I'll be seeing just as much of them as ever. Probably even more as I will be working part-time and a lot of it at home. Charles has a large place in Bucks and they'll have lots of space and a huge garden to play in.

Hope this is OK for you and that you will be feeling better soon. There's lots of food in the fridge and also lots of tins.

Enclosed new address and landline number,

Love,

Milly

Mark sat down and put his head in his hands. He wanted to weep but no tears came. He felt nothing except a rather dull pain and a huge tiredness. After a long moment of reflection, he knew what he had to do.

The flat in Russell Square, was not large. Just one bedroom and an American style living room/kitchen/dining room. It was comfortable, anonymous and convenient.

She did not like the decor – too much black leather and dark red – but then it was a bachelor's apartment.

Millicent made herself a cup of tea and sank back exhausted into the sofa. She felt so grateful to Charles for giving her this space and not insisting that she move in with him at once. But she was also sad. There was so much that she had loved in her home; and even bits of her marriage. It seemed like a very sudden wrench, even though she had known for ages it was going to happen.

Suddenly the bell rang. She picked up the door-phone. 'Flowers for Ms Crocker,' a voice said. She pressed the button and waited while the delivery man came up on the lift. It was an enormous bouquet of red roses. *How wonderful of Charles – he thinks of everything*, she thought, as she opened the envelope.

But the flowers were not from Charles. The card said simply.

'*Thank you – Mark.*'

She did something she had not done for many years. She burst into tears.

That night Mark had a strange dream. He was lost in the dark and he could hear, faintly, the strains of "Pratiranya". Then the music stopped and the dark shifted to a dismal grey. He saw that he was trapped by large, dark blocks. Suddenly a figure appeared. He knew it was Pratiranya. He was a dark angel with huge, blue-black, raven's colour wings. He was very frightening.

'Come!' he beckoned to Mark and led him to where there was a slight gap between the blocks. They went through a narrow gorge to where there was the glimmer of a faint light. Mark found himself on a bleak, open plain. There were no hills. The angel now began to fade. Just dimly Mark could hear a voice, 'There's more to go...' Then the angel disappeared and the dream died out. Mark woke up sweating.

Chapter 20

Telling The Children.

All Mark wanted to do now was to see the children. Nice, normal human beings whom he knew could comfort him just by being with him and enjoying the moment. They were a part of his life that no-one could take away. He felt that Millicent was right. He had neglected them and he should see more of them. With this in mind, he decided to go down to Brixstead a day earlier.

The thought of what he was to say worried him so he called in on the headmistress before going to the room where he was to pick them up.

Mrs Blainsley was in her late fifties, and showing years of experience with difficult parents and children. She was calm, efficient and kind but not too involved. Her sympathy was contained in discreet parcels.

'You don't need to worry about it,' she said. 'Over half the children in this school are from divorced parents. May I ask if you are having any issues over the arrangements – like, for example, property, or custody?'

'No – I don't think so.'

'Good – then it's much easier. It's also simpler when they're at boarding school, because they can have continuity.'

'That's good.'

'There are two golden rules to follow and you must make sure that your wife knows them as well. One is that you must never, never denounce your ex – even if you feel murderous! Even if they complain to you about her, you must never get sucked into that.' She smiled sympathetically. 'And the other is that you mustn't tell any lies. You know... like, "Mummy is very pleased that Daddy is going away". They'll see through it and you'll lose their trust. And, of course, if you have to come to some school function with your ex, there must be no bickering. That's the sort of thing that would really upset them.'

Mark winced at the thought of Millicent being referred to as an 'ex' but then that is what she was.

Mrs Blainsley took a sip of mineral water and continued. 'You don't tell them lies, but on the other hand you keep it brief. Spare them the details. Think about it from their point of view and what they want.'

'Thank you... you've been really helpful.'

He went to pick them up from their recreation room.

'DADDY!' Two voices yelled at him and his six year old daughter, Kate, flung herself into his arms. Her brother, Jonathan, the eight-year old, hung back embarrassed, but Mark hugged him as well.

Mark was moved to tears. Waves of love and delight poured through him. He had never realised until this point just how much they mattered to him and how much they gave him even though they were separated for most of the time. He couldn't speak for several minutes while Kate jumped up and down pouring out chatter about what she was doing. It was the first moment of light in the shadows that had dominated his life for the last few days. He did not admit to liking children as a general rule, but his own were different (as long as they were not squabbling, that is). But it was only in this moment he understood the extent of this difference and he knew that even when they were squabbling, he never stopped loving them. His life was going to change and now for the first time he began to believe that it was changing for the better. He would be spending much more time with them in the future.

He took them out to lunch at the local hotel and after much debating they chose hamburgers and chips, with sticky toffee pudding to follow. He settled for Dover Sole with peas and new potatoes. 'I've got some news for you,' he said as brightly as possible, 'there are going to be some changes. Mummy and I are going to live in separate houses and you are going to have two homes.'

'Oh… like my friend Sammy,' Kate said. 'Her mummy has six homes.'

'Are you going to have a divorce?' Jonathan asked.

'and one of those custard things?' Kate interrupted before he could reply.

'She means a custody thing… you know, they go with divorces.' Jonathan spoke with all the superiority of his seniority.

'Custardy pies! Custardy pies! Can we go to Jen's cafe this afternoon?' Kate put her hands on her legs and rocked from side to side with excitement.

'Yes of course. If you really think you can manage one after you've had all the pudding? Yes we are going to have a divorce.'

'Are you going to marry someone else?' Jonathan asked.

'No… but your Mummy is.'

'Someone we know?' Jonathan took another helping of chips.

'No… but he's looking forward to meeting you soon. He's got a large house in the country as well as a flat in London.'

Kate's eyes became round and shiny. 'Is it a house with a hundred rooms like the one in "The Secret Garden"? We've been having that at bed-time.'

'I should think not – but it does have a big garden and you'll be able to do all sorts of things.'

'Can we have pets? I'd love to have a puppy!' Jonathan said.

'And I'd like a pony. D'you think I can have a pony?'

'Look – you'll have to ask Mummy about that. I think it's

quite likely you will.' Mark reflected that the children were incredibly quick to spot the advantages of the new situation.

'And a rabbit? I'd really love a rabbit.' Kate waved her hands in the air.

Mark tried to visualise Millicent in a green quilted jacket surrounded by ponies and other pets.

'I'd think so,' he said again.

'Oh... Cool! We had rabbits here but the fox got them.'

The arrival of the sticky toffee pudding put an end to speech for the time being.

Mark, who had refrained from ordering a dessert because of the growing pressure on his waistband, now had a chance to say a bit more.

'Mummy wanted me to say that she will be seeing you just as much as ever, probably a bit more and she sends her love to you.'

'But what about the custody thing?' Jonathan persisted.

'Your mum and I are good friends about that. Custody cases happen when there are lots of quarrels. So what will happen is that she will have custody and I can see you just as much as I want.'

There was silence while they ingested this along with the sticky toffee pudding. Then Kate's eyes again became moist and shiny. She squirmed in her chair and then leaned over and touched his sleeve. 'But Daddy... won't you be lonely without Mummy?'

Mark found his eyes filling with tears from this unexpected touch of compassion. 'Of course not...' but then he remembered Mrs Blainsley's injunction, 'er... well... yes a bit, but not if you came and see me lots.'

'Really?' A smile spread across her face.

'And we'll do lots of exciting things, like the Zoo, and the London Eye and...' He had been thinking on his journey down about what they could do, and he reeled off the list.

London provided so much in the way of diversions and education.

Jonathan erupted with excitement, 'Daddy!… Daddy! Can we play Wigwam again?'

CHAPTER 21

Distraction

By the time Millicent returned fresh from Sweden and took the children away to meet their new stepfather, their good behaviour had diminished and Mark was quite glad to relinquish them. But his resolve to see more of them did not slacken. After they had left the house, the sense of relief soon faded and it began to seem horribly empty.

He was thankful that there was a lot to do in the gallery. The next event was the meeting with the men in grey.

The meeting was in the offices of a merchant bank and the group had already assembled as he entered. There was Max Finkelstein, Toby French Constance, Edgar Ordle, Peter De Vries and a couple of others. They wore immaculate grey suits with freshly laundered handkerchiefs in the pockets. They were ageless and had pale grey eyes behind gold rimmed spectacles and tight little smiles on tight little mouths. They were so powerful that they did not need to move much. You felt that empires could rise and fall at the flickering of one of their eyelids.

Today they were pleased with him. Charlene's show had been a sell-out. It was pleasing to report to them that everything had gone – nothing went to that graveyard of installation exhibitions, the local tip where those bits which could not be recycled would be allowed to perish in decent obscurity, deprived of the dignity of being called "Art". What the sanitary towel manufacturers had not taken had been scooped up by producers of piping and cotton wool, and also, to Mark's surprise, a tobacco company. The men in grey seemed particularly pleased about this. They seemed to take a great interest in the concerns of his clients.

Max Finkelstein explained, 'It's the shape of the tubing. That's the clever thing. Tobacco companies have to go in for subliminal advertising these days – they love anything tubular.' The others nodded in agreement. Mark was released without feeling any great sense of comfort because he felt miserable inside.

He grabbed at the small forms of compensation that fate now threw in his way; getting rid of the detested Lichtenstein and having the CD of Pratiranya. The trouble was that since his nightmare, he no longer felt like listening to it. He thought again about the fun his children had had, wrecking the orderliness of the house, and he thought of his plan to brighten up the kitchen.

In the gallery they were now setting up for the new installation. He now had a chance to speak to Garry.

'You know those plastic tomatoes they used to have in the fifties – to hold tomato ketchup. My granny used to have one. Do you know where I could get one?'

Garry thought for a moment, then he said, 'Yeah. I think I know what you mean. Do these tomatoes have ribs on the sides, a bit like the segments of an orange?'

'Yes – that's right.'

'Yeah – well there's a photographer's props place in Acton that'd probably have one. I've got to go there next week. Want me to try for you?'

'Would you? That would be great.' It would be his first gesture of independence for the house. It would brighten up the kitchen and no doubt please the children. He tried not to think about Louisa but not successfully.

Meanwhile, Louisa, lying on the hearthrug in her friend Elaine's flat, was choking back tears.

'You'll feel better lying down. I always had to when I was feeling sick. Stop it Woody.' Woody, who was in a high chair, had managed to grab a jar of jam which he held in his hand poised with readiness to drop. Elaine retrieved it just in time. 'Want a small gin?'

'No thanks. I'll be better in a mo.'

'You told him?'

'Yeah.'

'Do you think he'll pay up?'

'To be quite honest, I don't really care. Like, I'm going to have the child and I'll bring him up. I'll manage whatever happens.'

'Do you think you'll see him again?'

'Course. And anyway I know he'll look after me. He's good at heart like. He's been good to me over the years.'

'Like what?'

'It's not that he's given me lots of things like and taken me away and things, it's…' Louisa was at loss for an answer, lacking the nerve to say out loud that Mark was so good in bed. Instead she burst into tears.

Elaine got down on to the rug and comforted her. 'I love him,' Louisa sobbed.

'Yeah,' Elaine said and was silent for a moment. 'You're going to have to let him go you know. Know what I mean? Time you had someone who was more of a husband. It's what you deserve.' To bring about a distraction she asked. 'What d'you think it's going to be – boy or girl?'

'I've got a feeling it's a boy like – but I don't mind really. They said I could have an amino – whatsit if I wanted but I don't think I do.' She wiped her nose.

'I could try and find out for you by dousing if you'd like'.

'What d'you mean – dousing?'

'Oh… you know. You hold a string with a bead on it and ask it 'yes' or 'no' questions and if it goes clockwise it's 'yes' and the other way it's 'no'.

'Oh right.' The tears were forgotten now. 'I'd like to do that.'

So they got a string and a bead and Elaine dangled it over Louisa's stomach swinging it gently from side to side.

She asked if her baby was going to be a boy.

The string quivered for a moment and then slowly started to revolve in a clockwise direction.

'Wow! Yeah… it is!' Louisa was delighted.

'Perhaps… we oughter just check and ask about a girl?' Elaine was cautious.

So they did and the same thing happened.

Elaine burst out laughing. 'Must be twins – one of each – cor… that 'ud be a joke!'

Louisa found herself laughing as well.

Woody now put an end to further psychic questing by yelling for a drink and they ended up with more laughter helped by some gin.

By the time the evening ended, Louisa had resolved to get Mark out of her life. She would be unavailable on the phone and would not return messages. Well… just for a bit anyway. Like.

Chapter 22

Diversions

Jane, on arriving at the gallery in the morning, saw the envelope on the floor and sighed when she recognised the writing. Andrew seemed to have taken a fancy to writing to her rather too often and she was worried that he was becoming obsessed with her. Or worse – in love.

She opened the envelope and struggled with his untidy straggly handwriting. The letter was about arrangements for the exhibition and how much he was looking forward to it and how much it meant to him to be having a London show at last. It ended with a description of early Spring in Derbyshire:-

There is a willow outside my house. It hasn't come out yet but the branches are all green with buds. It waves its fronds in the wind against the blue sky, a bit like green/gold hair and I wish I could paint it. But I can't. Storms are more my kind of thing. I'm thinking about you and looking forward to seeing you, Best wishes, Andrew.

She showed the letter to Freddie, later in the day when they met for tea at Patisserie Valerie.

'He seems to be writing to me too often. I don't like the feeling that I'm raising expectations I can't fulfil,' she said.

Freddie broke up the palmier into little bits. 'I love the bit about the willow,' he said. 'But you're not falling in love with him are you?'

'No, there's no danger of that. Andrew is a strange man and he just treats me as an audience. I don't recollect him once asking me anything about myself.'

'But you find him interesting and you're concerned about him?'

'Yes.' She sipped her tea. 'I like listening to him talking. And I really want to help him.'

'But you've got this faint feeling that you're sinking into a pool of treacle?' He munched on a fin of palmier.

'I don't want to give him ideas, that's all.'

'It shouldn't be too difficult for you to write a firm and business-like letter. Would you like a piece of this – it's so good but I don't think I can manage it all?'

'Oh yes please.'

'What you have to tell him is that you'll do everything you can to make his show a success, but he must face the fact that it's not likely to happen and you don't want to raise his hopes.'

'Yes… about this or anything else.'

'That sounds good. You're not really falling for him are you?'

'No. The funny thing about being an audience is that it keeps you away. There's no involvement – you're just a spectator.'

'I'm relieved to hear that. People like Andrew are dangerous. They can attract you like a candle and then burn you up.' He took another sliver of palmier and munched it thoughtfully.

'Right… you are so right. But I would so like to get him the recognition he deserves. He's a really good artist you know,' she sighed.

'You can only do what you can do. It's no use worrying about it. Now I've got a proposal for you. I've been asked to paint some boats in Whitby and I wondered whether you would like to come with me.'

'Oh that would be lovely; but when?'

'End of next week. You'll have to take some time off the gallery – we'll go for three days.'

'But I can't close the gallery for two days!'

'Look... you're not doing too much business at the moment. You've got an assistant. You could get her to come in for one extra day and close the gallery on the next. Say it's being refurbished which covers everything from replacing fuses to repainting.'

'I suppose I could.' She was hesitant.

'I think it would be good to get away for a little. The gallery is getting you down.'

'You're so persuasive, Freddie. OK I will.'

For Mark, the days that followed were hard, but mitigated by the incessant activity of his life to which was now added the efforts of his friends to distract him with every sort of diversion: films, theatres, operas, dinners and parties.

The main difficulty was the mood swings. He went from being resigned and philosophical; from looking endlessly on the bright side, to being acutely angry or damply depressed in the flash of a second. Mostly he was depressed.

He went through the delicate process of adjustment to the exigencies of single life, becoming adept at defrosting the croissants and thankful for the fact that he could at least trust the toaster now that the oatcakes had gone. The excellent Mrs Kiridopoulos, the Cypriot housekeeper, was happy to come in earlier and take over the business of organising the shopping and sorting his clothes. She didn't complain about his muddles or having to pick up his underwear from the floor.

The nights were hardest. It was not that sex had featured very highly in his life with Millicent; it was just that her presence, acid and tense though it was, had been part of his emotional furniture. He was used to her noises, smells and movements. He missed her more than he thought possible.

Sushi did her best to comfort him. He allowed her to sleep on the bed and she snuggled against him, purring with pleasure at the new privilege. Sometimes she even brought him a special offering like, for example, a dead mouse. 'Ugh… not another installation, Sushi!' If she could have replied to him she would have said modestly, 'Well, just a little something to let you know I care.'

He dreaded telling Louisa about Millicent, knowing that this would raise hopes he could not, he just could not, fulfil.

Amongst the welter of mood swings, a new idea was forming. It came rather faintly at first but then it came again. At the same time as looking after Louisa financially, he had to let go of her physically. If he could not face the thought of marrying her, then the least he could do would be to stop standing in the way of her finding a husband who could support her and her baby in the ways she needed and deserved. Curiously enough, although he missed her dreadfully, there was something rather comforting in the idea. He could let go of her gradually. It didn't need to be explained.

The next day, Princess Seraphina again glided through Little Venice. There was an orchid reclining snugly on the pale green leather of the passenger seat with six delicate, white blooms nodding sagely behind the cellophane wrap. This time when the great car glided quietly to a stop she was acting under instructions.

Unfortunately the blinds were down on the Retro Gallery. A notice on the front door stated that it was closed for refurbishment and would re-open next Monday.

Blast. He swore quietly and jumped back in the car. He knew now that he absolutely had to see Louisa. He dreaded telling her about Millicent, but as Princess Seraphina glided quietly on to Bayswater he said, 'I have to grasp this nettle.'

Taking the orchid in his arms, he rang Louisa's bell.

She now came to the door looking disconcerted. A smell of burnt lentils met his nostrils.

'Oh. It's you,' she said, turning to let him in. 'You can't stay, I'm afraid, I've got someone coming to supper and I'm in the middle of cooking.'

Louisa's cooking was wildly unpredictable. Sometimes it was superb, but sometimes it was extraordinarily awful. He wondered what other ingredients were destined for the burnt lentil stew.

Mark handed over the orchid. 'Oh, thanks. That's nice,' she said, rather awkwardly putting it on a table.

He said, 'It was one thing I wanted to give you. The other is this.'

Louisa's resolve was now put to the test, but although she saw it coming, she was a little slow in raising her arm to ward him off. He took her in his arms and hugged her.

There was a long silence between them. He could feel her breasts now even larger and firmer than before and even more fitting for the little piece of Elliot, which he loved to recite to her.

> *'Grishkin is nice, Her Russian eyes*
> *Are underlined for emphasis,*
> *Uncorsetted her ample bust*
> *Gives promise of pneumatic bliss.'*

He could never understand why she hated this so much – it always made her pout, but now she was crying and although he did not admit to such a thing as crying in public, his eyes were watering and his heart was beating very fast. 'I'm sorry,' he said over and over again. 'I'm very sorry. And I've already told you I'm going to going to take care of you. You know I won't let you down.'

'Yes,' she sobbed.

Her silence and her forgiveness were almost worse than a recital of grievances. He felt full of remorse. Another second longer and he would propose to her.

'I'll go. It was stupid of me to call in without ringing you. I'll give you a call in the next few days. Shall we have lunch somewhere?'

'OK.'

He leaped down the stairs and back into the all-embracing comfort of Princess Seraphina. As the car drew away he saw an elderly Vauxhall draw up behind him. A man in a corduroy jacket emerged and went up the steps. He wondered whether this was Louisa's friend. He was torn between relief and jealousy.

In the car he realised that he had not told Louisa about Millicent, but then he began to feel that it didn't matter so much. It didn't matter that Louisa wanted something from him that he could not give. What mattered was that he should do something to make up for it and this is what he intended to do.

CHAPTER 23

On Primrose Hill

It was Sunday and Mark went to a lunch party given by one of his patrons at his mansion in Holland Park.

It was a massive affair with sparkling wine, eyes and jewels. Beautiful women swam round him in shoals. It was becoming increasingly clear that there were a number of contenders for the position vacated by Millicent. Also he was being continuously congratulated by the wealthy and successful on his amazing flare for publicity and brilliant taste.

'You're a frontier man, aren't you?' A husky voiced blonde woman spoke, 'Always right out there in front – a step ahead of everyone else. How do you do it?'

He was back again amongst the company of the courtiers who could see the Emperor's new clothing and positively adored it.

Unusually today he didn't enjoy the attention. What had happened recently (and particularly yesterday's scene) had put him in a reflective mood. He sat in the hall on the stairs and played with a little Chinese girl who had been adopted by a member of the family. They had a game with a soft rubber ball which he found he could bounce all the way down the stairs if he got the angle right. She laughed and laughed and cried 'Agen… Agen!'

As soon as was consistent with politeness, he left the party.

It was a fine spring day, if rather showery, and as he drove through Regent's Park on his way home he decided to take a walk up Primrose Hill. He parked his car near the Zoo and walked across the bridge by the birdcage to reach Primrose Hill. He would walk up the hill and down the other side where he would take tea in one of the cafés in Regent's Park road.

Regent's Park was full of flowers and blossom. The scent of wallflowers was still wafting over him as he climbed the hill. There were cherry blossoms, pink and white, flying in the wind and forming little snowdrifts. Small dogs played futile games with balls thrown by their owners; joggers jogged; nannies and, occasionally, even parents played with small children. It was all delightfully normal with the bracing wind adding to the charm.

Then he saw her – Jane. She was coming towards him in a pale green, silken, raincoat that revealed in the gusts, a fine pair of legs.

There are moments in life when you know things so strongly that you do almost feel apart, detached as though you were watching the events of your life played out on a cinema screen. These are the moments described by athletes when they are performing at peak level – the sensation that one part of you is moving as hard as it can, whilst inside is nothing but stillness. One such long moment happened for Mark. In that minute, he knew that Jane was meant for him. He wanted to surrender to her, to fall at her feet, swoon, anything. Of course it could have been the heady scents of spring on top of the champagne at lunch. Jane was someone he hardly knew. It was possible to make mistakes. All the same there it was – a powerful new sensation.

Jane was pleased to see him. She was smiling and asking how he was.

'What're you doing here?' was all he could blurt out.

'Why I live here. I'm just taking a bit of exercise.'

'Where d'you live?'

She gestured with her hands, trying to cover up her

shyness. 'I have a flat in Chalcot Road. Well, it's more than a flat really – the top two floors of a house. But what are you doing here?'

'Oh. I'm just having a walk, like you. I was on my way back from a lunch in Holland Park and I just thought I'd like some fresh air. I like it here. Perhaps I'll move here.'

Her face darkened perceptibly at this.

Hurriedly he said, 'I'm just going to have some tea at one of the cafés on the other side. Would you like to have some too?'

She hesitated for a moment and then said, 'Yes – all right. I've walked far enough. I was going to turn at the end of this path.'

They walked in silence for some minutes, then she said, 'And where do you live?'

He spent a few minutes telling her about his house and then said, 'My wife has just left me.'

'Oh… I'm sorry. Was it a terrible shock?'

'Well, yes it was, but to be quite truthful we didn't get on that well. I thought we did at the time, but now I'm beginning to realise that a lot of it was imagination and will-power. She's a marvellous person in many ways and she acted the part very successfully, but she wasn't really interested in my scene.'

'And you weren't interested in hers?'

'Well… yes you're right. She's a banker. Although I find bankers useful, I'm not really into the world of high finance.'

They reached the café. It was just warm enough for them to be able to sit down on the metal chairs outside. A crowd of interesting people filed by, like the cast of some minor film, which it is quite possible they actually were.

He ordered tea, which came in glasses with metal containers.

Jane said, 'You've been in the papers a lot recently; I've been reading about you.'

'Yes. In fact, there has been so much publicity that I'm now turning down radio interviews and making journalists wait months to see me. It wasn't like that at all in the early days.'

'You made a very interesting point about art and rubbish. I've been thinking about it..'

'Oh… well,' he said modestly. 'It was nothing. In fact it all grew up out of that conversation we had when I was stranded by my car.'

'Yes. I think it is quite a valid point about modern art enlarging the awareness and breaking the bounds of the picturesque. But it doesn't actually hold water.'

He was pulled up with a start. 'I don't know what you mean.'

'Well, you're saying that if you place an ordinary object, perhaps one with rather unpleasant associations, in a gallery setting, people will look at it again and find something more meaningful, perhaps even beautiful in it.'

'Exactly.'

'But the trouble is, it doesn't last very long. The next time you see a heap of rubbish it still looks like rubbish.'

'I don't know about that. Every time my cat brings me a dead mouse, I say "Installation". It always makes me feel better.'

She laughed. 'But that's because you've read that book.'

'What book?' He had no idea what she was talking about. All he wanted to do was to stroke her hair. A little gust of wind came and blew a strand across her eyes.

She pushed it back. *'Why cats paint.'*

'So you like cats?' he said as he watched a pair of out-of-work actors mince across the road.

'Sometimes.'

'So we do have something in common!'

'Not a lot.' She sipped her tea. 'You see, when you look at a really good painting, you feel so much better that everything outside looks more beautiful.'

'Really? Many people would find that there's a rather horrible contrast.'

'Only if you're neurotic.'

'I'd say most people are. Anyway, people enjoy what I'm doing in my gallery. That's why I find it so fulfilling,' he said.

A touch of anger flushed through Jane. 'Well... it might be good entertainment and that's all right... but in terms of art it's utterly meaningless. It's neither inspiring nor uplifting. I do go to the Tate Modern sometimes but not when I feel low because it only makes me feel worse. What do you do when you feel miserable and want cheering up?'

I buy an orchid and try to see Jane. He couldn't say that. 'If you must know, I get a tremendous kick out of pouring boiling water on empty yogurt cartons. You should try it sometimes. But then I don't expect you ever get really depressed.'

She looked at him for a long time in silence, thinking about Freddie and the Book of Blessings. She couldn't imagine Mark ever writing down three good events. But then maybe he had too many goodies to report.

They were distracted by the passage of a magnificent black lady in national dress, swaggering past with effortless ease – clattering beads, bangles and long gold ear rings.

'Wow,' he said quietly. 'That's panache for you!'

She nodded. 'I've just been to Whitby with my friend Freddie.'

'So that's why your gallery was closed.'

She bristled, 'How d'you know?'

'Oh... I just happened to be passing by yesterday... I couldn't help noticing.'

She recognised the lie and blushed. Again she had to push back the hair.

He adored this gesture. 'Jane...' he was rather hesitant, 'If you're not doing anything this evening... I wondered whether you… you wouldn't like to see a film with me.'

She shook her head sadly because she was not doing anything and would have loved to see a film.

'I'm sorry… but I can't,' she said at last giving him a look in which compassion and contempt were equally mingled. 'We're on the wrong side of the fence.'

'Why can't you? I know we've got different tastes and you're into a different sort of art from me, but it should be possible to be friends. I've a friend, Louisa, who hasn't the slightest interest in what I do. She doesn't go much more modern than Monet.'

'Oh I think I'd like her,' Jane giggled.

'But the point is that we're great friends.' He said this with a slight wince. 'Our differences don't matter.'

'You just don't understand, do you?' she said sadly.

'Go on. Explain.'

'How could I go out with someone who is cutting down the tree I am trying to perch on?'

'What d'you mean?'

'The thing is, I'm trying to run a gallery which barely covers its costs and may have to close. You recently sent me an artist, Andrew Silverstone, who I think is an outstanding painter, probably one of the best in the country.'

'So you should be pleased I sent him to you.'

'Look… I'm giving him a show quite soon because I've had a cancellation. If this had happened ten years ago, I'd have been able to help him get some recognition, but now it's different.'

'Andrew's important to you, is he?' he tried to conceal his mounting irritation.

She looked at him narrowly. 'Andrew's no more important than any other of the artists on my books. I'd just like him to have the success he deserves that's all… not a miserable fiasco of a show, with a few of his friends buying for three figures and barely covering his costs.' She was twisting her hands as she spoke with increased emotion and he could not help noticing how graceful they were and how lovely she looked with her flushed cheeks and bright eyes.

'Really?' Her prophecy about the show was very much what he expected.

Jane continued, 'No critic will come to his show. There'll be no reviews – no publicity of any sort. Only his friends will come to the private view. And there is nothing, just nothing, I can do because people like you have diverted all public attention and quite a lot of public money towards something that's worthless.'

He gripped the table and told himself to stay cool.

She continued. 'And another thing. I'm fed up with the pretence that you are doing this for the man in the street. The man in the street is being conned. All he's doing is helping you to sell meaningless rubbish to wealthy businessmen and large corporations. It's a total fraud that you are doing for the visual arts what pop music is doing for music. The great British public has nothing to do with paying for the stuff. Unless you count taxation, that is.'

Mark controlled his anger by breathing very slowly and reminding himself that this was the woman he loved. 'Look, Jane, you need to think about this. If I were to disappear tomorrow, d' you think your business would pick up?'

She narrowed her eyes and glared at him, momentarily at loss for words.

He continued, 'There's such a thing as reality and you have to accept it. You're in a cultural backwater. Look at Stalin – he was a dictator and he really tried to stop modernism. And he failed. Art's moving on and you can't stop it.'

'There's also such a thing as corruption.'

'What d'you mean – exactly?'

'You know perfectly well what I mean. About the star makers.'

'You've been listening to gossip.'

'Well why is that certain artists of no quality sell their paintings for outrageous prices, while equally good ones sell for a fraction of what they get?'

He twisted up his mouth, 'Hm… Marketing strategy.' He took a large swig of tea and gripped the table again.

'And the fact that a group of you get together with critics and museum directors and decide who the top flyers are going to be?'

He managed to stop himself from shouting *Oh bugger off!* But the idea now occurred to him that the best defence is attack.

'I'm sorry your gallery isn't doing so well,' he said gruffly.

She looked at him witheringly.

'Well… thank you for that.' She thought: *I don't think for a moment you're really sorry.*

'Look – You could do with a bit of marketing strategy yourself. I've been in your gallery and I noticed it had a rather dejected air.'

'Really?' He had hit her where it it hurt.

'Sales techniques, for example.'

'What d'you mean?'

'Your gallery's depressed because you're trying to hold onto something that's passed. Times have changed and you have to accept that. You can make it much more successful if you do. Lots of galleries like yours are actually making money and you want to learn from them.'

'You mean like my friends Derek and Marjorie who've turned their gallery into a gift shop-cum-café?'

It was exactly what he meant, and he elaborated on the various themes that occurred to him as he spoke. But inside a voice was telling him that it wasn't what he really wanted to say as he watched her listening patiently while she yet again brought the stray lock back to its refuge. His anger had now subsided as he talked in his usual glib fashion pointing with his hands to emphasise the various ideas. But what he really wanted to say was; *Jane you are as beautiful as you are intelligent and I just want to stay near you – I want to stroke your hair and sit and watch the sunset with you.*

Jane listened to his advice and calmed down. She didn't like being told what she should do – especially by someone she disapproved of, but she had to admit that there was some sense in what he was telling her. He was good at art promotion and she was lucky to have the benefit of his suggestions. He looked so nice when he spoke with enthusiasm. It was just a shame that he had got it all wrong. How could he not know?

He rambled on for some time until he could see her eyes glazing over and her attention wandering over to the people in the street.

'I've gone on talking too long,' he said. 'I'll have a think… there's maybe something I could do to help. Don't give up!'

She relented. 'That's kind.'

'No, you're the one who's kind – listening to me ranting on. Can't help it sometimes – ideas just keep pouring out.'

He leaned across the table and put his hand momentarily on the green silk sleeve.

Just for a second, their eyes met and a long minute passed. Then she drew back sharply as if assailed by an electric shock. 'Well… I had better be going now. Thank you for the tea. And the advice. You've been very helpful.'

She stood up..

Don't go. Please don't go.

But what he said was 'I think there really is… er… something I could do to help.'

'That's so kind,' she spoke stiffly, but she flashed a brilliant smile as she said 'Goodbye.' This was a reward and he felt overwhelmed.

He watched her as she retreated down the road. He sighed. It sounded as though Andrew was not the problem that he feared, but who was this Freddie who took her to Whitby?

She was thinking that she had to find something to do that evening, something that would stop her regretting her decision. Entries in the Book of Blessings (she didn't like this name but she and Freddie were unable to come up with anything else) were not going to take that long. But there were other things like organising the window boxes which needed some attention. Perhaps she could do that. And she wanted to look over some of the drawings she had done at Whitby.

Crossing the park on his way back to the car, he was caught by a shower, which a gust of wind thrust into his face. He smiled and brought out the only other piece of poetry he knew by heart:

'Western wind, when wilt thou blow
That the small rain down can rain?
Christ, if my love were in my arms
And I in my bed again.

Chapter 24

Interlude In Derbyshire

Two hundred miles to the North, the same rain blew in the face of Andrew Silverstone but it was much more bitter. He was cycling home from the shops with a bunch of wall-flowers perched precariously in the crammed shopping bag in his bike basket. He declaimed to no-one in particular, *"Oh Wild West Wind…"*

He burst out laughing. His favourite poem was totally inappropriate for Spring. He recited it nevertheless for he particularly loved the line: *"Destroyer and Preserver, Hear Oh Hear!"*

It expressed his feelings of triumph. Jane was coming the very next day to stay one night and collect the paintings for the exhibition. He had found the wallflowers in the local market and bought them as the final touch to his preparations for her arrival.

These had been lengthy. On the advice of one his friends he had spent five days cleaning the house. He had not noticed that it had been so dirty but when he got going, he found there was a lot to do. Now it shone in every corner. Well almost. There were a few small omissions (like the window sill behind the kitchen sink) that had somehow eluded his ministrations; but Jane was not likely to notice that.

He speculated about what he should provide in the way of meals, as she would be with him for lunch, supper and breakfast the next day. It was only right that he should feed her, when she was taking so much trouble, and driving so far, just for him. He prided himself on his culinary skills. He had three dishes all of which were a triumph.

The first was Corned Beef Hash, made with corned beef, onions, tinned tomatoes and baked beans. The second was Spaghetti Bolognese made with corned beef and tinned tomatoes and the third, his pièce de resistance, was Curried Corned Beef.

Andrew lived on his own. It was two years since his girl-friend, Zoë, who had flaming red hair and a temper to match, had finally quarrelled with him over the small matter of a burnt egg. He said this was rather a trivial matter, but she said it was the last straw and anyway a burnt egg in a ruined stainless steel pan with a melted plastic handle and the accompanying fumes was not a small matter, and furthermore, someone who could think of attempting to boil an egg and then forget about it, was not worth the effort. To which he replied that he was painting for God's sake. To which she retorted that if painting were to be the justification for such stupidity, then the time of her departure was overdue and stormed out, returning the next day only to collect her possessions. 'Anal retentive' Andrew muttered to himself. He did not miss her. She had no respect for Art.

Now, however, he had to admit he was lonely. Jane was a new and exciting possibility – an unopened book. Of course, she might not be free – they had not exchanged confidences.

She had told him that she was a widow, that was all. Since their hectic picture viewing day in London, he had thought about her a lot. He had also written to her, but it had not occurred to him to ask if there was any man in her life. The thought now began to obsess him.

He divided the flowers between two jam jars; one for the table in the living room and one for his spare bedroom. He took it up and looked round fondly. He had worked very hard to clean and clear it of clutter. He thought to himself that it looked very good and he ought to clean up more often.

Andrew lived on very little money. He had some part time teaching in the local technical college which brought in just enough to cover his mortgage and living expenses. He didn't even run a car. His mother liked to moan about how much he would be earning if he had remained as a solicitor, but he was actually very happy with what he had, feeling that he had been liberated from a nightmare.

His house was a basic late-Victorian workman's terrace cottage, with a slightly larger garden than the others in the row because his plot extended into the area behind the two blocks. On this his predecessor had built a large shed, which with the help of one his friends he had converted into a studio with a corrugated Perspex roof light. It was an excellent space as it gave him enough room to see his paintings from a distance.

Since Jane had promised him a show, he had thrown himself into his work with renewed vigour, terrified that she would find fault with either the quality or quantity. He need not have worried, for he had a huge stock of paintings.

He spent the next morning sorting them out. Although he was intending to stop and start cooking at a reasonable hour, he became so absorbed in this – looking at paintings he had done years ago and seeing new possibilities in them, that he had done nothing else when Jane arrived, much to his surprise, at exactly the predicted time.

'I got so caught up in the paintings. I haven't started lunch,' he apologised.

'Don't worry.' Jane had seen the kitchen and knew a little about artists. 'I think I'd like to go to a pub and have some sandwiches and beer. Wouldn't you?'

'Oh, yes,' he agreed thankfully. 'We could go to "The

Dove". It's just round the corner.'

Over their Guinness and cheese and ham rolls, he told her how much the exhibition meant to him and how excited he was.

Jane said, gently, 'Andrew, I tried to explain this when you first came to see me. The fact that I am giving you a show probably won't help you a lot. In fact you'll be extremely lucky to cover your costs. Don't get me wrong – I'll do absolutely everything I can, but it's just the way things are at the moment. Lots of galleries like mine are going out of business. We get no publicity, and no attention from the critics and the only people who buy the paintings tend to be the artist's friends and family. You do have friends and family in London?'

'Oh yes,' he said, looking rather crushed. 'I think you did explain this – but I got carried away. Look, it doesn't really matter. It's a step nearer recognition isn't it? And after all, it took Vermeer two hundred years to get established. Perhaps I'm lucky.'

'I just wish I could do more. All the public attention goes to the avant-garde stuff, you know – Mark Arniston Crocker and all.'

'Yes, it's terrible isn't it? I heard this joke at college the other day. It goes like this: question – "What is art?" Answer "Art is what artists do". Question: "What is an artist?" Answer: "An artist is a person who's been to Goldsmith's College".'

Jane laughed at this.

'Mind you, Mark did have the goodness to give me some advice yesterday on how to turn the gallery round. I think he's very good at business, but I won't be able to do it all before your show.'

'What did he tell you?'

'Oh, to change the name of the gallery and repaint the front and start a café and make posters and things for people to buy cheaply. He had a lot of good ideas.'

'He's right about the name. If you believe in what you are doing you are actually at the forefront. You could only call yourself "retro" if you were deliberately looking backwards. You're not doing that.'

'No. I suppose not.' Jane sipped her Guinness. She was tired after the drive and it made her feel better. She asked, 'What d'you think I should call my gallery?'

'I've no idea. Did Mark suggest something?'

'Gresham UK – perhaps the first step towards "Gresham International"?'

He laughed. 'Sounds trendy.' He paused and then asked hesitantly, 'D'you like Mark?'

Jane fidgeted with her napkin. She rolled it up and unrolled it while she thought what to say.

'...er...No. Not really. But I disliked him a bit less since yesterday. He did give me a lot of advice.'

Andrew felt so enormously relieved by this that he couldn't say anything else. Then he came to and offered her another drink.

'No, thanks. We've got a lot of work to do this afternoon and I have to keep my head clear.'

They spent all afternoon in the studio. Jane was practiced at selecting work but even so it was arduous. There was so much stuff and it was so intense. Some of it was over-worked, and some of it she felt was beyond her comprehension. She wished she had a partner who could advise her and reinforce her judgement.

Eventually she selected a group of possibles and then narrowed it down to the probables. After that there was the task of cataloguing, measuring and labelling everything.

She wrote the titles down in a book and put numbers on the

works, having learned to her cost the penalties for failing to do this. Then she sat down and wrote out the list for his benefit and gave him a receipt.

Andrew looked after her by plying her with coffee and chocolate digestive biscuits, and telling her about the paintings and what he was going through when he did each of them. He explained that it had taken a long time for him to reach the point when he felt he could exhibit, and when she saw some of his early work, which was very laboured and strained, she understood.

She finished writing the list and said, 'Goodness, I do feel hungry. I wonder, is there an Indian restaurant here? I'd love to take you out for a meal.'

'Well there is. But please let me take you. I was thinking of making a curry here, but I'd much rather go out.'

At the Monsoon Curry Paradise, he said, over a Rogon Gosht, 'You've learned a lot about me, but I know nothing about you. Tell me about yourself.'

My Goodness, Jane thought — *at long last — a question about me!*

'Well, what sort of things do you want to know?' she felt suddenly very shy. There was something a little daunting about his intensity.

'Well, where do you live, for example? Do you just sleep over the gallery?'

She laughed. 'I have a flat, well, what estate agents call a maisonette, in Primrose Hill. I'm really very lucky to live there.'

'And do you… live on your own?' It was the crucial question.

'I live on my own. No partner. But I do have a cat.'

'What colour?'

'Black.'

He took another mouthful of Rogon Gosht. 'Have you ever read "The Apotheosis of Tristram Swann"? That's got a cat in it. You'd love it. I'll lend it to you.'

'Really?'

Andrew now launched into a summary of the book.

Jane felt extremely tired. It was the easiest thing to do, to just let him ramble on. She liked stories, but Tristram Swann sounded as though it might be too complicated for her. She yawned and supported her head with her elbow on the table.

He noticed that she was nodding off.

'My goodness, you're tired. Let's go home.'

There was a slight clamminess in the bedroom. Jane got into bed as quickly as she could. As she slid her foot down between the sheets, it met something hard and lumpy. She reached down and pulled out a very ancient knitted teddy bear. 'Whose was that?' she wondered.

In the morning he made a pot of strong tea for her. There was toast made from sliced wholemeal bread that came out patchily browned from a battered and rusty toaster, and thick dark marmalade which she liked. Looking round the room, the wallflowers, the sagging sofa and chairs covered with Indian bedspreads, (a legacy from Zoë), the ornaments on the window and mantelpiece, mainly stones, some feathers, shells and dried flowers, she decided that she could become quite fond of Andrew. If only he could shut up sometimes.

When they had loaded the van, he looked intently at her as if trying to fix her features in his memory and held out his hand and shook hers. 'I can't thank you enough.'

'Well… we're in this together, aren't we? See you soon.' Then she was off.

She thought about him on the long drive back to London. Dear Andrew, so kind, so loveable. So brilliant and so talented; and obviously fond of her. She sighed. The voice at the back pointed out that in both of their recent encounters he had made her exhausted. So unlike Freddie, who made her feel energised.

CHAPTER 25

Louisa – Again

On the way back from Primrose Hill, Mark's spirits subsided; perhaps because he was returning to an empty house; perhaps the company of Jane coupled with the champagne and the heady scents of wallflowers and blossoms – the mild inebriation of early Spring – had now gone. He reached over and switched on his music centre. At once, the strains of "Pratiranya" blasted out. This time he was neither expecting it nor looking for it, but he had forgotten that he had put the disc in his player and had pressed the wrong button when he wanted the radio.

'Blast!' he said out loud and promptly switched it off. He didn't want to hear it again. 'I don't love you at all, Jane… that was all an aberration. I don't agree with you about art and I wish you wouldn't talk it about every time we meet. I'm sorry about Andrew's show but I don't expect he'll mind that much – he looked like the sort of chap who's not that interested in money anyway.' The trouble was that he had no feelings whatsoever about classical art due to over-exposure when as a small child, being dragged round galleries in Europe by over enthusiastic parents. It was not corrected by the insistence of one of the senior directors, when he joined the gallery, that he should attend courses at the Courtauld Institute. The idea that one could have uplifting experiences in front of an ancient masterpiece was anathema to him.

It occurred to him that things in his life had started to go wrong when he first heard "Pratiranya" and there was some way to go until they could be put right. He would do something about Louisa – that would be a start. But what next? He yawned. All of a sudden his life seemed empty. He didn't need to return to an empty house – there were plenty of invitations for that evening, but having decided to abscond in favour of taking Jane out, he felt that he couldn't be bothered.

Cheese on toast, conversation with his cat, (who agreed with him about Jane), a stiff whisky, a hot bath and an early bed-time sent him to sleep.

It was 11 o'clock the next day when he woke. On the spur of the moment, after making a few phone calls, he drove down to Kent and spent the rest of the day with his children, who Millicent had now returned to school after the end of the half term holiday.

By Monday, he felt more confident that he was free from his tiresome obsession. He strode into the office feeling pleased with this discovery of his liberation.

Michelle and Sharon greeted him with affectionate smiles. They took it in turns to work the word processor and paint their nails. This morning it was Sharon's turn for the paint-brush. Draped over the reception table in contrasting poses with heads turned to observe all-comers, they really were an installation on their own, he thought. Maybe they should be relocated to the middle of the gallery and have an exhibition rope all round them.

'There's been some messages for you,' Michelle said. 'Bad line – coming from Eastern Europe – just five minutes ago.' I wrote it all down for you.' She gave him the list.

'Ee looks tired, wonder who'ee shagged last night,' Michelle whispered to Sharon.

'Dya know what we did last night?' retorted Sharon.

Just a normal morning. He greeted the pile of papers on

his desk. Invitations, requests and queries. His diary showed the usual succession of parties, events and private views, although lunch was free. He rang Louisa.

'Harvey Nicks,' she said, promptly, when he asked her. He had thought The Basil would be more suitable for a quiet business-like discussion.

'But that's so old, like,' she said. 'Besides, although I'm feeling much better, – much less sick, like – I can't eat very much at any one point and I just like salads.'

This seemed reasonable so he agreed.

She was looking very good. Her pregnancy was not yet visible but her skin was fine and her figure firm. Her hair shone and her dark purple outfit set off the red lights in it.

'You look lovely,' he said.

'Yes, well… you know why,' she beamed at him and then asked, 'But how are you? I 'eard your wife left you. Like, was it a great shock?'

So she knew.

'Yeah it was, actually. I'm quite knocked out by it. It takes a bit of getting used to.'

'I'm so sorry.' She leaned over and touched his arm.

There was only one Louisa in his life. Someone who could give you sympathy when you had wronged her.

'Mark. I've got something to tell you.'

'Yes?'

'I was in a pub last night in Soho with some friends an' we 'eard a couple of guys talking, like. About artists and galleries an' such an' they mentioned you several times.'

'Yes … well… They would, wouldn't they?'

'But they kept on mentioning another guy, someone called Steffelgauze. Funny name, like. They said he'll knock spots of you. Ee's going to make you into a Retro gallery, like. I don't really know what that means but I thought I'd better warn you. This Steffelgauze guy sounds like an enemy.'

Mark laughed. 'Oh does he? I know a bit about Steffelgauze or Striffelperse or whatever. He's got some way to go if he thinks he's going to knock me backwards. I've got a lotta people behind me… a lot of interest in what I do and connections with all sorts of things that go on outside my galleries. I don't feel threatened by the likes of him. I don't think he's got staying power. Besides, the way things are at the moment there's room for both of us. It's a large field we're cultivating.'

'Oh well – that's all right then isn't it.'

'But thank you for telling me. Appreciate that. Always worth knowing what people are saying.' He gave her a big smile.

'Louisa…' He reached over and took her hand. 'I've been thinking. I'd like you to have a house of your own now. If you would like to do some house hunting and let me know if you find something you like… I'll buy it for you.'

Louisa flushed scarlet. It was an enormous proposal and it had come as a complete surprise. She could hardly speak for a moment.

'A house? But where?'

'It's up to you. Somewhere you feel comfortable. Something with a little bit of a garden perhaps, something further out of the city. Maybe Palmer's Green. I'll go up to 250K. You should be able to get something reasonable for that. I've done a bit of research with the agents'.

'But that's a huge amount Mark.'

'Houses are expensive.'

'You wouldn't mind if it was right out of London?'

'Well, no, I suppose not. But I would like to be able to go on seeing you. What are you planning to do?'

'I haven't really thought very much. I don't do much planning. Somehow something always just takes care of me.'

'Do you want to go back to work when baby is four months?'

She looked horrified. 'Well… nah. After going through all that I'd like to be with my baby and look after 'im. I suppose… if I had a house I might be able to let rooms to lodgers and live off that.'

'You don't want to go back to work? Millicent went back when they were four months old.'

'I might when ee's two.'

'Is it going to be a boy then?'

'Yeah.' (For although the doctor had assured her that she was not having twins, she clung to the belief that it would be male.)

'How d'you know?'

'It's just a feeling I have.' She picked at her salad, not wanting to tell him how she had found out.

'You'll have to have something to live off while you're not going to work.'

'Nah. I can manage on Social Security.'

'I won't let you do that. I'll give you a monthly allowance.' He found her utterly adorable. She had brought him a huge amount of relief, not minding about his lack of desire to marry her and being bowled over by his generosity. He just wanted to cuddle her.

'What did you do yesterday?'

'Me and Samantha and Lizzie went on the Heath. It was great but we got caught in a shower, like. We saw a couple in the bushes up to no good and they got awfully cross when it rained like. We killed ourselves laughing.'

'I suppose you couldn't take the afternoon off could you?' He couldn't, himself, really.

'Why not? They'll have to sack me soon anyway.'

In her flat, which was unexpectedly tidy and full of flowers, they lay in her bed and cuddled each other. He was infected by her happiness.

'I'll start house hunting this weekend,' she said as he started to go.

She added, 'Take care — you look tired. You should get some rest.'

He laughed. 'I don't need rest. I've just had some!'

When he returned to the gallery, he found a small clutch of weary but determined looking people waiting for him — Fartoos. *You can smell a Fartoo from a mile off*, he thought grimly, feeling a bit like a doctor, or an MP returning to his surgery. Why had his assistant not been dealing with them. Then he remembered — Hugo was off at a funeral. For a moment there flashed through his brain an image of Rembrandt, Vermeer, Van Gogh and Gauguin sitting there, and for another moment he thought he saw a penguin, a duck, a frog and a heron. The heron was a woman. The duck was the least ugly of the three males. The penguin had a bow tie and a blazer and the frog was really more a toad, raddled-looking with great bags under his eyes.

'I'm most awfully sorry,' he apologised in the customary manner. 'Had something to sort out — took much longer than I thought. Any of you have trains to catch?'

The penguin, the duck and the frog all muttered that they did. The heron who was a grey haired lady with a long neck, very pale green eyes and a long grey cardigan, said politely that she was quite prepared to wait. She was clutching something on her knee in a polythene bag that looked as though it might move if she let it go.

He saw the penguin first. He was a primitive painter in the manner of L.S. Lowry, only his paintings were all about the docklands. 'Not our style.' The duck did wishy-washy landscapes of ponds with little rowing boats in them and weeping willows, so he was well named. 'Not our style but thank you very much for showing them.'

The frog, or toad was a bit of a surprise. He wanted to show him a photograph of his prize object, which was a large, live flat fish in a very small rectangular glass tank which had a gold frame all round it. The tank just encompassed the body of the fish, leaving it no room for manoeuvre except slightly up and down. He said it was a piece of Living Art and he thought Mark might be interested in it. Mark was interested to the point that this was one of the first Fartoos who was not retro but installationist, but he found the exhibit utterly repulsive and cruel.

Helen Butterworth, the heron, was also a surprise. 'I just thought when I found this, that you would like it,' she said as she undid her parcel. What she revealed was an extremely life-like rabbit.

'Isn't it sweet?' She put it down on the floor and they contemplated it for a moment in silence. Suddenly, the bunny gave a large jump with a pitching motion that accurately reproduced the action of a real rabbit. It was still for another moment and then it did it again. And again, but each time the intervals between the hops were of a different length so you never knew when it was going to perform. Mark did like it. He found it hilarious. The longer he watched it the more he laughed.

'But... what the Hell? I mean, how did you come by this. Did you make it?'

'Oh no. My son was involved in a project in Scotland to conserve eagles. As they had to catch the eagles and were not allowed to use live bait, they developed these motorised bunnies.'

'And did they work?'

'Oh no. They kept falling over in the rough grass – and then the funding for the project ran out.'

'Love it,' Mark said simply. 'Don't quite see how we

could fit it into a show, but I think it's something we could use. I'd like to talk about it with some colleagues and see what we could come up with. Could we keep it for a bit and let you know?'

'Well, I don't think I could let you have it as it's my son's, but I can bring it in any time you want.'

'OK, fine. Give me your name and address.'

She fumbled in her ancient handbag and produced a rather battered card.

'But you live in Scotland?'

'Don't worry about that. I'm in London to see family very often.'

He did not want her to take the bunny away. He wanted one.

'Are there any more of them around? I mean, could I get one?'

'They only made a few. I don't know what happened to the others.'

'Well, they look intensely marketable. Imagine having motorised bunnies in your garden, without them eating your lettuces.'

'Yes. But I don't know anything about production.'

'That's not a problem. We'll be in touch about this.'

She took her leave. The second Fartoo installationist of the day and he had taken the unprecedented step of giving her a ray of hope, probably because she struck him as a not very hopeful sort of person, with just a rather casual, 'You might be interested…' Not a serious artist at all.

He worked late that night. There was a lot of stuff to catch up with. He sent off the rest of his staff and closed the gallery himself. Then there was a private view followed by a dinner, followed by a nightclub.

He managed to reach the radio button on the way home and was regaled to the strains of Acoustic Alchemy. What a triumph! What a wonderful life he was having. He had seen

Louisa and promised to look after her. He yawned.
    So why did he feel so miserable?

CHAPTER 26

In A Black Hole

The raised eyebrows of Michelle and Sharon now found their target. He was taking advantage of his bachelor status in the customary way. He might as well enjoy himself. There were plenty of curvaceous bodies and melting eyes at the parties he attended – hostesses who said 'Must you go now?' or girls who just looked at him and said 'Where?' It was fun; it was tiring, but although it fulfilled a need on one level, it left him aware of hungers in other areas that he perceived too vaguely to be able to understand. He just felt a sense of malaise as you do from any sort of excess whether it was from whisky, cake or chocolate.

He had held a meeting with the staff after the invasion of the Fartoos to announce a change in procedure. In future, if all the senior staff were absent, the girls in reception were to deal with Fartoos. Exhibits could be left and opinions would be given. If they wanted to meet with a director then they had to write in, in which case his secretary would know what to do.

Not that any could intrude at the moment, for the gallery was closed to the public while the new installation was being built. It was now a cheerful place. The boys were there, whistling, banging, drilling, sawing and making in-house jokes.

The new show was called "Black Holes; Light Spaces" and was the work of an artist called Barrowclough Cleaver who described it as "An Experience of the Truly Cosmic". Mark was not exactly moved by anything that vaguely approached

New Age mysticism and groaned inwardly when he first heard about it, but his backers had found massive sponsorship from a pharmaceutical company that produced tranquillisers, as well as from the usual sources.

When he understood the idea a bit more, he found it much more favourable because it was really rather frightening.

In fact the original title had simply been "Black Holes" but there was a suggestion that some of the more sensitive viewers might find this too claustrophobic, so they had added "Light Spaces" just to reassure. It was a clever combination of installation, video and audience participation in which the viewer found himself the object of observation.

The gallery was completely blacked out and there were projections of mysterious flying objects as well as distant planets and stars on the walls. Then there was a collection of boxes, most of which had the same proportions as a telephone box or an old-style confessional. You could get into these by opening the door. While you were inside, a red light flashed on and off. As you were looking at the light, anyone could open a set of wooden cupboard windows and look at you looking at the light.

There was one box, in the centre of the group, which was much larger and had a chair in it; this was the climax of the show. In this box, when the red light went off, after one minute of complete darkness, a video projection went up on the opposite wall of the box. It fulfilled the canon of the best performance art by being a continuous loop and by hinting at a meaning, which, of course, it lacked. It started with a barely perceivable dark rectangle, which gradually lightened. As it did so, one began to make out writing, that looked like the blurred words of a poem; but when it started to come into focus, it began to wobble and fade. It was written in mud, and this gradually swallowed the poem before one could see that it was actually nonsense. Then it all faded to darkness again.

The construction and wiring of this contraption was quite complicated and there was a lot of toing and froing and quite a lot of 'f-ing' and 'b-ing' before it was judged ready. The boxes got nicknames – the small ones were the 'Tardies', (this being the team's version of the plural of 'Tardis') – and the large one was the 'Pal' short for 'palace'.

One of the team, Garry, (which was his nickname because he was bald,) met Mark as he was crossing the floor. 'Would you mind trying out the Pal for me? I think I've got it right but I just want to watch the control panels with a punter inside.'

Garry was not known for his cheerfulness – he was usually taciturn – but this time he had a curiously broad smile on his face.

Mark went into the box and closed the door, which one had to do to make the light come on. As he did so, he saw an object on the chair. It was a large, red plastic tomato! Garry, bless him, had not failed him in his hour of need.

The red light now faded out but the projector did not come on. He waited in complete darkness for one minute. Then another. Nothing happened. He knew where the switch for the projector was; it was reached through a small trap door in the centre of the ceiling, above the chair. Carefully putting the tomato on the floor, he stood up on the chair and after some fumbling, opened the trap-door and found the switch. Then he stepped down, but as he did so, his foot landed on the plastic tomato. He lost his balance and fell, catching his head on the back of the box.

Before he lost consciousness, he passed out of time and into eternity. He felt as though he had been sucked out of his body and was travelling down a long dark tunnel on the sides of which were projected scenes from his life. A pampered baby growing into a cheeky little boy teasing his sisters – a schoolboy on trips to Paris being bored by the Louvre. Then the undergraduate – reflections on water, the smell of cannabis, alcohol, books, parties and women. The early days in the gallery; of charm and diplomacy, marriage; Millicent, the house, the children, Louisa warm, soft and tender. Success, parties, flashing lights, meetings, people, parties. He was drowning in a swirl of foam, as the sequence accelerated. Parties, people, flashing lights, The Arbuthnotts, the Strathpeffers, Henry Streffelgueze swept round the vortex. Then he saw and heard her – Jane, 'What you are doing is utterly meaningless.'

'*Yes,*' he thought, '*you're so right!*' He tried to get back into his body so that he could tell her but he only managed to say 'Jane' before darkness overwhelmed him and he lost consciousness.

When he came round he was in complete darkness. He wondered if he were dead and if he were, what would happen next. He groped about him and found the plastic tomato. He clutched it to him as if it were a shred of reassurance in the void. If he were dead, he reckoned, he would not have been allowed to take a plastic tomato with him.

A line of light appeared in front and lengthened into an L shape. The cupboard doors opened and a face looked down at him; a face that was familiar but puzzling for it brought no shred of recollection with it. Deep violet blue eyes under a mop of untidy grey hair looked down at him with great compassion.

'Jane's right,' was all he could murmur. 'She's so right.' Then his eyes closed again.

'Of course she's right,' said an elderly voice. The old lady continued as his eyes opened again. 'Young man, you're in a state of distress. Let me help you.'

He blinked again.

'Head hurts,' he said. 'must have passed out.'

'I think you're concussed. Look, have some of this. It'll help you.' She reached into her handbag and handed down to him a small eye dropper bottle. 'It's Rescue Remedy. I can't administer it myself as I can't reach you in there, but all you need to do is put a few drops on your tongue.'

He did this and was surprised to find that it was brandy. It had an instantly reviving effect and he began to sit up.

'Don't move. I'll go and get help.'

'Don't go.' Suddenly he needed her desperately. 'I'll come back instantly,' she promised.

Then the door was opened and he was surrounded by his staff. He was still clutching the tomato and the eye-dropper bottle, feeling rather foolish – but they were more concerned with his health. With help, he managed to get back onto his legs and, walking shakily was escorted to his office where there was a sofa he could lie on. Hazel rang the doctor.

The old lady saw him safely ensconced on the sofa and then said she would go.

'No,' he pleaded. 'Old lady... not go.' He found it rather difficult to speak.

'I don't expect you remember meeting me. It was a few months ago, on a train. My name is Lucy Bleddoes. I am an artist – painter. I came to this gallery in the hope of meeting you again and having a look at the current exhibition. When I found that it was closed, I rang the bell and one of the workmen let me in.'

While she was talking, he found his wits gradually returning.

'Train?' He couldn't remember and screwed his face up with the effort.

Lucy gently took the dropper bottle from him and replaced it in her handbag. 'You remember – we were going to Paddington. You kindly helped me with my luggage.'

Then it came back. 'Oh...Yes...You paint teapots, and roses... and... angels.'

Lucy beamed at him. 'There. You see, you are all right.'

'Do you really see angels?' He hadn't seen any in his brief out-of-the-body experience while he was unconscious.

'Not very often. And never in London. Mostly I see colours coming out of people.' Lucy looked round at Hazel, Michelle and Sharon and the rest.

Mark asked, 'What colours do you see round me?'

'None at the moment.'

He closed his eyes again.

Lucy said, 'You're very tired. You know London is very tiring and stressful. Why don't you come down to Somerset and stay with me? Lots of people come to stay with me. It's so peaceful and quiet. My house loves visitors and you need to rest for a bit.'

Mark thought about this for a minute and then he said, 'What's it like?' He had no intention of going away at the moment, particularly to visit an old lady he hardly knew, but he did not want Lucy to disappear. He wanted to keep her talking.

'Oh… I have a lovely cottage in creamy stone with roses growing all over it, and mullion windows and casements in the thick walls. My garden is a riot of colour at the moment. At the back there is a stream and beyond that, there's a field…'

She went on in this vein for some time and he closed his eyes and visualised this cosy-country-cottage sequence. Cliché it might be, but after what he had just been through it was immensely comforting, soothing and healing.

The doctor arrived and once again Lucy said she would go.

Mark said, 'Please give me your address,' and she wrote it down for him in his diary.

The doctor seemed to think that he was not too badly concussed but that he ought to be x-rayed and take this and the next day off, just to be on the safe side. Hazel took him to the Middlesex and after the usual interminable wait, he was attended to. They reinforced what the doctor said. He was not seriously damaged but must take a rest for a few days and he must not think of driving a car. And he had to see the consultant in a few days time, for further information and advice.

He simply stayed at home and cuddled Sushi. All his friends rang to give sympathy, even Millicent.

'Millicent!' He was so pleased to hear from her.

'I heard you had a fall. I was going to ring you anyway because we need to make some plans about the children and holidays and things, but I won't bother you with all that now. I expect you want to rest.'

'How are you?'

'Oh…well – adjusting to a new lifestyle. I'm giving up my job and I've accepted some directorships instead which will probably keep me just as busy. I'm still doing two charities and a school board.'

'And what about the house? I've heard it's rather magnificent.'

'You mean Galveston. It's amazing but it needs a lot of work. We can't move in for ages. We've rented a smaller house nearby so that I can supervise the work.'

'Katie wants a pony.' He picked up a pen and started doodling on his message pad. That's what is so nice about phone calls – no-one could watch you.

'Don't I know it. She'll get one, but it's a little hard to organise while all the conversion work's going on. But it's not too hard. I've got lots of assistance.'

He thought she sounded very bright. Rather too bright, in fact. He asked, 'And the Lichtenstein?'

Millicent laughed. 'Touché. It's all packed up in the coach house. I'm going to lend it to a museum for a bit. Charles likes Ruysdael.'

CHAPTER 27

Edwin's Surprise

It was a sunny day and Jane entered her gallery feeling optimistic. Her optimism was justified, for a couple entered the gallery with the obvious intention of buying. Only they wanted a lot of talking and explaining although the pictures on display, which were all of flowers, did not need much elucidation.

While she was talking, she noticed another figure enter the gallery. This was something that happened so often. The gallery could stay empty all day and then suddenly there was a crowd. People seemed to attract people – perhaps she should turn it into a coffee shop.

Eventually the business was settled and she turned to greet the other visitor. To her surprise she saw that it was Edwin. 'Edwin!… how nice. I haven't seen you for ages.'

'No… er… well,' his speech was hesitant as usual, but at least he was not carrying flowers – she was safe.

Jane said, 'You're looking very well Edwin.' It was true, he looked radiant.

'I've… got some good news for you.'

'Oh yes?'

'I've… met the most wonderful woman. She's agreed to marry me. I'm just so happy… I had to come and tell you!'

'I'm so pleased for you, Edwin. Just what you wanted.'

'Yes… at last I've… er found the new Lady Crailing.'

'Lady Crailing? What d'you mean?'

'Oh,' he looked embarrassed. 'I never got round to…er telling you. Partly because I don't like people knowing…

but also because I was going to tell you... when we were engaged... I'm actually an earl.'

'Well... there's nothing wrong with that is there?'

'I don't like it very much... though. People want things from you all the time.'

Jane said comfortingly, 'Why don't we sit down and have a nice cup of tea and you can tell me all about your new lady.' There was work to do in the gallery, but Edwin's story sounded intriguing. She made mugs of tea for them both and they sat down.

Edwin said, 'I had a nice simple life working as a librarian in Worcester... and then... much to my surprise I inherited this... title from a distant cousin. I'd never met him, in fact.'

'Well... if you don't like it you can always renounce it, can't you?'

'Yes... I suppose so. But the point is that I can't...get rid of what came with it.'

'What was that?''

Edwin let out a big sigh, 'A Gothic pile in bad repair in Staffordshire. I've tried to sell it, but I can't... no-one wants it. It's not quite large enough... for an institution but it's much too...big for the average family... I can't even pull it down – although I did get permission to pull down the servant's wing... thank goodness.'

He paused and drank some tea before continuing, 'First earl, who made a fortune in biscuits... donated to the... er... correct political party... got the title... and the second was a spendthrift and because of untimely deaths... and infertility, it came to me... it was almost as bizarre... as "Kind Hearts and Coronets".'

'How amazing,' Jane said.

'Yes... er... well... er... It's a terrible house. High ceilings and badly proportioned rooms... dark paint and wallpaper...

all rather dilapidated... but mind you... it has got the most magnificent... staircase... I can just see Henrietta striding down it... in a black tunic with thigh high boots and a large hat with a red feather.'

'Henrietta? is that what she's called?'

'It suits her... she's quite extraordinary...'

'Tell me.'

'I... I still can't quite... believe it. Very tall and commanding. She's been an explorer in Africa... done all sorts of things... but now she's a sort of art dealer. I met her... at a private view.'

'Well...' Jane finished her mug of tea. 'I must congratulate you! I can see why you want a wife! Has she seen your stately home?'

'Not yet... but we're going there quite soon... she's very busy... at the moment.'

'But tell me Edwin,' Jane sounded a bit severe. 'How long after meeting her did you propose to her?'

'Oh... about two weeks... we just seemed to fall into each other's arms.'

'And you think you can share your whole life with someone based on just two weeks?'

'Well... er... yes... it was a feeling of... knowing that we were meant for each other!'

Jane was not so sure about this; it seemed more likely to be a combination of desire and imagination. But she did not want to hurt his feelings. He was so vulnerable.

Edwin now picked himself up and made ready to go.

Jane said, 'Thank you for telling me all this. Do bring her into the gallery – I can't wait to meet her.'

Edwin assured her that he would. Then he said, 'Oh and Jane... please don't mention this to anyone else. We're keeping it under wraps just for the... er... time being. We'll announce it in... two months time.'

Jane gave him her promise. 'But Edwin, do you mind if I tell Freddie. Freddie's like a brother to me and we share everything.'

'er... Yes... if you think he can... keep a secret.'

'I can promise you that – he's very discreet.'

After Edwin had left Jane rang Freddie and told him.

'That's mind blowing,' Freddie said. 'To think that if you had accepted him you could have been a countess by now.'

Jane giggled. 'Or at the pace Edwin works at I might even have been an ex-countess by now. But I can't wait to meet this Henrietta lady.'

'I think I've heard of her,' Freddie said. 'One of my friends mentioned her to me. She goes to a lot of parties and loves dressing up. But tell me, did Edwin say anything about being in love?'

'Not exactly. There was something about knowing that they were meant for each other, but no mention of affection between them.'

'Hmm,' said Freddie.

'But mind you – Edwin isn't the sort of person who talks about his feelings much. He might be deeply in love, for all I know.'

'Yes... well...' said Freddie and they left it at that.

Edwin lost no time in bringing Henrietta to visit Jane.

'What a lovely gallery,' Henrietta said. She was wearing a pair of purple velvet trousers with an emerald green cloak over it; her outfit was completed with a small black Trilby on her head. She was not beautiful, neither was she in the first flush of youth. But she was both good natured and impressive. Jane found herself liking her. 'I hear you are in the art business yourself?'

'I am indeed. But my line's a bit more contemporary than

yours. It doesn't matter. I've wide ranging tastes myself. I'd adore it if, in my travels, I found a Van Gogh. But that's not likely is it?'

'Yes well – wouldn't we all! Would you keep it? I'm not sure I would – it would be just worth too much and I'm sure I couldn't afford the insurance!'

A small group of Japanese visitors now entered the gallery. Edwin, seeing that Henrietta and Jane wanted to go on talking, gallantly went over to them and started chatting.

'I think I'd keep it for a bit – just for the fun of it.' Henrietta laughed. 'But tell me Jane, Edwin says you feel a bit persecuted by Mark Arniston Crocker?'

'Do you know him?'

'He's a very old friend – I've known him for years. I don't think he would willingly do you down, you know – he's very kind hearted. His staff love him – they've all worked with him for years.'

'He told me his wife had just left him.'

'She was a cow. He never said a word against her but I think she gave him a dreadful time. She was always going on at him in public.'

Edwin now came and discreetly touched Jane's elbow, 'They want to… er… buy that small sunset.'

'Excuse me a moment,' Jane said. 'I must go and deal with them.'

She went and talked to the Japanese group. It took some time because of the language difficulties, but eventually the sale was made and the red spot placed on the sunset.

She felt pleased and went back to Edwin and Henrietta. But just as she did so, another visitor entered. This one was not such good news, being one of her regulars, a lonely old man who just wanted to talk about himself and his dreadful watercolours.

This took some time but he left in the end and she went back to Henrietta and Edwin who were now preparing to go.

'The perils of running a gallery! You have to be a sales girl one minute and a therapist the next. It must be more fun to be freelance like you.'

'It has its advantages – but also drawbacks.' Henrietta drew up her cloak round her, 'Look Jane… I'd really like to talk to you some time without being interrupted. Would you like to have lunch with me – one day soon?' And she gave Jane her phone number before they swept out.

The following week Jane met Henrietta at the restaurant at Liberty's.

They greeted each other affectionately. Henrietta was in Royal Blue – a long skirt and a tight fitting short jacket made her look taller than ever.

'So how did you get on at Edwin's dream palace?'

Henrietta gave her a look. 'Didn't he tell you?'

'No… I haven't had time to ring him.'

Henrietta made a grimace. 'It's all off,' she announced.

'Oh dear… I feared that might happen.'

'It wasn't just Lostock Hall. That was bad enough. It was Edwin's attitude that was the problem.' She picked up the menu and began to scan it. 'I say I'm most frightfully hungry – let's order something before we get into the gory details.'

They ordered salads. Henrietta spoke. 'Lostock Hall isn't quite as bad as Gormenghast… but it's getting that way. On the other hand, it has huge potential. Huge character and quite a lot of charm. It's just so neglected and sad and damp and empty. It reeks of must and ancient cigars. Edwin told me that the dry rot had been treated and there was a lingering hint of chemicals in the air to underline that – but I wondered. He gets it cleaned and dusted but the windows need painting and some of them need replacing. I could go on and on about the dilapidations but that's enough to give you the picture.'

Jane agreed and asked, 'But what about the grounds – is there a nice park?'

'The gardens are grassed over and regularly cut – so they're not too bad, but there are lots of overgrown shrubs at each others' throats – so bits are a bit like the Sleeping Beauty's garden.'

'It sounds charming.'

'Yes… well it is in a sort of way. But what got me finally was that Edwin's ancestor had started building a miniature steam railway. All the track has been laid but he ran out of money before he could get any rolling stock. There's a wonderful amenity there – local kiddies would love it. But could I get Edwin to see this?'

'Oh dear.'

'And it was the same with the house. There are all sorts of things you could do with it and I gave him a lot of my ideas – like running holidays for wealthy Americans who would like to stay with an English Milord – you know, that sort of thing. And there are grants you can get to do up historic houses.'

'Yes… I've heard about this from one of my friends.'

'The trouble is Edwin just doesn't want to do anything.' She paused as their meals arrived. 'Not that we quarrelled exactly. He just went very silent – was in a huff. He went damp like the house. And in the end I said I thought it wasn't really going to work – our thing, and he agreed and brightened up. Thank goodness I had the sense to keep quiet about it until I'd seen Lostock!'

'It's a shame. I'm very fond of Edwin, but I can see what you mean.'

'Yes… I thought it seemed ideal because we complemented each other. He's soft and gentle and I'm quite tough.'

Jane laughed at this. 'Well… at least I've got something out of it – a new friend.'

And they spent the rest of the meal talking about other things.

Before they parted Henrietta said, 'By the way, I don't know if you've heard, but our friend Mark has had a fall.'

'No, I hadn't. Tell me.'

'It seems he fell in one of the installations that was being built for the new show; he was concussed.'

'Oh dear – perhaps I should ring him…'

'It might be an idea.'

CHAPTER 28

A Country Idyll

Louisa now rang Mark. She was bubbling over with delight as she told him that she and Elaine had found a house in Stoke Newington with three bedrooms, a garden and a lovely stained-glass door into the back. He advised her on the practicalities of house buying, making an offer and having it surveyed.

'I'm so pleased,' he said. 'It's made my day. I'd like to come and see it but I'm stuck here at the moment.'

'What happened? You all right?'

'Oh… haven't you heard? An accident in one of the cabins in the new show. Fell and was concussed.'

'How did that happen?'

'It was weird. I had this strange experience. I was out of my body and saw my life go by from a distance. And when I came round, I wasn't sure if I was still alive. There was an old lady looking at me through a window and for a moment I though it was God. Then she helped me by giving me some brandy in an eyedropper bottle. Funny way to carry brandy.'

Louisa laughed, 'I think it's a sort of homeopathic remedy, like. Elaine knows.'

He told her how it happened.

'I think I'm all right, but I keep on having dizzy fits and my head hurts. The doctor says I can't go back to work until they stop. Everyone keeps telling me I must go away and I think I'd like to go and stay with the old lady. She says she's got an idyllic cottage in Somerset.'

'Sounds like a good idea.'

'But the trouble is…' He trailed off as though he had lost the sequence of his thoughts.

'The trouble is what?'

'Well the doctor says I mustn't drive at the moment.'

'You could go by train. You've been there in a train before, haven't you?'

'And there's another thing.' He spoke hesitantly.

'Yes?'

'Well, she's an artist. I think she might be expecting me to look at her pictures and give her an opinion and I know I won't like them and I don't want to cause offence when she's been so kind to me.'

'Oh Mark!' Louisa laughed. 'You're a stupid old thing. Course she won't be offended. Not if she's seen your gallery – she'll know what you're up to. And anyway, you can surely find good bits to praise in them. You were going on the other day about seeing beauty in rubbish, like.'

'Don't make me laugh, it hurts!' But he felt better.

It was not like Mark to be so sensitive about the feelings of other people, or quite so concerned about his ability to smooth over differences of aesthetic approach, but his customary confidence had been shattered by his fall. The last two days had been depressing. His head still hurt; he was confused and suffering from attacks of giddiness, while his doctor forbade his return to work or travel and told him to rest, as did everyone else. The irritating thing was that anything done with his eyes, reading or watching television, seemed to increase the pain in his head. Days were spent listening to the radio and playing discs and tapes. He felt as though he would never feel better. Life had changed.

The only bright part was being able to place the plastic tomato on the countertop where it looked superb amongst the stainless steel and the white tiles. However, he felt he had paid too high a price for it. Life had played a bad joke on him and gone sour. He stared endlessly at the blank space on the wall left by the Lichtenstein and speculated about what to put in it.

More and more the idea of the country began to appeal. But he lacked the courage to pick up the phone and ring Lucy – while the more he delayed the decision to ring her, the harder he found it to do.

There were plenty of alternatives to Somerset. One of the reasons that he and Millicent had never considered buying a house in the country was that they had friends and family in almost every visitable county in Britain and if they wanted a quiet break they enjoyed staying in hotels, especially those with Jacuzzis and swimming pools. This saved them from all the trouble of running a country house when they were very busy and had two properties abroad anyway.

They had delightful friends with Georgian manor houses, sheepskin coats and four-wheel drive vehicles. Women who were always laughing and sparkling; large country kitchens with comforting Agas, pheasant pâté in the fridge, well-stocked wine cellars, superb gardens and a horse or two in the stables. Why not go to one of these for a bit – much more space and comfort than a cottage?

There was a ring on the doorbell. Answering it, he found an enormous bouquet of flowers supported by two arms covered in turquoise leather under which appeared two legs clad in purple suede.

'Hallo!' Charlene's voice sounded from under the flowers. 'This is from me and the boys.'

He was delighted to see her. 'Come in… come in.'

He told her what happened, about being sucked into the hole and watching a resumé of his life. And then was rescued by Lucy Bleddoes.

'You should go there,' Charlene said at once.

'Yes.' He paused as he took the bouquet and put it on a table. 'But, not supposed to drive at the moment and can't face the train journey.'

'Not a problem,' she said firmly. 'I'm not doing much at the moment and I've just bought a Porsche what wants exercising. It's bright yellow and it's dead brill. Where did you say she lives?'

'Somerset. Near Yeovil.'

'Bloody Hell! I've got a sister in Somerset. We could go there day after tomorrow and I'll stay with Brenda. Look, why don't chya ring her now? Come on.'

And so it was arranged; to Somerset he was to go.

Now he was sitting in the sun on a deckchair counting his blessings. The orchard at the back of Lucy's cottage led down to a stream, which provided a pleasant and soothing gurgle in the background. Her cottage was more beautiful than he could have imagined, in spite of containing every country cliché except for thatch.

He had arrived the previous day. Lucy had been very quiet, taking care of his basic requirements and insisting on his resting. Rest and silence, interspersed with a little attention were what he needed at the moment more than anything. He felt cherished without having any demands made on him and soon began to realise just how tired he was and, in fact, had been for a long time. Lucy had a gift of being able to appear at the right moment with food or drink or the recommendation of a walk and then disappear. She said hardly anything and he felt no urge to talk. It was something entirely novel in his experience – this consideration that seemed to have no strings attached.

The remarkable thing was that this was someone he hardly

knew, having only met her twice. He couldn't understand why he felt so comfortable with her. Even his worry about her paintings seemed to be taken care of, for they were not visible in any of the rooms he had so far seen.

When they were having their evening meal that night, Lucy judged it a fit moment to break silence.

'Now you are looking a lot better,' she began, 'I wonder if you might be able to answer a couple of questions for me.'

'Go on.'

'I wondered whether you might be able to explain exactly how it is that you came to be lodged in that contraption in a state of concussion, clutching a large plastic tomato.'

'Yes, I can see that you would find that puzzling. The thing is… don't quite know where to begin. It's really quite a saga.'

'Well let's find a beginning and we'll start there.'

So he told her everything, although not entirely in sequence. About hating the Lichtenstein, about his dream and about his feelings for plastic tomatoes, his teenaged experience at the party in Hendon when he had squirted the only attractive girl in the room with tomato ketchup. About Millicent and her departure and about his feeling that the plastic tomato in the kitchen would somehow assert his sovereignty over this territory. The rest was easy.

Lucy Bleddoes closed her eyes and smiled an appreciative smile. 'Now I understand – at least, I think I do. A bit like Saint Paul seeing through a glass darkly perhaps,' she said. 'More wine?'

She poured out some more.

'What was the other question?'

'Who is this Jane, who you told me so emphatically, as you came round, is RIGHT.'

'Jane…? I don't remember. Or perhaps she was someone in a dream.'

He sipped his wine thoughtfully.

'Your memory must be a bit damaged.'

'No... I don't think so.' His head was starting to hurt again. "Jane" rang a bell in his head but he couldn't bring a precise picture to the surface. It worried him.

'I think... perhaps you are not ready to talk about Jane yet. You haven't really forgotten but there's something you don't want to let out. Don't worry about it. Forget that I asked. It'll come back to you in the next few days. You don't have to tell me.'

She led him into her sitting room and they listened to some Elizabethan lute music on the Bang and Olufson, which she referred to as her "gramophone", and then she told him to go to bed.

He retired to the comfort of his room, which had a soft deep bed and its own bathroom. Being off the dining room, it was downstairs and secluded. Mention of Jane had stirred something in him. He dozed off but permanent sleep refused to come, because he was worried that his memory might be affected by the bang. This was the first evidence of it, for so far he seemed to have reconnected successfully with all the strands of his pre-fall life.

Sleep became increasingly remote. Restlessly he got out of bed, opened his curtains and window and looked out. A full moon caught the blossoms and leaves on the apple and pear trees, embossing them with silver against the deep blue shadows. Small movements and rustlings in the distance suggested birds settling or possibly even rabbits or hares playing and over it all he could just hear the gurgle of the little stream. Something small and dark slowly wended its way across the lawn. It was a hedgehog going about its business in the discreet darkness of the night. He watched entranced.

And then something hit him. 'Jane...' he said, 'Jane. You

are so right… it is meaningless…' It had come back, the last missing little piece of memory. He returned to bed and went to sleep with a little smile on his face.

The returning sense of well-being was still with him in the morning. Over coffee in the dark green, gold-edged French cups, basking in the glimpses of sunlit garden through the deep-set windows, he said, 'Feel so much better. I… I don't think I know how to begin to thank you for all this.'

'It's nothing. It really is a pleasure for me. And you are a very undemanding guest. I don't have to take you sightseeing or anything. I just boss you about and go on with what I have to do.'

He remembered something. 'But I've been here three days and I haven't seen your paintings yet. When are you going to show me?'

'I didn't want to bother you when you were so tired. But now you are better, I think I could inflict them upon you. We will go upstairs when you have finished your breakfast.'

So she took him up to her domain on the upper floor. The studio was in the end room of the house and stretched its full width, above the sitting room. She had cleverly removed the ceiling and opened it up to the loft, revealing the tie beams and inserting a roof light. 'Now you see why I am so thankful that this is not a thatched roof. I couldn't have had this skylight. I wouldn't have been able to have it on the front of the house either, but I've managed to get away with it, being out of the public eye.'

The studio smelled delightfully of hessian, old wood, apples, linseed oil and genuine turpentine. He turned his attention to the paintings.

It was much as he expected. He was underwhelmed. They were 'nice' paintings – loveable in many ways with soft colours, blurred outlines and thick textures and he could see why she had no difficulty in selling them. But they left him cold. He managed to praise the colours.

'But where are the angels?'

She drew aside an old bedspread from a pile of canvases and pulled out a large painting. Like the others, it was thickly painted with heavy textures and many glazes and it was hard to make out to begin with, but then you could see that there were teapot, flowers and fruit in the bottom half of the painting and something like a freshly plastered wall above it. Only it wasn't smooth like a freshly-plastered wall but lumpy and matted with a mass of different shades of gold, ochre and pale earth colours. Then, gradually, it formed itself into an angel.

He gasped. It was magnificent. It took him to a region he had never previously visited, somewhere strange and yet familiar, where time did not exist and everything seemed to be pulsating with a golden light.

'Sit down,' Lucy said and he sank gratefully into a wicker chair.

It was some time until he could speak. The vision faded with the same gentle ease as the disappearance of a rainbow.

'What happened?' he asked Lucy.

'That's what I was going to ask you. What happened and what did you see?'

'It all happened quite suddenly. There was nothing there in the background of the painting and then there was an angel. It's still there now… But the rest of the stuff has gone.'

'What was that?'

'The golden light and everything. And the intense feeling of joy… it was very strange… very strange. Felt as if I knew everything and everything was all right. The strangest thing though was this light that came out of everything – as if it was lit up from inside – even the space between the objects seemed to be pulsating… and full of gold filaments. When I closed my eyes the gold filaments were still there. Reminded me a bit of patterns you get in clear water and strong sunshine.'

'And then it faded away?'

'Yes… It's gone now… It was so beautiful… Everything seemed to be part of me and yet separate. It was so strange… but so wonderful, so joyous. Do you know what it all meant Lucy?'

'Was there anything else that you felt?'

'Yes… I had a funny sort of sense that I had been reprieved.'

'You saw my angel and that drew you into a vision.'

'Yes… but what did it mean? It was so vivid – so powerful. I'd like it to come back.'

'You just had an intense experience of Art, that's all'

'Do you mean that's supposed to happen every time you look at a painting?'

'No… sadly. It doesn't happen that often. In fact for most people, it never happens at all. But you should get a tiny, watered down version of that – that's why people go on about Art being uplifting. You were just extremely lucky and got the concentrated version.'

'I see.' He thought about it for a moment, 'It's not something that I could possibly forget. But it won't come back?'

'There's no knowing. As I've said, you can get bits of it. Now you are very tired and I think you should have a rest.'

That evening as they sat at the table he said, 'I can tell you about Jane. It came back to me last night. Jane is someone I love. I've been trying to lock up these feelings and tell myself they don't really exist because I know that she doesn't really like me. She runs a gallery which deals in the sort of art that you do and it's not very successful and she feels that people like me are undermining her business. Perhaps we are. I don't know.'

'Oh…' Lucy sounded surprised. 'I think I have met her. She has a gallery near where my nephew lives – near Paddington.'

'Yes… that's right.'

'She's lovely and she's got very good taste. I enjoyed the paintings she was showing.'

'And she's going to give you a show?'

Lucy straightened her back. 'No, of course not. I don't actually want one in London. Yeovil every two years is quite enough for me.' She poured them both out another glass of wine and then said, 'Anyway I don't believe you would be deliberately undermining anyone. You're caught up in the tentacles of a trend, if it can be said that trends have tentacles. It wasn't really your creation but just the product of the times.'

'That's comforting.'

Lucy said, 'It is just possible that you might want to change things a bit.'

CHAPTER 29

Kite Flying

Jane rang Freddie to tell him the latest about Edwin.

'Just what we thought,' Freddie said.

'Yes, alas. Edwin is a dear, but such an ass. It was an affaire of the mind, not the heart. Henrietta doesn't seem the least put out. I actually rather sympathise with Edwin. I wouldn't want my home turned into a health spa or a holiday home for rich Americans – would you?'

'No – but what concerns me is Edwin. It's a bigger disappointment for him isn't it?'

'Yes of course. That's why I'm ringing you. I'd like to ask him to come kite flying with us on Saturday and I wanted to OK it with you first.'

'Oh, that's a nice idea, definitely!'

So Jane rang Edwin.

'I'm sorry to hear your news,' she said.

'Oh… ah… yes. Well… er… I'm not that downhearted, actually. By the end of the… weekend I had been… so… er… deluged with ideas… I couldn't think… and when she said she thought it wouldn't work… I was so… er relieved… er.'

Jane cut him short. 'Freddie and I are going kite flying on Saturday and we'd like if you would come too.'

'I'd love that' he said.

So Edwin, who had already met Freddie in the gallery, joined them.

It was a sunny day on Parliament Hill and Jane and Freddie

had brought the kite, which they owned jointly. Kite flying is great fun in the early stages of the flight when you have to get it into the air. This is the time when it can swoop to the ground if the wind is a little unsteady, but once it rises a certain height, it hovers calmly in the thermals and the whole business becomes less exciting but perhaps more calming and philosophical.

They lay on their backs on the grass and took turns to hold the reel, watching and enjoying the patterns made by the swirling tails against the pale blue sky. 'It's just like fishing,' Edwin said. 'Fishing in the sky... how I wish...' he trailed off.

'Go on,' Jane said. 'Wishes are allowed. Who knows, the Great Kite Master up there might just be listening. But I know what you are wishing. You want a wife, don't you.'

'Oh,' he sighed. 'How did you guess?'

'Edwin,' Freddie spoke rather sternly. 'We'd all like to find a partner, but you have to let things happen and not try so hard.'

'What do you... mean?'

Jane gave a tug on the string and spoke. 'It's no use proposing too early in a relationship. You have to wait and let things build up. You have to fall in love properly.'

'No... it's different when you've got... a big house just waiting for a... wife to run it... I think... if I can find the... right woman...then the love will...build up.'

'I thought you'd found that with Henrietta.' Freddie let out some string.

'Henrietta... that was different. She never stopped talking. She never... stopped having ideas... and some of them were terrible.'

'I can see that she could be a bit bossy,' Jane said.

'But I'd still like someone... who could help with the house.'

'You mean you want a house manager?' Freddie asked.

'I... thought I did... but now – to tell the truth... I'm not so sure.'

'It sounds a bit like sleeping with the housekeeper,' Freddie said.

'How long d'you… think I should wait before proposing?'

'At least a year.' Jane said, 'Would you like to hold the string now?'

'Thank you.' Edwin took the string gratefully.

'Have you ever been in love Edwin?' Jane asked.

'Er… well… no. I… loved my Teddy Bear when I was small. He got lost… and… then there was my teacher, Miss Roseveare… and then… the girl in the greengrocer's… no-one since.' He sighed, then brightened 'I met someone this week… actually who might do'

Jane and Freddie said together, 'You haven't proposed again, have you?'

Edwin shook his head rather sadly.

Freddie spoke sternly, 'Edwin – it's my opinion that you're trying too hard. You're trying to light a fire and cook on it all at once. You have to wait until it's going properly before you get involved in proposals. Propositions are another matter; but proposals…'

'But how am I to find someone?' The kite took a little dip at this point and Freddie rescued the string.

'Well,' Freddie was practical. 'There are agencies you know.'

'And you could always advertise in the lonely hearts columns,' Jane added.

'Or you could go to Russia, or Thailand and get one there, quite easily.'

'I'm not sure I want… a foreigner… Can you imagine one at Lostock Hall? And have you… ever met anyone who made a satisfactory relationship through an… er… advertisement?'

'Yes, I have,' said Freddie. 'But it wasn't hetero. And it took a long time.'

Jane said, 'Edwin, you've burned your fingers with

Henrietta. But it's taught you a lesson.'

Their discussion was now abruptly ended as a large dog bounded up to them and enthusiastically tried to lick their faces. Edwin drew himself up and said in an unexpectedly commanding manner, 'Leave off! Pestilential hound... Go on... GO!' and the dog, rather to their surprise, slunk off.

To change the subject he addressed Jane, 'How about you Jane? Has that... dreadful fella... left you alone since... you refused to have lunch with him?'

'Well... not exactly. We met completely by chance one afternoon on Primrose Hill.'

'He's been stalking you?'

'I don't think so. He was coming from the opposite direction. It was just one of those things. He didn't know I live in Primrose Hill and he just happened to be taking a walk there.'

'So you cut him dead and walked on with your head high and your nose in the air?' Freddie said.

'No, I actually let him buy me a cup of tea. We had quite a discussion.'

'I bet you did.'

'I told him that what he was doing was utterly meaningless, in terms of art... and...'

'Go on.'

'He told me at one point that I had a closed mind and there was a lot I could learn from the modern art movement – particularly about marketing.'

'Yes... well, that's not surprising because... marketing is what it's all about really. Not art,' said Edwin.

'Yes, that's true. But he had a point because he went on to give me some very practical advice about the gallery.'

'And are you going to take it.'

'Just as soon as I can. I'll think about it of course. It may be that some of the suggestions are more feasible than others.

But it was kind of him wasn't it?'

'You sound as though you are becoming... er... partial to him. I don't like this at all.'

'Don't be so Gothic, Edwin. You have to allow the enemy to score on some points. Anyway, I again refused to go out with him and he didn't press the point. He told me that his wife had just left him and he obviously felt a bit sad.' Jane was silent for a moment while she watched the kite. 'I'm probably going to phone Mark because Henrietta has told me that he has had an accident and been concussed.'

'Good idea.' Freddie said, 'He's done something for you.'

Edwin who seemed to have a patriarchal concern for Jane said, 'Just don't get carried... away by compassion. I've heard that he has a mistress... as well, so I don't expect he's that bothered by the loss of his wife.' The kite again gave a downward lurch and Freddie had to pull hard to get it up again. They all watched this manoeuvre in silence and then Freddie said, 'Maybe we've all got closed minds,'

Edwin said, 'Look... I've had my wish. What about you two?'

'Yes... Freddie, what about you?' Jane looked at Freddie.

'A white McLaren,' said Freddie who was unable, or unwilling to give voice to his deepest desire... 'Jane?'

'Oh... that's easy. I'd like Andrew's exhibition to be the success it deserves to be. I'd like the critics to come and make his reputation and I'd like it to rescue my gallery's financial position.'

At this the kite gave a great twitch, sending its tail swirling and spinning into graceful arabesques.

Edwin laughed. 'That's a sign... the Great Kite Master... has heard your wish.'

'Shall we reel in?' Freddie asked. 'I think it's time we had some tea. Any ideas where we should go?'

'I think,' Edwin said, 'that it should be Patisserie Valerie.'

'I think,' Freddie said, 'that first we should all purge our closed minds by a brief visit to an avant-garde gallery; just to see what it is we have to learn.'

If Jane was rather silent during their descent from the hill, it was because she was trying to digest the news that Mark had a mistress. It cut into her with a pain that increased the more she thought about it. She felt that he had somehow behaved dishonestly by enlisting her sympathies over the break-up of a marriage that wasn't, by any account, too successful. But how could he have told her when he hardly knew her? Maybe if they had talked longer he would have admitted it. Or maybe not. It irritated her that she should have this reaction. Mark meant nothing to her – so why should it annoy her so much to find that he behaved like the average sort of man that he was?

'All right. Here we are,' said Freddie.

The taxi had dropped them off outside a pair of ramshackle houses in a terrace in Camden Town. 'This is the purge I have chosen for us. This should prise open our clenched minds.'

'Is this really it?' Edwin was a little dubious.

'This is it. Mrs Egglesdrop's Sooper Dooper Play House.'

'We have to pay to get in,' Jane said.

'It's all right. This is my treat,' Freddie said firmly. 'Noses down and tackle this in the spirit of adventure!'

'Oh rather!' retorted Edwin. 'We shall be the epitome of... jollygoodchaperie!'

The two houses had a blue door on the left and a red door on the right. The one on the right was marked "Entrance". The blue door had nothing on it. The windows were covered with opaque paint so it was impossible to see in. Freddie led the way and they found themselves in a narrow corridor, at the end of which sat an imposing lady with bright emerald hair.

She took Freddie's money and then in a deep and commanding voice ordered them to go up to the top floor. Having done this, they passed through a succession of rooms from top to bottom, in each of which was some kind of an exhibit. There were three bedrooms in which a giant, a pantomime horse and a mermaid reclined on the beds. In the bathroom there was a giant lobster, and in the toilet a snake curled gracefully.

There were tables hanging from ceilings and chairs without legs and odd bits of human limbs protruding from walls or bookshelves.

As they went from room to room, they found themselves laughing. It was outrageous and incongruous. Mrs Egglesdrop had taken a conventional terrace house and turned it upside down. It made a mockery of the sort of aspirations that affect that section of society which would love to own just such a terrace house in Camden Town. In one room there was an ostrich with its head buried in a sofa; in another there was a large egg, which they found would revolve when they touched it.

'I wonder what would… happen if you cracked it,' Edwin said.

'Go on,' said Freddie, 'I expect everyone else has had the same idea.'

By now Jane had wandered through to the next room. 'Look at that!' She exclaimed, 'Oh my goodness!' The room had a padded floor and on it was a collection of teddy bears, having a tea party. Only of course it was not tea that they were drinking but heavy spirits and beer. Their sizes ranged from eight foot to five inches.'

'I love teddies,' Edwin said and after a moment's hesitation pushed over the biggest one and fell onto it and hugged it. 'This is blissful… Come on, you try it.'

So they all rolled about among the teddies, feeling a

revival of childish innocence. When they had had enough they went down to the ground floor where they were handed a collection of Victorian masks, which covered their eyes but not their mouths, and told that they had to sing. There was quite a large group of people also wearing these masks and a pianist played old fashioned tunes on a jangly piano. They joined in the songs and they each had to sing a solo. They found that although the masks distorted the sound, the change of identity gave them a sort of new confidence and all three produced sounds and melodies that surprised them. Then everyone took their masks off and although they were now strangers again, the ice had broken and there was a lot of talk and laughter over cups of tea.

'Well,' Jane said, when they eventually left. 'I have to thank you Freddie. That was fun. I haven't laughed so much for ages.'

'But do you feel your mind has opened?'

'Not exactly,' Edwin said. 'It was Dada… there's nothing particularly new about that.'

'Yes… well it was Dada plus installation, plus audience participation,' Freddie said.

Jane said, 'It was very clever. Very well put together.'

'It was therapy!' Freddie said.

'But was it art?'

They replied in unison. 'NO!'

'What was it then?' Edwin asked.

'It was a circus,' Jane said. 'Entertainment. I'm glad we went. Do you think I should have some events like that in my gallery?'

'No,' Edwin said. 'You stick to what your heart is in… You'll be all right. Seeing this has made me realise… the difference. There's a lot to be got out of… entertainment… it's something we all need. But art is… something else.'

CHAPTER 30

Fool On A Hill

'What you said about change… been thinking about that.' They were sitting at breakfast and Mark was enjoying the spectacle of steam rising out of the dark green coffee pot on the hot-plate on the table.

'Yes?' said Lucy.

'I… just don't know what I'm going to do. I feel like I'm in charge of a huge train travelling at great speed in the wrong direction and I don't know how to turn it. I don't even know how to stop it, for that matter.'

'Could you get off it?'

'I'd love to do that. Love to go on staying here. Be a complete dropout. It's really idyllic. But you'd get fed up of me and I know I have to get back. There are things to do.' He paused and took a sip of coffee. Lucy didn't do croissants, but somehow it didn't matter.

Mark continued, 'I adore doing what I do. There are so many people involved and I love working with them. I love all the excitement and the parties and the press conferences. I just can't throw all that away. I just can't.'

'It's possible that you don't really need to. I mean, there might be some bits you could throw away without having to ditch the whole thing. Perhaps you might be able to steer the gallery in another direction.'

'Well… you won't let me promote your painting!'

'Now Mark – we've been through all that!'

In a curious way he was quite relieved that she was so

adamant. For although he loved her dearly, it was only the angel paintings that he really admired and his desire to promote her work was to do with other factors, like gratitude. 'When I banged my head and got concussed, the idea came that Jane is right – what I'm doing is rubbish. If that's really the case, then I shouldn't be doing it.' He sighed. 'But it's such fun!'

Lucy was quiet for a long moment. 'It's fairly complicated,' she said at last. 'To be perfectly honest, I don't really know what you should do. You have to follow the dictates of your inner self – but I know that's not much help when there are two voices arguing different things.'

They sat in silence for a moment. Mark liked this so much about Lucy. They didn't have to keep up a conversational flow.

Lucy said, 'The answer always comes in the end. At least it has for me. Even if you make a wrong decision, you learn about it.'

'How?'

'When things go wrong for you.'

'Always? You mean every time something bad happens it's the result of a wrong decision?'

'Sometimes it is – sometimes it isn't. It's not so easy to know. But looking at it from a different perspective can be useful. It's an idea to work on. You have to just wait and see. And not worry too much. My feeling is that you'll be all right.'

There was nothing he could say to this so he was silent. Then an idea struck him. 'Lucy?'

'Yes.'

'Would you... or could you be prepared to part with that angel painting? I'd really love to have it and it would take up a space in my house that needs filling.'

'Would you really like it?'

'Yes, of course.'

It was Lucy's turn to be embarrassed.

'It's one of my best paintings… if not the very best… I'm not really sure I want to part with it. On the other hand there are things I need to do for the cottage… so perhaps I could let it go.'

'How much?'

Lucy named a price.

'Much too little. That's outrageous!'

And they went through a process of reverse bargaining, which caused a lot of laughter, until they found a price they could agree on.

'At least that's settlement on one thing. But do you really not know what I should do next?'

'I've already told you – I haven't the foggiest idea.'

'At least what do you think I should do now?'

'A much better question. I think you should go up a hill.'

'Up a hill?'

'Hills are remarkably good places for problem solving – that's why so many hermits and monks live on them. The air is purer and the increased oxygen helps one to think straight. Unfortunately, Somerset is not especially well endowed with hills – but there is one at Glastonbury. I think you should climb the Tor tomorrow.'

'But Glastonbury's a hippy place – I'm not into New Age Mysticism.'

'Glastonbury is a lot older than all that. You would meet it on your own terms. It has a very strong presence. And it so happens that my friend Marjorie will be going there tomorrow; she always goes on Thursdays to see her grand-children. I could easily arrange for her to give you a lift.'

So it was settled. To Glastonbury he would go.

Marjorie was a restful person to be with because she

chatted brightly all the way about her family and garden and asked him no questions. The town was alive with flowers and flags; there was some kind of puppet festival going on. In the main street, an unpacked Punch and Judy stall was looking more like an installation than anything else in its wrapping of thick bubblewrap.

It was cheerful in the blustery showery day. The showers were not heavy and the sun was bright.

He found his way to the Tor. As Lucy had told him, he found that it did have a strong presence. Perhaps this was due to its position, rising out of the Somerset levels – or perhaps to the tower on the top. There was a sort of fairytale quality about it. You could imagine knights in armour and princesses and monks even if you had never heard any of the legends. There weren't any other hills he could think of that had towers on top – a few castles perhaps on crags, but no mysterious towers.

He climbed up the well-constructed pathway listening to the singing of a thrush, followed, further up, by the exuberant, soaring notes of a skylark. There were dandelions, daisies and little blue speedwell all around in the grass.

It was not a long climb to the top and the activity was pleasant and soothing – but all the same, it exposed an alarming degree of unfitness. *When I get back, I'll regularly spend time in a gym. And I'll go to bed earlier. And eat more sensibly.* He promised himself.

But if he had expected any great mystical revelation or any repeat of his experience with the angel he was to be disappointed, for no new doors opened in his perception.

He passed under the archway in the ruined tower and looked up to the sky. Once through the other side he stood on the grass, opened his arms to the wind and addressed God.

He spoke silently in case anyone should hear for it was a

busy place, 'God, what is the answer? What am I going to do now? Just where am I going?'

God was not at home, however, and had omitted to leave a message on his answering machine. Perhaps this was just as well. Mark could not have endured an angelic voice of sympathy telling him, *God is experiencing an unprecedented number of calls at the moment; please try later.* And anyway like most of his friends, his belief in the Deity was sporadic and dependent on exigency.

It was too cold to stay long on the top, because of the sharp wind, but he found that a little way down he was sheltered. He sat on the grass and then lay back and dozed for a while.

He was not alone. There was an endless procession of people and he enjoyed watching the diverse costumes. Long, trailing, tie-dyed skirts and long, unwashed hair, alternated with short "en brosse". Sometimes it was hard to work out which gender a person was. Almost everyone had a gem or a piece of fine metal stuck into some part of the face or body. There were nose rings and eyebrow, lip and navel studs. A few stalwarts wore vests that exposed extraordinary tattoos of dragons, unicorns or butterflies. It occurred to him that these hippies had pre-empted the name "New Age" in the same way he and his colleagues in the art world appropriated "Cutting Edge of Modern". It was an interesting idea, but not exactly a great revelation.

One couple in particular attracted his attention, partly because they were such a weird juxtaposition. The girl was short, fat, bubbly and blonde and the man was tall and thin, sunburned with long straggly hair and a pointed beard. They had a large paper bag with them and were picking up discarded crisp and confectionary packets. 'That's a good idea!' he called to them. 'Yes – isn't it?' said bubbly-blonde. 'We always do it when we come up here. We're going to recycle most of this.'

'Oh… how?'

'We use it in our puppet theatre, for sets and costumes and things. We're puppeteers.'

They sat down beside him. He asked them their names. 'I'm Rainbow and this is Willow,' said the girl.

'Willow and Rainbow what?'

'Rainbow and Willow Peacetree. We chose our names ourselves. They represent our auras.'

'Do you like working with puppets?'

'We love it. We have a van that everything fits in and we travel round the country all the time. Willow does the scenery and I make the puppets. Would you like to see our show? We're doing one this afternoon.'

He thought that he would – he was not meeting Marjorie until four, so he had time on his hands.

He might not have descended from the hill with any great revelations but he noticed that his head had stopped hurting. He felt better and calmer.

The puppet show was unbelievably awful. That is not to say that there were no good bits in it. If it had been an installation, he probably would have liked it; but with puppets, you somehow expected to have a beginning, middle and a resounding end. This play suffered from too many ideas, too much of what he could only call "New Age Guff", too much noise and, oddly enough, too much violence; perhaps because it was trying to follow in the wake of Punch and Judy. However, perhaps his criticism was unfair for the children loved it.

The puppets themselves were grotesque and clumsy, but the box proscenium was a wonderful mass of rich colours and textures as was the scenery. It was full of lightness, using gauzes, delicate draperies and murals made of a patchwork of textiles and scraps of brightly coloured paper. He took Willow and Rainbow's leaflet, with a vague feeling that somehow, somewhere, he might be able to make use of this talent.

In the morning Charlene came to fetch him. He invited her in to meet Lucy and view his new acquisition.

'Wow!' she said. 'That's quite something. Wish I could paint like that. What'yer going to do with it? Put it in the gallery?'

'I'd like to. But right now it's going in my house. I've got a blank wall waiting for it. Do you think we could get it in the car?'

There was just enough room behind the front passenger seat. He embraced Lucy. 'I can't thank you enough.'

'I am not going to tell you to "take care",' said Lucy, 'because this has become an impossible cliché. When people tell me to take care, I reply "live dangerously". But all the same…'

They laughed at this.

On the way home, while Charlene chatted gaily about her nieces and nephews and her new idea about designing some tee shirts, he had another idea about something that he could do for Jane.

Back in Canonbury, he unpacked the painting and installed in on the wall in the space left by the Lichtenstein. He lay back and admired it. It was beautiful and calming and it looked just as good in his house, or if anything, even better because there was more space around it.

The visionary experience he had had at Lucy's did not return but he didn't mind. He had some memory of it each time he saw the painting and he felt that he enjoyed it more every time he looked at it.

All he wanted now was to see Jane and tell her. Tell her that she was right, and tell her that he loved her. But the events of the past few days had shaken him up. He had lost all his confidence. He could not pick up the phone and ring her, neither could he jump into Princess Seraphina with an orchid and rush off to Little Venice. It was the same diffidence he had experienced when he wanted to ring Lucy – only more so.

He just could not do it.

CHAPTER 31

Breakfast With Jane

Jane found it difficult to ring Mark. Freddie, who had noticed an alarming increase in the number of mentions of Andrew in recent days and feared that with the excitement of the impending exhibition, he might be making a comeback, kept on encouraging her to ring. Eventually she did so only to be politely informed that Mark would be away until the following week.

On his return, Mark was suffering from the same problem. The blockage was still there. Every time he thought about picking up the phone, he saw a picture of her refusing him. Now that he had some understanding of the reasons for her rejection, he felt totally inadequate. Many, many times, the idea came and each time he stretched out his hand to the phone, another voice said 'No. Don't'. Confused about his future and denied the pleasure of telling her about the extraordinary chain of events that had changed his life, he felt utterly depressed and dejected.

When his phone rang, he picked it up in an automatic way, expecting to hear yet another of his socialite friends recommending their particular cure or inviting him to stay.

But... it was Jane! He couldn't believe it. 'Jane!'

'I – I'm just ringing to say that I heard about your accident. I'm very sorry about it...' She trailed off, not knowing quite what to say next. There was a silence at the other end and she wondered if she had done the right thing or whether she had upset him in some way. Then Mark spoke.

'Jane. I'm so glad you rang. I wanted to speak to you so much.'

'Are you all right?'

'Yes. I'm very all right. Jane, please could I talk to you – I want to tell you about something that has happened. It's something that you might be quite pleased about. I owe you an apology.'

'An apology?'

'Look. I can't really explain it all over the phone. Please could we meet somewhere and talk about it.'

'I'm terribly busy at the moment. We're hanging a new show tomorrow – you know what that's like.'

'Breakfast?' he said hopefully. 'You must eat breakfast.'

Jane did not eat breakfast most days when she went to the gallery. Breakfast was a luxury for weekends, but there was a note of urgency in his voice, almost of desperation. 'All right,' she said. 'I'll be at that café in Regents Park Road at 8.30 tomorrow morning. But I won't be able to stay long.'

'It won't take long. I'm just so grateful to you. See you then.'

He rang off.

It was a cold and misty spring morning. Jane added a scarf to her raincoat and wore sensible shoes to keep out the damp.

The café was unexpectedly crowded. Mark was waiting for her on a bar stool by the bar, with just one empty seat which he was keeping for her. It didn't seem to be the best place for a long intimate discussion.

He was overjoyed to see her and jumped down from the stool. He only just managed to stop himself from giving her a big hug. 'Jane!' He beamed with delight as she climbed onto to the stool. 'What's it to be. Cappuccino and croissant?'

'Caffe latte and croissant, please.'

He ordered for both of them and then fell silent, which was uncharacteristic. There was something different about him

– the confidence seemed to have diminished. Jane decided to help him out.

'My friends and I visited an installation exhibit near here last week and… we loved it.'

He looked puzzled. 'Oh… why?'

'It was such fun. We laughed and laughed.'

'Don't tell me you've had a mystical experience and been converted to avant-garde art?'

'Not exactly… but there's something to be said for entertainment, isn't there?' He laughed.

Their coffees arrived. Mark spoke rather quickly and softly, not wanting to be overheard, 'I had this bang on my head and it all went dark and I heard you saying that what I was doing was rubbish and then, while I was away I thought I saw an angel shimmering out of a painting and it's all made me see things differently.' It was a condensed version but the place was crowded.

'Phew,' said Jane, coolly. 'But how did you fall? What happened?'

He told her, as briefly as possible, about his fall and then said, 'I owe you an apology.' He felt convinced that she did not believe him.

'What an earth for?' She stirred the foam on the top of her latte.

'I got it wrong. What I'm doing is rubbish.'

'I'm not so sure.' Jane sipped her coffee. 'There's nothing wrong in making people happy, is there?'

'I think – it's the business of wrapping it all up in pretentious prose that's the trouble.'

'Anyway, where did you find this great revelation?'

'I stayed in Somerset with an old lady.' He told her about his vision of the angel and then added, 'I think she knows you.'

'Oh really?'

'Lucy Bleddoes'

Up to this point, Jane did not have the slightest intimation that he was telling the truth. But the mention of Lucy somehow put it another scan on it, 'Lucy came to my gallery when I was feeling rather low. She said some things that helped me.'

'She's a remarkable lady.'

'So what are you going to do now?

'I don't know,' he sighed. 'Lucy said I had to work it out for myself. I think it might be possible to steer the gallery in another direction. I'd hate to give it up.'

Jane looked at her watch. She could see his eyes imploring her to believe him and she wanted to think things over by herself. 'I've got to go,' she said.

'You don't trust me?'

Jane laughed. 'If anyone asks me that I always say "No".'

He drank his coffee. 'It's rather what I feared.'

'No,' she said. 'It's just rather too big a lurch in the plot for me to accept at the moment, especially when I'm very preoccupied with getting Andrew's show off the ground.'

He wrenched himself out of his own morass of feelings and asked calmly, 'Preparations going well?'

'As well as they can in the circumstances.' A shadow came over her face. 'That's an artist who needs more in the way of recognition than I can provide.'

'Are you in love with him?'

'That's not really any of your business. Andrew's a good artist and a man of great integrity.' She glared at him. 'Now I really must go.' She got off the stool and pulled her coat round her shoulders. 'You've told me a good story – I'm not sure if I believe it. But I'll think about it.'

Once again a long look passed between them. This time he told himself – *she might not believe me but at least she's not in love with Andrew.*

'Might we meet again – somewhere quieter and talk some more?'

'I don't really know… I'll have to have a think. Thanks for the coffee. Bye Now'. And she was off.

Mark now knew exactly what he was going to do for her.

Chapter 32

A New Revelation

Jane felt bemused.

On the one hand she wanted to believe Mark; on the other it seemed so unlikely. He could have reasons for wanting to deceive her.

She wanted to believe him. It was a good story – but it just seemed so unlikely. In her experience, people did not change their whole mindset just because of a bang on the head and a vision. Mark did not have a very good record as a teller of the truth. Yet, on the other hand, there was something about his manner which rang true. He really did seem to be changed. Also there was just one factor which made it more plausible, and that was Lucy Bleddoes.

She tried to resolve her fluctuations by saying, 'Oh well... time will tell'. The problem was, she didn't want to wait. She needed to know now exactly what had happened and whether she really could trust him. She was beginning to want this.

Fortunately, Andrew's exhibition was approaching and she was also looking into the possibilities of implementing some of Mark's suggestions. It was a relief to be busy.

It was Andrew's show, opening next week, that was the big worry. Andrew had been irritatingly fussy about minor details – there were many phone calls and letters telling her all about his doings, but when she thought of Andrew she thought of integrity. He might be a bore but he was unshakeable in his conviction that he must not show his work until he was ready

– no matter what inducements he was given from people anxious to help him make use of the optimum moment. He was convinced that the show would be a brilliant success in spite of Jane's cautions. She was touched that his mother had even paid for a new suit for the special occasion.

Irritated with Andrew and irritated with Mark she was snappish with Freddie who had called in to see how things were going.

'What's up?' Freddie asked. 'You're not your usual cheery self.'

She sighed. It seemed too difficult to explain.

'You're not veering round to Andrew are you? You've been talking about him quite a lot.'

'Oh no... far from it. I can't help talking about him because he's demanding a lot of attention. And it worries me that he's living in cloud cuckoo land about his chances. He seems to be on a high at the moment and I dread to think what will happen when he crashes.'

'Look darling. you're doing all right as you are. You don't need to perform miracles. The art scene has changed and so have the avenues to success. You can't alter those, not unless you're God that is, but I think you've got the enterprise and the courage to recognise a good piece of advice when you get it and act on it. You should be pleased about that and not be worrying about what you can't do.'

Jane did not answer.

'Anyway he might not crash,' Freddie said.

'Optimist! You know as well as I do what the chances are.'

'I suppose I should.' Freddie was silent for a moment.

Jane could remember some of his less successful shows. 'But all the same it feels a bit tough on poor old Andrew.'

'Oh screw Andrew.' Freddie was getting impatient. 'He'll survive. After all, I've had a few lousy shows in my time.'

Jane picked up a small piece of paper and said nothing

'Are you sure that's all you're worried about?'

She silently fidgeted with the paper. 'I had breakfast with Mark the other day.'

'And how did that go?'

She rolled the paper into a tight scroll and then unrolled it again.

Her silence unnerved Freddie. 'What's really up? Something's bugging you?'

She sighed again. 'I can't make out what's going on. One minute I think one thing and then the next I think differently – I just don't know. He's had a fall, got concussed, went and stayed in the country and had a vision.'

'Yes... so?'

The paper was rolled up again... an expression of anguish passed over her face, 'as a result, he's changed his ideas about avant-garde art and says he got it wrong and I'm right.'

'My Goodness! But that's not a bad thing is it'

'If it's true, it's a very good thing. But how am I to know? He could be lying... trying to trap me into having a relationship.'

'I see... I can see that it must be difficult for you.'

'Andrew for all his failings has this blazing sincerity and I can't help thinking what a contrast with Mark.' Again the paper was unrolled.

'I think...' Freddie spoke in a tone of great compassion. 'I think it's a case for tender love and care. I'm not only going to take you out to dinner tonight but I'm going to drag you off to a party. It's high time you had some distraction from these two men.'

Just then the phone rang. Jane picked it up. She answered briefly and blushed. 'Yes... yes... OK... yes... tomorrow... fine.'

'That wasn't Andrew I take it.' Freddie noticed the brevity of the call.

'No. Only some joker who said he was the art critic of the Sunday Times and wants to see the new work before the private view.'

'Perhaps he isn't a joker.'

'Wouldn't that be amazing! But he sounded like a joker.'

'You better be here, just in case.'

'Oh... I will.' The paper was rolled into a very tight scroll.

'So where is this party you want to take me too?'

'It's at the house of an artist in Notting Hill. I'm sure you'd like them – Bill and Janet – great friends of mine who've just moved back to England. But... there's another reason I'd like you to come...' He trailed off, suddenly and quite unexpectedly shy.

'What's that?'

'Jane, I've met someone. It hasn't got very far yet but I know he's going to be there and I just want you to meet him.'

It was unusual for Freddie to talk about his love life – so much so that she had stopped asking, though this did not stop her from wondering.

'Oh, Freddie!'

She did not like parties but she loved Freddie enough to overcome her reluctance. 'That's so nice. Of course I'll come.'

It was a shabby house, but not too different from the one Jane was living in and the party was in the large first floor room at the front. It was dimly lit, crowded and noisy with music and chatter. One of the things she hated about parties was the eternal hope that she might meet her ideal partner, a hope that was always dashed. She looked around to see if this imaginary paragon was there and once again he wasn't. She decided to make the best of it.

Freddie introduced her to a young man, Robbie, with brilliant dark eyes, high cheekbones and a bright expression.

She liked him a lot and was pleased for Freddie. Robbie told
her he was a dancer and loved his work and they had a brief
conversation about it, before she was swept away by a noisy
group of his friends.

Freddie rescued her and took her to meet her hostess,
Janet. 'Have you got a drink?... Have you got something to
eat?' Janet was preoccupied with hospitality. Jane reassured
her. 'I hear you have a gallery?' Janet said.

Jane told her about the gallery and invited her to visit.
Then another clutch of people swirled in between them and
she was cut off.

In an attack of shyness she retreated to the kitchen. There
was always something so comforting about kitchens in a
house where there was a party going on. You could hear
people talk for one thing and it is a much easier place to get
to know strangers.

This kitchen was attractive. It had dark blue paint on the
walls and clever lighting to compensate for the dark. The
countertops and appliances were white and the floor was blue
and white checks. There was a large abstract painting on the
wall with lots of crimson, scarlet, oranges and pink, giving
just the complimentary colours that the cool walls needed.

A large girl, rather heavily built, wearing a pinafore made
of patches of velvet, was sitting at the table drinking orange
juice. 'Have one of these,' she smiled and offered Jane a dish of
stuffed vine leaves. Jane took one gratefully. 'I've been doing
this all day – handing out samples of food.' The girl laughed.

'Why... are you a caterer?' Jane was relieved to find the
room so empty.

The girl laughed. 'Nah... I work for Forbaggio's, the
cookshop in Ken High... like. We've been demonstrating
some of our lines for parties. There's a very pretty cake tin
with a daisy on top, so we made lots of lemon cakes, like, and

handed them out. We find that when we give customers food, they get the idea very quickly.'

'I love Forbaggio's. I've bought some great platters there,' Jane said. 'Do you enjoy working there?'

'I love it but I won't be there much longer.' The girl coloured slightly and then as if to change the subject hurriedly said, 'What do you do?'

'Oh, I run an art gallery.'

'Oh do you? I've got a friend in the art trade. You might know him.'

'Oh – Who?'

'Mark… he runs an avantgarde gallery in Cork Street. I don't like the work much though.'

'Not Mark Arniston Crocker?'

'Yeah… that's the one.'

'Of course.' Jane was surprised – she had not expected to hear this name.

'Yes… that's right. You know 'im then?'

'Not very well… I've only met him a few times. Do you know him well?'

'Yeah, I'd say so. I've known 'im for about five years.'

It was clear to Jane that this was knowledge in the biblical sense.

'What do you think of him?' asked Jane.

'He's very nice. At first you think he's all brash and boastful, but when you get to know him you see the other side. He's much more sensitive than you think. He's got a lot of heart… good at taking care of people, like. He's always doing lots of things at once but he manages to take care of people who need him.'

'I suppose he's good, well, he's really very good at promoting his sort of art, but it's not my sort, that's all.'

'Oh, I agree,' said Louisa. 'I don't go much more modern that Monet.'

Something about this stirred a dim recollection for Jane. 'I think I agree with you there… Tell me, what's your name?

'Louisa – what's yours?'

'Jane… Mark mentioned you to me. It's quite funny because I said I'd like to meet you. Isn't that odd?'

Louisa laughed. 'Funny old world, like! By the way, he had an accident recently – he fell and bashed his head on one of his installations. He's all right now though.'

'Yes, I know,' Jane said. 'Have you seen him since his accident?'

'No – just spoken on the phone.'

'Did he sound a bit changed?'

'Well yes, now you mention it… excuse me a mo… I've got this cramp in my side – need to stretch like.'

She got up out of her chair, stood up straight and raised her arms in a big stretch. 'There… Ooh that's better. Little thing's starting to move around like.'

With a sense of shock Jane noticed the pregnancy.

'Louisa,' she said as calmly as she could, 'Is… er… Mark the father?'

Louisa sank down into the chair and nodded with a little smile.

'Ah… there you are! I've been looking for you everywhere.' Freddie burst into the room looking excited and happy. 'Robbie would like to come to the next show – have you any spare invites?'

Jane fished in her handbag and brought out a couple of invitations for the Private View. Louisa saw what she was doing and asked about it, so Jane gave her one. The room was now full of people and it was impossible to continue their conversation. She quietly made her way out. The shock of Louisa's revelation had killed the party for her.

CHAPTER 33

A Race

Jane returned home in a state of acute distress. Time would tell, she had said repeatedly – and now it had. She knew that he had wanted to tell her more than time allowed at their breakfast, but even so she felt angry. So angry in fact that she didn't know whether she wanted never to see him again, or to confront him with the fact that he was a cheat, a liar and not be trusted.

She knew it would be a long night and occupied herself with minor chores, like pruning and watering the geraniums, in order to postpone going to bed.

Before she did this, she glanced at her answering machine. It was flickering away. 'Nigel Detchant, Observer art critic. Could I please come and see Andrew Silverstone's work as soon as possible. Ring me – this is my number...' Another joker. She burst into tears. But she knew she would return the call.

It was a long night. Eventually, before dawn, calmer voices began to intervene. It wasn't quite fair to blame Mark for not telling her. Perhaps there was some explanation which left him in the right. Perhaps; but then she sank back into gloom and the misery of another deep disappointment.

By the following Saturday her anger had cooled although she still felt upset. It was a cheerful sunny day and Saturdays, when her assistant Ardelle was in the gallery, gave her a freedom which she always enjoyed.

In the afternoon, she decided to take her usual walk up

Primrose Hill. She still felt disappointed and sad, but more or less resigned. It was the way of the world and she had to get used to it. She was glad she had been so severe with Mark at that breakfast. Despite an enormous impulse to give him all her trust, she had insisted on time, waiting, and 'taking a lot to convince'. Her prudence was completely justified.

Just then she saw him. He was not alone but was walking up the hill towards her with two children at his side. He looked animated and happy with his hair tossed about by the breeze. Despite her anger and her resolves, her heart gave a little flip when she saw him. *I have been ambushed again*, she thought with a momentary shiver of excitement. And then she felt angry. He shouldn't have tried so blatantly to see her like that.

Mark waved and then walked rapidly up to her. 'I was so hoping to see you… I knew I couldn't count on it. How are you?'

'I'm fine,' she said, angrily avoiding his eyes.

'This is Jonathan and this is Kate… we've just been to the Zoo – it's Jonathan's birthday treat – what he asked for. And we thought we might go to the ice cream place in Chalk Farm. This is my friend Jane, folks, say "How do you do?"'

The children said "How d'ya do", politely and Jane returned their greetings while continuing to look away from Mark.

It was obvious to him that something was up and his brain worked quickly to provide a solution. He addressed the children,

'Would you like to have a race. I'll give a prize to the one that can get to the top first.'

'It's not fair,' Kate pleaded. 'Jonathan can run faster than me.'

'So we'll give you a bit of a start.' After a certain amount of argument they agreed on a ten yard start for Kate and then they were off.

'Now,' said Mark quietly and firmly. 'Tell me what's biting you Jane.'

'I went to a party last week and met Louisa.'

'You met Louisa. So?'

'She's expecting your baby.'

'Yes. Think I know that.'

'Well... are you going to marry her?'

'No.'

'You're behaving like a complete and utter bastard! How can you?'

'I've behaved like a bastard. I told you. Louisa has been my girlfriend for a long time. She loves me. I can't marry her because I don't really feel that way about her. Oddly enough, although I used to feel guilty about this, I don't feel a trace any more. Come to understand that if you marry someone you don't really love, then you really can't make them happy. Baby wasn't my idea. I made it very clear to her, but she wants it. As it's my responsibility I'm taking care of her. Bought her a house and I'll go on looking after her for as long as she needs.'

'But why didn't you tell me?'

'Hell, Jane. You didn't really give me much time. Of course I would have told you and a lot more if we'd had more time together and I was hoping to meet you today and suggest that we find some time soon when we can.'

'I see.' Jane was not really mollified by this.

'Jane... I've done so much thinking recently. Realised what I was up to with Louisa doesn't reflect to my credit, but as I've told you I'm doing what I can.'

'So what were you up to?' she asked disdainfully.

'Louisa was my prop for a lousy marriage. She gave me the things I couldn't get from my wife. I used to feel quite smug about this – the two women were such a good foil for each other, I thought I'd got it worked out really well. But now I know that this was a big lie. OK for me but not for them – was hurting them both. Louisa especially. Should have got out of that marriage long ago.'

'So why didn't you?'

'I keep on asking myself that... I suppose it was because on the surface level Millicent and I worked very well. Looked good together, gave great parties, beautiful house, and successful careers. The envy of our friends. But it was all a big fake. We enjoyed the acting, but underneath we were miserable. And then there was always the fiction of the children to explain why we should stay together. But...'

At this point, there was a distant scream. Kate having reached the summit just behind her brother, had fallen. Mark ran up the hill to comfort her and Jane, out of some sort of instinct, followed.

The little girl was not badly hurt but she had fallen on the path and given herself a nasty graze which was bleeding slightly.

'She needs to have it washed and dressed,' Jane said, cursing inwardly. 'You better come round to my place and we'll do some first aid.'

'That's very kind of you – is it far?' He was dabbing at the wound with his handkerchief.

'No, just round the corner.'

Kate had stopped crying by now but she was still sobbing occasionally.

'D'you think you can walk, Katie, or would you like to ride piggyback?'

Kate indicated sniffily that riding was the preferred alternative.

'OK, up you come.' He knelt down and she jumped onto his back.

'You can pretend I'm an elephant like the ones we've just been seeing.'

'I wish you were a' elephant.'

The walk to Jane's house was not long but the heavy

burden made it seem so. They twice had to stop and rest. 'I'm not used to being Elephant' he said.

When they got to the house, they had to get Kate upstairs to the first floor. Once again Mark had to recognise how unfit he was.

'I'll get water and first aid stuff,' Jane said and disappeared upstairs to her bathroom.

'It's a nice house,' Kate said. 'I like the smell.'

Jane returned with the hot water, antiseptic and plasters.

Mark insisted on doing the treatment himself so she contented herself with opening up a piece of Elastoplast ready to go on the wound. She watched as he tenderly sponged his daughter's knee with the soaked tissue.

Jonathan meanwhile looked on, silent and bored. So Jane engaged him in conversation, asking about which animals he had liked best. They drifted round to the subject of pets and both children brightened up as they talked about their newest acquisitions.

Then Jane said, 'When we were small, when we had a fall our mother used to give us "Bump Medicine" – it was always something sweet. Would you like some?' It was a question that needed no reply. She went to the kitchen and fetched some chocolate biscuits.

Kate and Jonathan helped themselves enthusiastically.

'Thank goodness I've got these. I always have some in hand in case Freddie comes.'

'Who's Freddie?' Mark asked casually.

'Oh… he's one of my artists. He's a great friend. Like a brother to me in fact… now shall I make some tea for us all?'

Something about the normality of these simple exchanges – something about the children and having them in her house – something had an soothing effect on her temper. She found herself softening towards Mark – he obviously adored his children and she was beginning to think about the reasonableness of what he had told her. She had not been fair to him – he had not been given time to tell the whole story. She felt sorry for her behaviour. And yet she felt angry with him for stalking her on the hill. Angry and, if the truth were known, just a bit excited.

Mark, who was feeling frustrated about not being able to continue their discussion, sensed that Jane was relenting. The atmosphere in her house was so attractive, with its light colours, natural materials and plants everywhere. He asked what the smell was and she pointed out the white Jasmine in the pot by the large window.

He sat back in his chair once the operations were over and felt his spirits rising as she brought in the teapot and cups.

Eventually, however, he felt they were imposing on her.

'We've got to go now. I'm going to ring for a taxi to take us back to the car and then we're going to the ice cream place in Chalk Farm. You're welcome to come too if you'd like.'

For a moment, Jane was tempted to say 'yes', but then she remembered that for all his sweetness, plausibility and tenderness to his daughter, she still didn't trust him and it was best to keep out of trouble especially when she was so busy with the gallery. 'I'm sorry, I can't, I've got to do something else.

'Well, thank you for everything. It's a lovely house. I'll hope to see you soon. Say "Good bye" children.'

And then as the taxi arrived he gave her a quick kiss on the cheek.

Freddie rang to to ask how she was. At least, that was his pretext but actually he wanted to know what she thought of Robbie.

'He's lovely. I could go for him myself. But that would mean fighting with you and I'm not sure I'd win,' she said.

Freddie laughed. 'I'm so pleased. But are you all right. You left the party early?'

'Oh… I was a bit upset because the girl I was talking to turned out to be Mark's mistress.'

'Well there's nothing wrong with that is there?'

'She's pregnant.'

'Well, that's something that happens when you're straight, isn't it?'

'He's not going to marry her,'

'I don't really know why this should worry you so much. Is it really any of your business?'

She couldn't explain. Neither could she tell him about the afternoon's encounter. 'I had another visit from a critic.'

'Sounds a bit hopeful'

'Yes… I was so depressed when I got the message, I didn't believe it – but now, I think it's possible. He came last week. There wouldn't be two hoaxes would there?'

'What about the first one – d'you think that was a fake?'

'Not sure. He sounded quite convincing and spent a lot of time.'

'Odd,' said Freddie, 'but you know it's a huge thing to get a preview crit. It gives people more time to see the show if it's reviewed before it opens. To get one is unusual – but two – amazing. I feel hopeful all the same.'

CHAPTER 34

The Deptford Krakatoa

Due to open on the Saturday after the one in which Jane had met Mark and the children, the Deptford Gallery had been under construction for months. For the best part of a year, contractors had been toing and froing, grinding and roaring, demolishing and reconstructing, creating every sort of irritant in the way of noise and dirt. It had not been straight-forward as building projects hardly ever are and the opening date had been postponed several times. But now at last it was ready.

The publicity build-up had been immense. Press releases, interviews, press conferences, radio and television appearances as well as pranks at the openings of other installationist exhibitions.

Henry was correct in his claims that his project would make the average installation look puny by contrast. He had the advantage of a huge space and a long run-in for the preparations.

The theory was quite simple. Scientists today are obsessed with the fundamentals of creation – the unified field and the Big Bang – now seen as the source of everything. So an exhibit entitled BIG BANG would reach down to the most fundamental level of art. And the great thing for gallerists was that at this level you didn't even need to bother with artists because what you are dealing with is Virtual Art. All you have to do is provide a large dark space which you can black out, and pour laser beams and weird sounds all round. The onlookers should feel a sense not only of awe, but complete displacement. They might come in calm, but they would go out quaking. Not only that, but if they read the handouts properly, they would have life changing experiences and relate to themselves in an entirely different way.

The interior of the building, which was three floors high, after being stripped of its original layout had been rigged out with platforms, gantries and staircases – the effect a little like a Piranesi etching. There were also mysterious cubes about the size of a small house, with doors and trapdoors and booths containing loudspeakers and projectors.

It was no easy task to coordinate the sound effects and the lighting – the huge streams of pure coloured light that went round the vast spaces and the squeaks, crackles, whines, beeps, bangs, roars and hums that slowly increased in volume until it reached the threshold of what was safe for the ears. And then nothing.

Henry was a bad employer. He demanded long hours of work and refused to pay overtime. When the chief sound engineer, an Indian called Govinda, took an afternoon off to attend an Indian festival, Henry lost his temper and told him that he was a typical Indian slob, adding with a sneer, the question; did he expect Ganesh to do the work for him? Govinda closed his eyes, said nothing and was silent for the rest of the day.

Somehow in spite of everything his team of sound and lighting engineers managed to get it all together. The dress rehearsal, which was also the preview for the critics and had taken place on the previous Thursday, went off perfectly. It was as one onlooker said, "utterly discombobulating".

The great night came and the audience filed in eagerly anticipating the thrills, shock and pain. "The foundational experience" as one publicist described it.

The doors closed for the start of the performance. The lights went down and it became totally dark. There was a distant rumble of a drum, and then the light show started. Tiny sparks of dim light swirled round. But there was no accompanying sound. Henry began to worry. Then there came a distant whine – he relaxed. The whine was accompanied by a drone and gradually expanded into the sound of bagpipes. It was the Dagenham Girls Pipe Band playing "Amazing Grace" loud and clear. Henry was beside himself with fury.

He rushed to the control booth where Vince, one of the technicians, was frantically pressing buttons on the computer. 'It's no use,' he said after enduring a string of expletives from Henry. 'Someone's gone and changed the soundtrack – and we don't seem to have it backed up.'

'Where's Govinda?' Henry roared at him

'Yes… where is Govinda? He don't seem to be here sir, he was in earlier but he seems to have gone off.'

'Well can't you get hold of him?'

'His mobile's switched off.'

The Dagenham girls now gave way to the "Dance of the Sugar Plum Fairy". The audience had started to giggle because it somehow complemented the lumpy, amoeba type shapes now being projected,

Henry let out another string of expletives and roared at Vince to get hold of Govinda.

'I can't sir,' he said apologetically. 'When he was in earlier to check the systems, he said something about going to India to see his family. I didn't think he meant quite so soon.'

Gradually the obvious sank into Henry's anger crazed mind.

'You think he sabotaged this deliberately? MY GOD! When I get hold of him I'll kill him.'

The "Dance of the Sugar Plum Fairy" was now succeeded

by a selection from "The Sound of Music" as the light projections became harsher and brighter. The laughter that had
only affected a few people now spread like wildfire through
the auditorium. People began to dance and even to sing some
of the numbers.

Henry could hardly speak. He stamped his feet and
punched the air with clenched fists. 'Stop it… can't you. Stop
it at once!'

'Sir… the only way I can stop it is by turning off the
electricity. And that would mean the alarm going and the
building having to be evacuated.'

'You mean everyone – in the whole building?'

'Yep… that's right. It's a health and safety regulation in
case of fire.'

'We can't do that. What the Hell can we do?'

'Well… why don't we just let it go on as it is. They seem
to be enjoying it. It'll take all week to make a new soundtrack but what I'll do is make an announcement and promise
them a free ticket for next weekend's show with the original
soundtrack.'

Henry did not like this idea one bit, but he accepted it
grudgingly for want of anything else.

'And you don't need to worry too much about the
publicity… you know… the critics came to the preview and
they were pretty well impressed.'

'I suppose so.' He fought down his anger and allowed
himself to be slightly mollified by this thought.

The light show was now reaching its climax. A tremendous
outburst of showers and fountains of lights of all colours – it
was like being in the middle of a spectacular firework display.
"The Sound of Music" gave way to the Pachelbel Canon,
which was followed by "Let it Be". The audience joined in
the singing or else just clapped. Then it was all over and the

lights went up. Vince found a microphone and addressed them from one of the balconies. He apologised for the glitch and promised them free tickets for the next performance with the original sound track. One man shouted up that he liked it as it was and there was a round of clapping.

Meanwhile, high above the cloud banks, with the seat belt sign switched off, Govinda leaned back in his seat and smiled as he anticipated his vegetarian meal. The Deptford Krakatoa had become a damp squib.

CHAPTER 35

Henry Strikes Back

Henry was too angry to sleep that night.

By breakfast the following morning he was ready to kill. But at least, he kept telling himself, the critics didn't see it.

His manservant, Clint, brought in his breakfast of black coffee, waffles and maple syrup. He took a large swig of black coffee, a mouthful of waffle and picked up the first of the pile of Sunday newspapers by his plate.

But his sneering smile of anticipation soon faded.

Both the Sunday Times and the Observer carried rave reviews about the work of a totally obscure artist called Andrew Silverstone who was showing his work at a totally obscure gallery in Little Venice. The Sunday Times reported the fiasco opening of the "Big Bang" in a brief item the news section. The Observer did not report it all. The Gossip columns in the gutter press made fun of it, but only briefly because another earthquake took up most of the space.

'Where's Stanches?' Henry asked. He had two servants – Clint who looked after him in the house, and Stanches, his odd-job who took care of things outside.

Stanches now appeared looking very abject, having been warned by Clint of his master's mood.

'Stanches, I want you to get over to the Retro Gallery as fast as you can. They've knobbled the critics. You're to find out how they did it, and how much they paid. Understand?'

'Yes boss.'

'Right. Now go.'

'Now?'

'Now.'

Stanches hesitated a moment.

'Please. I go at once if you say. But no good now. Gallery will be closed. Today Sunday. This… England, sir.'

Henry swore at length, while Stanches and Clint stood by impassively. They were used to his rages.

'All right… tomorrow then. I'm going to boot out that gallery and whoever paid the bill. It can wait a little if necessary. Find out what's going on. OK?'

'OK.' Stanches slunk away. Clint apologetically brought in some more waffles.

At about this moment, the phone rang in Jane's home.

'Jane!' It was Andrew sounding very emotional. It was this emotional strain in his personality that she found slightly forbidding.

'Andrew how are you? Getting ready to come down?' She was as polite as possible but she didn't like being disturbed on Sunday mornings. There was an awful lot to do before the opening of a show and she liked having a morning to herself to potter about in her dressing gown, drink coffee from her cafetière, listen to the Brandenburg concertos and repent the follies of the previous night – not that a trip to the cinema with Freddie counted as a folly, but this was the general pattern of Sunday mornings in Primrose Hill.

'Jane…' There was a long pause before Andrew could bring himself to speak. 'Have you seen this morning's papers?'

'Not yet… why?'

'Both the Observer and the Times have given me previews. It's fantastic. I don't know how you did it, but it's wonderful. They've both said such kind things. Congratulations.'

'No!' Jane said, 'I don't believe it! I thought they were

practical jokers when they each came round last week. But I showed them the work – they didn't say much, just made notes and went away. Oh, God, if I'd known I'd have given them some coffee at least.'

'Well listen to this; "I was bowled over by the quality of these landscapes" and "They come in the tradition of Constable and Turner, but they are expressed in the vernacular of our time".'

'That's tremendous. I've got the papers here; I'll look at them right now. It's wonderful news Andrew, I'm very excited.'

Indeed she was. She had a strong suspicion that she knew who was behind this. It could only be Mark. It was a new ingredient thrown into the seething melting pot of her emotions, for she was still angry with him – not so angry about Louisa but more angry about the fact that he had ambushed her on Primrose Hill.

She sank into her armchair not knowing whether to laugh or cry. It was good news. Good for Andrew – exactly what he deserved. Now he might begin to make some money from his paintings and her gallery would also benefit. But Mark had set this up. He must have known about it yesterday, when she attacked him about Louisa. She now began to feel an increasing amount of remorse. She also began to see that it was possible that Mark really might have changed – *just a little bit perhaps*, she said, grudgingly to herself, and then, he could always change back again. It could just be temporary aberration.

The more she thought about it, the more she remembered that Mark's expression changed whenever she mentioned Andrew. She had watched him while she praised Andrew's integrity. It was clear that he was jealous of him. If he had done this, knowing that it would help Andrew, then he must have overcome some inner resistance. This was certainly a sign of some sort of paradigm shift.

She arrived at the gallery early the next morning in order to be there before the hanging team arrived.

William and Pete, her faithful hangers, who were both out of work actors, arrived almost immediately and began unpacking their gear. While they were doing this there was a ring at t he door.

An ugly little man stood there. 'Can I see pictures?' he said.

'I'm very sorry, but we're closed today for the hanging. The exhibition opens tomorrow – do you see this poster?' Stanches shrugged his shoulders and slunk away.

'I suppose we ought really to hang on Sundays,' Jane said. 'But Ben always believed in having a day off.'

'Quite right,' Pete said. 'I didn't like the look of that feller. Looked like he was up to no good. If I was you, I wouldn't tell him anything.'

'Yes… I suppose this is the price of fame. The down side, you could say, but I didn't think I could have any enemies.'

'There's a lot of jealousy in the art world.' Pete had years of experience of hanging shows. 'Looks almost like you could have annoyed the mafia.'

'The mafia? Isn't that a bit melodramatic?'

'Could be. It's a strange old world isn't it? Let us know if you want any bodyguards,' William added. Then they all had a mug of tea.

When she arrived back at her house she found a bouquet of flowers – white and pale pink roses with eryngiums, waiting for her on the stairs. The downstairs lady must have taken it in.

There was a note for her;

"Dear Jane,

OK I confess. I could have found another route from the Zoo to Chalk Farm on Saturday. I just wanted to see you so badly.

I've had to do a lot of thinking recently. Do you remember when I first came into your gallery and you were playing that song "Nasty Man" — you decided that I was one. You were right.

It now doesn't seem so smart to hurt people by telling lies. You go on doing it and you can't get out of it. I don't want to hurt you. I just don't. I don't want to be a nasty man any longer.

So, I've decided that the best thing I can do is to leave you alone and not bother you — even though I'd love to talk some more with you. You have my phone number.

These flowers are to say "Thank you" for being so kind to us.

Best wishes for the exhibition!

Mark"

This made her want to cry.

Back at the penthouse, Stanches reported to Henry. 'Boss is a woman. Wouldn't let me in. Said they were hanging the show.'

'What's she like?'

'Pretty enough.'

'Hm... we could go for her. It would be quite easy to rub out the show, destroy the gallery and the paintings. But that'ud only give her a huge amount of publicity. It u'd only hurt the artist and that's not the point. What we want is the backer. In fact there's probably a backer's backer. I think the next step will be to keep an eye on her. It's probably her bloke who knobbled the crits. I always deal with the man at the top. Keep a watch on her an' we'll see.'

CHAPTER 36

Andrew's Opening

If Jane had wanted to ring Mark, to find out exactly what he had done and give him the thanks he deserved, it would have been very hard for her, because the week became frantic.

Even if it had been calmer, she would have found it very hard to ring Mark. She was completely at a loss as to what to say. She now regretted that she had been so hard on him at their last meeting but she found it impossible to communicate anything to him. The more she thought about it, the harder it became to do anything. Perhaps she should write a letter. When she thought about it, increasingly this seemed to be the right solution. The trouble was, not only finding the time to do it, but also knowing what to say. There was plenty of feeling – she was grateful, she was sorry, she understood now about Louisa, etc., but the whole business of arranging these thoughts in a neat compact form without sounding stupid, phased her. She now wanted purely and simply to see him and talk but had the same lack of confidence that he had felt about contacting her.

The exhibition was open to the public on Tuesday and the Private View was in the evening of the same day. Normally on the opening day there were very few visitors – usually friends or relatives of the artist who could not make it in the evening. This gave her ample time to get everything ready. But today was different. Freddie looked in. 'I just came to see if I could help!'

She hugged him. 'So you were right!'

'Just for once!'

'No – more often than that!'

'Get champagne for tonight – there's going to be something to celebrate!'

People kept on arriving. They even bought paintings. And then Andrew came looking excited and making fusses about the way the paintings were hung. Jane was so grateful for Freddie and his gift of tact.

Journalists and reporters came wanting to interview her and the photographer, whose name was Maureen, arrived to record the whole exhibition. And then the sinister little man. As soon as she saw him, Jane had a quiet word with Maureen. 'Can you get a shot of that man without his noticing? He's a bit menacing and I'm taking precautions.'

Maureen agreed.

Stanches came up to Jane and started talking.

'This your gallery?' he asked.

'Yes.'

'Good pics.'

He had a strange rather hispanic accent which she could not fathom. Jane said, 'Yes, I'm glad you like them.'

'Good reviews!' He rubbed his nose.

'Yes, and so I should hope. They're really very good paintings.'

'How come they came here?' He sounded sneering and scornful.

She was prepared for this. 'Well, you see, I sent them a very high quality reproduction of one of the best paintings along with an invitation to the show, as well as the details of the artist. They came because they were impressed with the quality of the work.' She pointed out the painting that had been used for the invitation.

'Bit of a surprise for you... eh?'

'Not a bit.' This was technically true because when they

arrived she still thought they were jokers.

Jane pushed back a strand of hair that had fallen across her face,

'You seem to be very interested in the critics. If you want to know why they came, why don't you ask them?' She beamed at him.

He disappeared soon afterwards.

Maureen packed up her gear and came to say "Goodbye".

'By the way – I got shots of that ugly little man, while you were pointing out the paintings to him. I'll have them for you tomorrow. If you think he's been bothering you, you should go to the police.'

'Yes, I'm thinking of doing that – but the trouble is that there is so little to tell them. He hasn't done anything wrong exactly.'

'Nevertheless, it's always worth taking some pre-emptive action – even if he's just a harmless loony!'

The private view was unlike any of the previous ones. The paintings were sold out in the first hour. It was unbelievable! Andrew was dancing with delight. His optimism had been vindicated. All her forebodings were false. He was now made and she had done it. She should have felt triumphant, but instead she was withdrawn and nervous.

A lot of people came. Andrew had more friends than she had anticipated and some must have been gatecrashers, but then she realised that as usual she had sent out nearly a thousand invitations to everyone on her list. This time they had come.

She was surprised to see Louisa.

'I had to come. I just wanted so much to see them,' Louisa said.

'Would you like to meet Andrew? He's over there?'

'Oh yes… I think he's great, like.'

But Jane got buttonholed. A young man who looked vaguely familiar was telling her a long saga about how his life had changed since he had come into her gallery when he was feeling low because his girl friend had dumped him. 'It started me off looking at paintings... I go to the National Gallery every Sunday. It's wonderful stuff isn't it... I'd really like to study art now.'

And then Edwin being tall, thin and possessed of the ability to slip easily through a crowd sidled up and hugged her. 'Edwin, how nice to see you – where have you been?'

'Oh... in the country... sorting out issues... about rats... and bat surveys... all rather boring. I say... isn't this a wonderful show! Congratulations! So many people here... I can't really see the paintings... I'll have to come back... Is Freddie here?'

'Yes, over in that corner. He's got good news too! '

Louisa touched her arm gently. 'I'm not feeling too good and me phone's run out of puff... like. Could I use your's to get a taxi?'

'Yes of course'. But it was easier said than done. Her phone was in her desk on the other side of the room. It's hard enough getting through a semi-inebriated crowd when no-one knows who you are, but if they do they all want to talk to you – near impossible. Fortunately Edwin was still by her side so she turned to him, 'Edwin, can you get this lady a taxi – she's not feeling too good.'

'I'd be... er... delighted,' said the gallant earl.

The party took a long time to subside and Jane felt very tired by the time they had all left. On her way home, she thought she saw the little man again. She went straight up to her window and looked out, where she saw a small shadowy form disappearing round the corner.

The next morning, before opening the gallery, she went straight to Paddington Green Police Station. A rather tired looking blonde police woman took notes without making too convincing an appearance of interest in her story, but then Jane was not aware of the number of stories the police woman had had to record. People in the area were up to no good – spying on each other with telescopes, bugging lavatories, spraying toxic chemicals and breeding all sorts of nasty creatures like scorpions, tarantulas, pythons, boa constrictors and even, on one occasion, a rhinoceros. If it was all to be believed, then London back gardens were more dangerous than the Amazonian jungle. Jane's story was dull by comparison which might make it genuinely connected to criminal activity but it did sound a bit like a loony.

'We'll keep this on file and see what turns out,' she said. 'Of course if you had a picture of the man, it would helpful, because then we could match it up to our records.'

'Oh, but I do… I came round here first thing because I didn't want to be followed if I left the gallery. But a photographer's coming in this morning and she has some.'

The policewoman brightened up. 'If you can let us have it as soon as possible that would be helpful. And anything else you can provide which might shed light on it.'

Jane thanked her and left.

When she arrived at the gallery and opened it up, she rang Freddie.

'I didn't have enough privacy yesterday to tell you – there's something a bit disturbing going on and I've had to go to the police.' She told him about the little man and being followed.

'Is he there now?' She looked out.

'Yes – he's just arrived and he's outside, leaning against a wall – smoking.'

'Would you like me to come round?'

'I don't think there's any point, at the moment. Perhaps later. Maureen's coming in this morning with some photos and I'll need to get them to the police station without being followed.'

'Let me know when you want me and I'll come straight round. Oh, by the way, I've got an invite to a party at the Tate Modern on Saturday. Robbie can't come because he's performing and I just wondered if you'd like to be my guest. They do quite lavish do's.'

'At the Tate? How come you get invites to that?'

'One of my clients is a merchant banker and he has a lot to do with big finance companies which have a lot to do with sponsorship and the party's in their honour. My client doesn't go for avant-garde art so he gave me his invite. It will be quite amusing, I think… and the food is always amazing. Do come.'

Jane opened her mouth to say that she couldn't because parties were not her thing and anyway, she'd had enough of them recently. But she found herself agreeing for the simple reason that Mark would probably be there.

As she put the phone down a visitor arrived. To her surprise, she saw that it was Henrietta.

'Darling! I just had to come… I've heard so much about the artist. They look wonderful! How clever of you to find him!'

Jane was pleased. They talked for some minutes and then Henrietta asked, 'But tell me – why are you being stalked by Henry Streffelgueze's man?'

'Henry Streffelgueze?'

'You know that phoney, who'se just put on an exhibit in Deptford which was a fiasco – you must have heard of him surely?'

'Yes, now you mention it I have. But how d'you know all this, Henrietta?'

'Ah,' Henrietta fished in her handbag and found a small piece of paper,

'That's quite a story. You should go to the police – that

man is up to no good. I met him on Henry's doorstep once. He struck me as sinister. This is his address, though I don't know his name.'

'I've already been to the police. But I haven't been able to tell them much and I'm not sure they even believe me.'

At this point someone else entered the gallery. Jane said, 'Ah, here's Maureen.' She went and greeted Maureen and led her to Henrietta. 'This is Henrietta who knows who the stalker is. Have you got the pics?'

'They came out well enough – not brilliant mug shots – but I had to be discreet.' She pulled some photos out of her bag.

'Yes… that's him. 'Henrietta said. 'Would you like me to take them to the police station.'

'Oh… yes please. But won't he recognise you as you leave? And then he might follow you to the police station.'

'We'll distract him,' Maureen said. 'We'll go out and ask him if he'd like a cup of coffee. He must get awfully bored out there all day!'

So that is what they did. Jane and Maureen advanced on Stanches who turned tail and walked away down the road. Henrietta was able to leave discreetly and take the material to the police.

Chapter 37

Tate á Tate

'It's no use. Me hanging out. Dame's gettin' suspicious. Only person came wot I knew was – tall dame, friend of yours. If I go on watchin' they'll tell police.'

Henry's eyelids drooped over his eyes. He looked increasingly suspicious. 'So what d'yer suggest Stanches?'

'No idea. Unless we go for dame herself. Could do with gettin' clobbered.'

'Yeah… it's time for some action.' Henry spoke slowly and thoughtfully.

'A heist?'

'Why not. OK we'll clobber her.'

'Wanna me to get the boys? It'll take a few days. They're busy at the moment.'

'OK.'

Jane wore an outfit of deep crimson for the party at the Tate. As Freddie had promised it was a grand affair – there was pink champagne and Filipino waitresses handing round delicacies arranged on mirrors decorated with baby orchids. There were sculptured quails' eggs, radishes cunningly disguised as fly-agaric mushrooms and small bundles of parma ham stuffed with mozzarella and asparagus. At first she thought these were just any kind of nibble, like sausages or stuffed olives, then she saw that they were also things like smoked oysters and lobster. In fact it was some time before she understood that these were not just appetizers but a whole dinner that was being served in bite-sized pieces. Bits of pheasant, artichoke hearts, fried baby aubergines, and small roast potatoes, were followed by strawberries sandwiched with thick cream and tiny meringues – the latter being the only items that were not on sticks.

Everyone was there. The whole crowd of wealthy semi-celebrities – the fans of the Emperor's new clothes: Clive and Vareena Suetonius, Ethel Grulk, Nancy Rataffia, the Arbuthnotts, Brünnhilde Strathpeffer as well as Albert, Caroline and Peter Gorbal Shlumbacher, the Browne Sakis and the Smiths. She knew none of them. She kept on looking round for Mark but he was not there.

In between the crowds and the platters of food, the exhibits were just visible. She couldn't make them out – they looked a bit like enormously blown up photos of a dissected cow's intestines. Which is probably what they were – the show was called, simply "Inner Reality".

What could have happened to Mark? She wandered round the huge space feeling more and more out of her element. She did not like the Tate Modern. It always felt cold and like some vast railway station in which all the trains had left and none would ever come back.

Suddenly, just when she had given up all hope, she saw him. He was some distance away and was surrounded by friends. He looked rather sad but handsome enough in a well-cut dark blue jacket with a high Indian collar. She wondered if he would see her. He was so far off, it seemed unlikely, but then he looked in her direction. He saw her at once and started to move towards her.

When he caught up with her, she gasped and blushed, not knowing where to look. He also appeared to be at a loss for words. For an eternity in the flash of a second they held each other in their eyes. It was enough. Then he, coming to his senses said, 'Jane! What a nice surprise. I didn't expect to meet you here.'

'I... just thought...,' she started.

But they were like two beings stranded on different tectonic plates. Huge surges of people swept them in opposite directions. Brünnhilde Strathpeffer bore down upon them with all the delicate sensitivity of a steamroller in a lettuce bed. 'Mark, darling! How wonderful to see you again. Are you all right?' She embraced him effusively.

Mark introduced her to Jane but she continued imperturbably. 'Mark, Darling I've been meaning to ring you. We want to invite you to accompany us to "Harrybells" to help convalesce. I know you need a bit of tender love and care. Everyone does at times. Albert and I would be so delighted. You could see the terraced rockery we're building and the bedded out sundial just about to come out in its full glory. The Strathmiglos are coming and the Higginses; I know you would love them.'

Jane felt helpless as she and Mark were slowly drifting further and further apart.

She turned away and decided to find Freddie and tell him that she had had enough. She searched for him with her eyes but he was not visible at that moment. Just then there was a firm hand on on her shoulder.

It was Mark – he must have somehow leapt across the widening gap. 'Quick' he said, 'We have to get away. There's a quiet corner, I know. Come with me.'

He led her down a passageway that she had not noticed and they found a staircase and sat on it.

He said, 'I didn't expect you to be here.'

'Freddie brought me. But I came because I wanted to see you.'

'How are things? The show was a success from what I've heard.'

'Yes – but it's been a worrying week,'

She told him about the little man and Henrietta's intervention.

'Ah… yes. That does sound like Henry Streffelguese. He doesn't like success. And particularly when his own show has been a flop.'

This wasn't what she had really meant to talk to him about – but it was just the way things came out.

'I…' She started to say what she really wanted. But at the same time two things happened. Mark started to say something with equal hesitance and her phone started to ring.

He looked at her reproachfully. 'Mine's switched off.'

'I can't risk that. It could be an emergency.' She answered it.

'Oh my God…' Her expression dropped. 'Really?… Oh no!… I'll come right away.'

She turned to Mark. 'It's the police… the gallery's been broken into.'

CHAPTER 38

Towards the Imagist Revival

'We'd better get you there at once,' Mark said. 'My car's just outside.'

'I must tell Freddie – he'll be looking for me'

'Look – to save time, I'll go and fetch the car and meet you at the front entrance, while you find Freddie.'

It was easier to charge through the throng singly. She found Freddie without too much trouble and told him her news. He was shocked but quietly pleased that Mark was taking charge of her. 'I'll come along later,' he promised.

Mark had the car at the front entrance waiting for her as planned. They set off at the maximum pace that was consistent with legality. 'Now tell me... I'd like to know exactly what Henry's man asked you.'

She told him.

'And what did you tell him?'

'Oh – the truth. I sent the critics good publicity. And when two of them rang me to make preview appointments, I assumed that it was a joker.'

'That was smart of you.'

'But I know who it really was.'

'Oh – really?' He sounded rather cool.

'You... I have to thank you for doing something really big.'

He laughed. 'It was nothing. Only I didn't want you to know.'

'It wasn't nothing for me, or for Andrew, for that matter. The whole thing was a wonderful surprise.'

'But then this. It looks as though Henry is out to get me. He's had it in for me for ages – spreading rumours that I was about to fail, and doing disruptive pranks at private views. You heard about the fiasco of his exhibition in Deptford?'

'Yes.'

'Well – the funny thing is that the joke turned upside down, because the public loved it. Also one or two critics who missed the authentic performance at the preview came to the first night. They only do performances at weekends which means that there has been a little time for the enthusiasm to spread by word of mouth and local radio and small press – with the result that people are beginning to queue up.'

'And you feel happy to be part of this scene?'

He sighed, 'Not any more. It's all lies. A pop singer is held up by his fans – but the general public has nothing to do with the success of an installationist – that's all PR and funding from questionable sources.'

'Yes but the Deptford thing sounds as though the public got a say in it anyway.'

'True. But an exception that proves the rule. Also the critics have ignored it, which is bad news for Henry.'

'So what are you going to do now?'

'A good question. Jane, I've thought and thought recently and I've come up with an idea.'

'Oh yes?' She swallowed. *Must keep him talking and not think about what we're going to see.*

'I want to steer the gallery gently round to a sort of art that is more positive – more life enhancing.'

'How would you do that?'

'Well – it's no use having fantasies about giving Lucy a show, if she wanted one, which she doesn't. Or even Andrew, for that matter. We have a certain tradition of modernism and I can't go back on that. And then my gallery is very large. We have space that needs to be taken up with three dimensional items.' They stopped at some traffic lights and he looked at her. 'I hope I'm not boring you. You must be thinking about your gallery.'

'No... no. This is distracting. We'll be there soon enough. Tell me about your idea.'

'Angels,' he said simply. 'But not Lucy type angels. Contemporary twenty-first century angels. In three dimensions.'

'And you think you can get away with that? It sounds a bit like getting a liner to make a U-Turn in mid-Atlantic'.

'I hope so – it's not so much a U-Turn, more a gentle veering in a new direction. But I do see that the idea will have to get over a number of hurdles.' He opened the glove compartment and took out a small pack of peppermints. 'Would you like one? I find they help after a heavy meal.'

'Oh – thanks.' She took one and he continued. 'You see, when I stayed with Lucy I went up Glastonbury Tor and met two lovely hippy puppeteers. Went to their show and fell in love with their creativity. They had made funky modern angels with bright cheeks and wearing red high heels. Funny and cheerful – you could say they were "jolly", and not the least sentimental. But what got me was their environment. Proscenium and the stage decoration was what you might call "Street Gothic" – lots of arches and pointy shapes, all decorated with small bits of coloured paper which they collect from discarded rubbish – like sweetie papers.'

'Goodness – that sounds interesting.' Jane tried to visualise the funky angels. But there was something about the tone in her voice that told him she wasn't totally engaged in this conversation. He fell silent while he negotiated Clerkenwell Road. Then he said, 'I can tell you're thinking about the break-in.'

Jane said, 'I can't help it. I don't understand why anyone would want to do it.'

'Henry's crazy and also rather sinister. We don't know what he's really up to. When we had the incident in my gallery, it looked just like a prank. We discussed going to the police, but there wasn't any evidence of criminal activity. Henrietta's had a fling with him and says he's definitely a fake, but what he's really up to, or why, is anyone's guess.'

'I see.'

'I think he's out to get anyone who diminishes the publicity he wants for his gallery. Your show came on about the same time as his and he lost the attention of the Sundays. I suspect that he guessed that someone had talked to the critics on your behalf and sent his man to find out and to spy on you – and when they couldn't find anyone, they decided to hit you. That's partly why I'm coming with you – I want to explain this to the police.'

Jane did not feel like saying anything more. She felt too churned up.

When they reached the gallery they found it all lit up. There were two policemen and the usual small crowd of disaster watchers. Jane went up to one of the policemen.

'I'm Jane Gresham – the owner.'

'Good you got here so quickly. There's a bit of damage and we want to keep the mess for a few moments while the forensic man does his bit. But the paintings don't seem to be damaged. They got your computer. We'd like to ask you a few questions.'

'Yes and my friend here has an idea who it was and why.'

The policeman talked to her and told her that they had contacted the 24 hour service that boards up damaged shop windows. He made sure that she was insured and again advised her not to clear up the mess but wait until the forensic people came. They told her that it had been reported by a passer-by who had witnessed the break-in from the end of the road and that it had happened very quickly.

The mess was appalling. Mark helped her sweep up some of the glass splinters, made sure she rang the right people and stayed with her until the temporary repair people arrived. Then he waited while they boarded up the shop front. They had a cup of tea and she felt suddenly very tired.

'It's not as bad as it could have been, you know,' he said. 'At least the paintings haven't been damaged.'

'Yes – but my computer…'

'You'll probably get a better, newer one from your insurers. Did you have any vital files on it?'

'Well… my mailing list. But I do have it on my card index file – so that's OK. I suppose I'm lucky really.'

'And they can replace the glass tomorrow so you won't lose out on having it open.'

She nodded and gave a big yawn.

'You're very tired. I'm going to take you home now the place is secure.'

'Thank you.'

She got into the car. Too tired to speak on the way home, she was grateful for Mark's silence. He stopped the car outside her house and got out to open the door.

'You want something to help you sleep. Been a shock for you. Hot milk with a dab of whisky works best, d'you have any?'

She shook her head. 'Just milk'

He dived into the car and took a small hip flask out of one of the compartments, 'Always carry some in case of emergencies.'

'That's very kind.'

'See you soon. Sleep well!'

He kissed her lightly on the cheek and then got back in the car.

By the time Freddie arrived at the gallery, she had already left but he came the next morning with a bouquet of lilies.

'I'm so glad to see you.' She hugged him effusively.

'Was Mark well behaved?' he asked anxiously.

'Oh yes, he was a perfect gentleman. Very kind and thoughtful. It's just that… I don't know him as well as you. You're part of my family.'

Freddie looked thoughtful. 'Tell me what happened exactly. And let's do some clearing up. Looks like it was quite a party.'

'Talk of the devil… here he is.'

Mark was carrying more flowers. Mixed roses and gypsophila.

'My goodness.' Jane was pleased.

'You can't have too many flowers at a time like this.' Mark again kissed her lightly.

Jane turned to Freddie, 'And this is Freddie – who has helped me on so many occasions.'

'Yes I've heard about you. You like chocolate biscuits.'

Freddie laughed, 'How did that come out?'

'My little girl hurt her knee on Primrose hill and Jane helped us in the emergency. By the way Jane – you made an awfully good impression. They loved your house. But mostly they loved your biscuits!'

Jane laughed, 'But the biscuits were only chocolate diges-tives – nothing very special.'

'I think my poor little rich kids have never had anything other than Fortnum and Masons.'

They all laughed at this.

Shortly afterwards Mark went outside to make a couple of calls.

'He's very nice you know.' Freddie said, 'I really do like him.'

'Yes.'

'And he's obviously smitten with you.'

'Yes,' Jane sighed.

'So what's the problem?'

Jane sighed again, 'Well... it's a bit like that old song, "Will you still love me tomorrow?"'

It was Freddie's turn to sigh. 'I know what you mean,' he said.

The window repair team now arrived and started work. Shortly after this, they had a visit from a plain clothes police officer.

He told them the latest news.

The upturn in the fortunes of the Deptford gallery was short lived. After the previous night's performance there was a police raid. The police had known about the real purpose of the project for some time – they were just waiting for the optimal moment to strike when they could arrest the largest number of the suspects.

"The Big Bang" was a false front, concealing the real function which was to provide space for what was an enormous money-laundering brokerage. The backers were a New York cartel with links to organised crime in many countries. They needed to find a respectable home for vast quantities of money. In order to present a convincing façade, the gallery had to become a front runner in the art world. Henry was trying to catapult it into supremacy over the other galleries by whatever means were in his power: tricks, sneers and slanders, extensive publicity and thinly disguised bribes, such as offers of loans of villas in Barbados or the Seychelles. The trouble was that when Henrietta had first exposed Henry as a fraud, the rumour had gone round the art world. There is nothing critics dislike more than to be shown up as fools, so their reluctance to review "The Big Bang" was not entirely due to Mark's intervention on behalf of Andrew.

When the police raided the Deptford gallery they found a large underground office with many files of potential investments in shady companies, as well as equipment for forging invoices and fake identity papers. They also found quantities of foreign currency and even some gold bullion.

Henry was an accomplished criminal with considerable ingenuity and creativity, but his Achilles heel was his anger. It blinded him to the dangers he was facing if his gallery failed to make its mark. The fiasco of the opening and the attack on Jane's gallery were his downfall. The police caught him just as he was about to make his escape while the news filtered through to his backers.

Jane's spy, the little man, Stanches, was a Bolivian with links to cartels from that country. He had been under observation for many months but the police had not known who his boss was until Jane had given them the vital information – the missing link with Henry Streffelguese. The police had found Stanches at Deptford and were confident that they would find the computer. But the gallery was huge and it contained many hidden passageways and caverns, where business could take place without the knowledge of the general public. It was an absolute rabbit warren and it would take time to search the whole thing.

The detective took statements from Jane and Mark and then reassured Jane that she would be safe from now on. 'I know it probably doesn't feel like it, but you've been very lucky. You could've been attacked. I'm glad you've had an escape!'

With that he departed and Mark left shortly afterwards.

'I do like your Mark,' Freddie said, rescuing a tiny fragment of glass that was lodged on the chair.

Jane sighed. 'I like him too. But I just wonder...'

'You mean you don't trust him? It looks as though he's in love with you.'

'Possibly... but it's like that old song again.'

Freddie and Jane waited until the new window had been fitted and then went out for a late lunch/tea of soup, sandwiches, scones, jam and cream at the local pub.

'Feeling better?' he asked,

'Oh, my goodness yes!'

'It's a lovely day – why don't we do something ordinary – like kite flying?'

So they took the kite up Parliament Hill.

CHAPTER 39

After The Party

'So they got him,' Henrietta said. 'How satisfactory!'

It was two days later and Henrietta, Freddie and Jane were sitting outside Café Veronique, one of Freddie's favourite places.

'Did they ask you for a statement?' Jane asked Henrietta as a waiter brought up the cappuccinos and éclairs with which they had decided to celebrate.

'Yes, of course,' Henrietta said. 'Just like they did with you. But although I've read about it in the papers, there's a good bit missing.'

'I don't know much more than you. I hardly know anything about money laundering. It's not my problem.' Jane thoughtfully stirred the foam on her cappuccino.

They laughed.

Jane wanted to talk about something else but Henrietta was relentless. She now asked, 'Did the police get everyone in the gang?'

'Apparently,' Freddie now spoke up. 'But they didn't get the New York backers.'

'I think Henry was very clever and creative, but what he didn't do was to mug up on American avant-garde art. He'd done his homework on Young British Artists, though. And the European ones.' Henrietta took a bite from her éclair.

'Yes, you showed him up there. And you provided a missing link. They'd been watching Stanches for some time, but didn't know the connection with Henry.' Freddie delicately cut his éclair into small pieces with a fork. He added, 'But what was really his undoing was his temper. If he hadn't decided to attack Jane, he might have got away with it. Though he'd have had some trouble with his backers over the flop at the opening.'

'But what I don't understand,' Jane said, 'was why he had to build up all this publicity for his gallery. He could have just run a discreet operation from a sugar mill in Deptford, without attempting to catapult himself into a front runner in the art scene.'

'No... that's not the way it works.' Henrietta started to pick up her éclair for another mouthful. 'There are such huge amounts of money involved. If, for example, you were to put £200,000 in your bank account, the Inland Revenue, or your accountant would be down on you like a shot. But if you were running a gallery where insubstantial things were being sold for vast sums, then you'd be high and dry.' She took another bite of her éclair and they were all silent for a moment. Jane caught between the two modes of tackling éclairs, compromised by cutting hers in half and lifting the sections with her fingers.

Henrietta said, 'By the way, did you get your computer back?'

'No – not yet. But I'm not too worried. I haven't lost any records and I'll get a more up-to-date one on my insurance.'

Freddie said, 'The police found all sorts of things in that place – forging equipment, foreign currency, gold, even a vicuña coat with a gun sling in its lining.'

'How do know all this?' Henrietta took a swig of her cappuccino.

'The detective told us, when he came to visit. I asked if I could have the coat but he said no...'

Henrietta laughed, 'You'd have looked so good in that outfit!'

'You look so good in yours,' Freddie said.

'I'm just glad it's all over,' Jane said. 'Are you about to go away somewhere interesting, Henrietta?'

Henrietta thought for a moment. 'Er... Only Kazakhstan.'

CHAPTER 40

A Dignified Retreat

Although the physical damage to the gallery was quickly repaired, Jane's emotional wound was not quite so easily mended. She felt she had been assaulted. Her friends were supportive and rallied round with diversions for her; operas, theatres, films and meals. Freddie took her to the revival of "Blithe Spirit" which she found hilarious and Andrew to "Death in Venice" which she loathed.

She felt confused and churned up about Mark, wanting to see him at one moment and not wanting to, the next. She decided that the best way to deal with this was to let go. She had had a bad experience with a previous boyfriend who had jilted her and could not face the possibility that this might happen again.

When she was a child, sometimes she used to cross a field to reach her school. Occasionally she was menaced by cows – innocent curiosity but threatening all the same. She found that the way to deal with this was not to run away but to move away slowly and gently and soon enough they would lose interest and turn away to lick their backs or graze on tussocks of tasty grass. This seemed to be the best way to deal with Mark.

Mark felt concerned about her but was anxious not to put pressure on her. It was a novelty for him to love someone whom he was not sure could return his affection. He had to deal with this on his own.

He was increasingly lonely. He cut down on most of the parties and listened to music or went to the cinema or theatre on his own. He thought endlessly, but without reaching any conclusions.

Time passed.

It was now summer. London was full of the scents of the buddleias that sprouted out of the buildings everywhere, as well as the dust and the exhaust fumes. A young niece from Australia came to stay and provided a welcome diversion. They went everywhere together, and when he had the children they went boating in Regent's Park on a sunny day when the ducks and the herons were in full squawk, and the water smelled of mud and reeds. As they passed under the bridge someone waved at them. It was Sharon from the front office looking rosily animated with her boyfriend. Everyone seemed happy that day and the children managed not to fall in… but it was a close run thing.

Primrose Hill smelled of buddleias as well, but there was also a rich diversity of plants in the back gardens and window boxes; Lavender, Nepeta and Russian Vine being the most powerful. In the evenings there was the buzz of al fresco dining; rosemary, grilled steaks, minted peas, roast garlic and wine. It was immensely civilised.

Jane was pleased to see Edwin who called in at the gallery. 'I haven't seen you for ages what have you been up to?'

'I've been in darkest Staffordshire, sorting out mildew… and planners. It's so refreshing… to be back in London.'

She told him her news.

'My goodness… how awful for you'

'Yes it was, but I'm all right now.'

'By the way… I've got news for you! He looked down a little bashfully.

'Oh Edwin!... no... not another proposal?'

'No... that's the... er... clever thing. I haven't proposed... this time I've taken your... and Freddie's advice.'

'You mean you've fallen in love?'

'Yes... actually. It's a completely new sensation... head over heals... right down to my toes... and fingertips... I'm in love. I feel quite giddy at times.'

'How wonderful... that's such good news. Congratulations. Do I know her?'

'Well... actually you do. In fact you... introduced her to me... it's Louisa.'

'What a surprise... that's marvellous. And does she... er love you?'

'I think so... We're awfully happy together.'

'Have you told her?'

'Not yet... but she's been to the country with me and seen the horrors. I don't want to tell her until... she has agreed... to marry me.'

'She's pregnant!'

'Yes – I know. If we marry... I'll have a ready made heir in hand.'

'Doesn't that worry you?'

'Why should it?'

'Well, suppose you have a child of your own.'

Edwin looked at her and shook his head sadly, 'That's a possibility... but... not very likely.' He looked down and as he didn't go into any further details she didn't feel like asking him.

He looked up again and said, 'I just love her so much... she's so sweet... and cuddly... and I love the way she's got her flat arranged.'

Jane gave him a big hug. 'I'm very, very pleased. If I weren't tied to the gallery just now, I'd suggest we went out for a drink to celebrate.'

Edwin reached down into his shoulder bag. 'I thought that... might be the case. So I brought something with me!' He produced a bottle of Prosecco.

Later on, Freddie came. 'How's it going?' he asked, hugging her.

'Not too badly.' She told him the news about Edwin. Freddie laughed.

'He gets off the mark quickly, doesn't he?

'Yes – but at least he hasn't proposed. And this time, I think it's quite serious. He really is in love.'

'Well... that's very nice.' Freddie rubbed his hands together. 'Actually I came in to ask you what you'd thought about holidays this year.'

'Well – I'm closing the gallery for the first two weeks of August and I might go and stay with an aunt in the West Coast of Ireland.'

'Do you do much business in the second two weeks of August?'

'Not a lot. We'd do more if we catered for tourists and sold cheap prints of London and the Scottish Highlands.'

'So why don't you close for the whole month? Lots of galleries do. It's a dead month for selling fine art.'

She looked at him with a big smile. 'Freddie – I can see you're plotting something.'

'Well... I've been feeling for some time that there's not quite enough colour in my palette and so I've booked an apartment on an island in Croatia for the last two weeks. I was going to take Robbie, but he's been offered a tour with a troupe he's wanted to be in for ages – so I wondered if you would like to come instead. You can have your own room.'

'Freddie... that's a wonderful idea. I'm having some

improvements done in the gallery and it might be good if I were out of the way.'

The aunt in West Cork was nice, but to escape to the sun and the Mediterranean was much more appealing.

'Good... I'll count you in. Must go now – have a hair tinting appointment in Baker Street.'

He kissed her and left.

It was a day of visits from friends. The next one was Henrietta.

Jane was tempted to tell her that she had just missed Edwin, but tactfully restrained herself.

'Darling,' Henrietta unburdened herself of a small rose bush in a pot.

'I've only just heard about it. I'm just so sorry. They should have arrested him earlier.'

'Well – it's thanks to you that they were able to. They told me that his connection with Henry S was the missing link. I'm very, very grateful.'

'Mark told me how clever you had been to think of getting that photo done. He told me the whole story.'

'Oh yes – Mark. How is he?'

'Seems rather low at the moment. Hasn't been on the social round at all. Rather quiet and withdrawn. He hasn't really been himself since that bang on the head. Maybe, it's just taking time.'

'Yes... I've found it takes time to get over a shock.'

Henrietta ran her hand through her copious hair. 'I have heard a rumour that he's in love with some woman who can't return his affection.'

It hit Jane in that area behind the chest, 'Oh really?'

'Well it's only a rumour. But he's also been seen boating in Regent's Park with a sexy young bird.'

This hit Jane again, but this time it was more like a stab.

Somehow she managed to control the pain. 'Well, it's good that he's got someone isn't it?'

'Sure.' Henrietta reached in her bag for the lipstick. 'He's been through quite a lot in one way and another!' She laughed and Jane laughed with her.

But she felt like crying.

'I've gotta go.' Henrietta repaired her lipstick. 'Meeting a friend at the Bewdley Gallery. I haven't seen the latest Jason Crowpick everyone's raving about.'

'Oh yes?' Jane choked back the tears. 'I don't think I know that name.'

'Oh it should interest you because he's an installationist who's now doing imagist paintings. So it looks as though there might be a trend towards more figurative stuff.'

'Really – what sort?'

'It's called "Christian Martyrdom". All based on the tortures the early Christians suffered. Mind you, I have heard it said that Jason has about as much talent as a commercial pub sign painter.' She rearranged her scarf as she prepared to go.

Jane thought it sounded horrible and crossed it off her mental list. But she could not comment on the exhibition, she was numb with shock.

'Bye,' said Henrietta. 'See you soon.'

She hugged Jane, blissfully unaware of the blow she had just dealt. Jane found both the hug and the innocence comforting.

She had been meaning to ring Mark when all the hubbub had died down but there was now no way she could. She said to herself, *I was right not to trust him. Thank goodness for my caution – saved me from a nasty bump.*

She even wrote this down in her Book of Blessings; but, all the same, it was agony.

CHAPTER 41

Doña Isabel

The visit from his Australian niece cheered Mark up. Samantha was a jolly girl who embraced life with a total enthusiasm. Although by the end of the week he was tired of her rather loud Australian accent, her baseball cap and the shorts that revealed legs not worthy of exposure, he missed her when she was gone.

He now felt almost more alone than at any other time of his life. This was strange because he was surrounded with people – there was a backlog of stuff to deal with in the gallery, and his social life, which was inextricably bound with his business concerns, continued. But he couldn't face the parties. So he reduced the amount of time spent on them – making an appearance and then leaving quickly. It was harder though with the dinner parties but he dealt with this by refusing most of the invitations or making excuses for the ones he had already accepted. It was not a lie to say that he 'had to do something that evening' even though the something consisted of sitting in the kitchen talking to the cat while he ate a sumptuous feast of baked beans on toast. His digestive system improved from this restricted diet – he no longer suffered from feeling bloated.

He thought constantly about Jane. At their meeting in the Tate, she had seemed to be softening towards him. When they had sat together on that staircase he could feel warmth flowing between them. And then she had received that horrendous message. He had helped her as much as he could

and she had thanked him politely but there was no suggestion of a future meeting and he felt that he must stick to his
promise not to put pressure on her.

The nights were hard. He would fall asleep all right but
then wake after a few hours and find himself unable to go
back to sleep. His brain would not let him go. He speculated
and apologised and thought up useless plans, but the realisation was sinking in that she was not going to phone him.

One night when he had made himself a cup of tea, he
turned on the radio and started trawling for some acceptable
distraction. Rather to his surprise he tuned in to the last stanzas
of "Pratiranya". He put out his hand to turn it off and then an
odd thing happened. He discovered that once again he liked
this song. It had been the prelude to a change in his life.

Jane or no Jane things were going to get better. He could
change the direction of his gallery – he could steer his ship
into more favourable waters – he could free himself from lies.
He was so pleased with this revival of affection for the song
that he would have played his CD but then he remembered
that he had left it in the car. He could play it tomorrow.

He started thinking about the process of change and the
effect that his vision in front of Lucy's angel had had on him.
He wondered whether he would ever have anything like that
again. Although Lucy had cautioned him about looking for
it, or expecting it, he thought it might be an idea to look at
some more art and see if it could revive the memory of that
experience. His gallery was not too far from Trafalgar Square
– he could go to the National Gallery during his lunch break.

For Mark, to set foot in the National Gallery was a bold
and daring step. He had been put off Classical Art by over-
zealous parents, force-feeding him at too early a stage in his
life – followed by school trips organised by an art master
who would pronounce Rembrandt as "Rombron", (and Van

Gogh as "Von Heugh"). Something about the tone and whole bearing of this man, made Mark associate old masters with thick, heavy brown paint. He paid lip service to the idea that they were "great" but the truth was that they were, for him, utterly brown and boring.

So, on his first excursion into these hallowed precincts he avoided "Rombron" and settled instead for Goya's portrait of Doña Isabel de Porcel which reminded him of Jane.

He had no mystical experiences. All that happened was that he thought her eyes were very like Jane's. And yet in spite of this anti-climax, he left the gallery feeling more rested and calm. He decided that it was an experiment worth making and that he would come again.

He went again, the following week. Doña Isabel became a starting and finishing point for his sallies into the Art of previous centuries. It was a sort of oasis from where he could stride out into the desert of Great Art and return to be refreshed after massive helpings of Titian, Tintoretto, and others. He even found he could tolerate "Rombron" in small doses. No visions came, but the feeling of calmness and acceptance seemed to increase.

One day, looking at the Rembrandts, he began to sense a sort of sweetness he couldn't quite explain. It was to do with love, but only in a general sort of a way – nothing to do with what he felt about Jane – more to do with feeling that you wanted to give something to the whole world and not unlike the feelings that you can get on a sunny spring morning when all the birds are singing.

After this he went back to Doña Isabel and sat down and closed his eyes. He thought of Jane and the fantasy grew that if he could visualise her, Doña Isabel would melt away and Jane would gradually emerge from the frame smiling gently and with hands outstretched towards him.

He sat for some minutes in this pleasant haze but then he realised that someone was looking at him. He opened his eyes and saw... her!

Jane sometimes did business with a framer in St. Martin's lane. It was nice to go into the National Gallery afterwards and look at some of her favourite paintings. She was surprised to see Mark sitting in front of the Goya portrait with his eyes closed. He had lost weight and looked tired – but strangely peaceful.

She felt it would be sensible if she were to leave without drawing attention to herself, even though her heart was beating so loudly that she thought it must be audible. But just as she passed him his eyes opened. He said nothing for a few seconds, his jaw dropped open and his eyes moistened. Unsteadily he rose to his feet. 'Jane...' he whispered, 'I can't believe this... I was so wanting to see you...' And then his eyes watered so much that he couldn't speak – the tears running down his face.

He tried again. 'Jane...' sniff. 'Jane...' It was all he could manage.

She took him in her arms and they kissed. It was not possible for them to do anything else for she was crying as well.

(There is absolutely no truth in the rumour that at this point Doña Isabel was seen to wink. Although at least one attendant swears he saw it.)

It was not a long kiss – they were in a public place. Jane drew back and then laid her head on his chest. She could not stop sobbing for several minutes.

He said gently, 'I think we could both do with a cup of tea, don't you?'

She nodded and hand in hand they made their way down to the tea-room.

'But I can't understand...' she said, pouring out tea for them both, 'I heard that you were in love with someone and that you had a young blonde girl friend.'

He laughed, 'That just shows you shouldn't listen to gossip. Yes I am in love with someone. She's sitting opposite me now. And as for the young blonde – that was my niece, Sam, from Australia. Stayed with me for a week and was good fun and great with the children. She had a whole stock of "knock-knock" jokes which kept them laughing. I don't do incest, actually – even when thwarted in love.'

'I see.' Jane looked as though a great weight had been lifted off her. 'But why didn't you ring me?'

'I was trying not to hassle you – felt that you were rather delicate after the ordeal you'd been through. Wanted to like anything, but something kept stopping me. It's just that in the past, in the bad old days I would have pestered you frantically – but now I have to think about what it's like for you.'

'What it's like for me is... that I feel confused. One minute I want to throw myself at you and the next, I want to hold back. I was badly mauled by my last relationship – my boyfriend jilted me very suddenly in favour of my best friend and it's left a scar.'

'You mean you still can't quite trust me?'

Jane buttered a fruit scone before replying. 'I just don't know. Anyway what made you come into the Gallery this afternoon – I thought this sort of art wasn't your scene?'

'It wasn't in the bad old days, but since my stay at Lucy's I've had a feeling that I might have missed something, so I come here sometimes just to see.'

'And have you found it?'

He laughed, 'Well I found you for one thing! But yes and no. I haven't had a repeat of what happened at Lucy's, but I have, in a rather dim sort of a way begun to see things I didn't see before.'

'What sort of things?'

Mark also buttered a scone. He scratched his head and thought for some time. Then he said, 'It's not so much a matter of seeing things because of course you do see more things if you look carefully. It's more a matter of feeling. '

'What do you feel?'

'It's hard to describe, but I feel calmer and more optimistic. It's a bit like being higher up on a mountain and finding that you can see a bit further. I'm more aware of my failings and the results of my actions. I've also fallen in love with Doña Isabel because she reminds me of you.'

Jane looked at him intently and they were silent for a brief space of time. Then she said, 'I think you're telling the truth. What are you going to do now?'

'Right now I've got to go back to the gallery and work on something for a meeting tomorrow. It's almost August and holiday time. I'm closing the gallery for the whole month though I won't be going away for all of that time. When am I going to see you again?'

Jane thought for a long time before replying. She wanted to see him again but, on the other hand, she felt overwhelmed by the sudden rush of emotion. She wanted to let things settle down and find out what she really felt. Could she now trust him? He was still working for a corrupt business. Was he really able to steer his gallery into a purer, cleaner mode?

Mark spoke without waiting for her reply. 'I think this is something that can only be sorted out with time.'

Jane breathed a sigh of relief, 'You're right... all this seems to have happened so suddenly. I just need some space to think things through.'

'Are you going away in August?'

'Yes, for the whole month. I have an aunt in the West of Ireland and then Freddie is taking me to Croatia for the last two weeks. Are you going away?'

'Taking the children to Corfu for the first two weeks and then I'll be back here – there are things to organise. Might be selling the house – I don't feel comfortable in it any more.'

Jane sat up in her chair,

'So… we may not meet again until September?'

'That's what it looks like.'

'I think… that this is helpful.'

He leaned across the table and picked up her hand, 'My darling Jane, I don't want to be parted from you ever again… but if time is what you need, then you'll have it. A small present in return for what you've given me today.'

'Don't make me cry,' she said.

CHAPTER 42

Toothpaste

Mark returned to the gallery feeling distinctly more cheerful. He also felt a surge of enthusiasm for classical art, though whether this was due to Doña Isobel or Jane's kiss was hard to say.

He had worked carefully on his proposals for softer, sweeter installations and would be discussing them the next day with his backers, the Men in Grey. He felt that things were now going his way.

'There's been a message for you,' Hazel told him. 'The toothpaste man wants to come and see you about an exhibition. He's rung up several times but always when you were out.'

'Toothpaste Man?'

'He's the director of a company that makes toothpaste and he wants to see you about the possibility of an installation. Apparently he was deeply impressed by Charlene's show and the impact it had on the sale of tampons.'

'What does he think we are? A PR firm or something?' Mark snapped.

Hazel raised her eyebrows at this. He was not behaving true to form as in the pre-bump days. There was something both sombre and touchy about him. She was not surprised that Sharon and Michelle had invented a love affair for him – his mind seemed to be elsewhere a lot of the time. She asked cautiously, 'Wouldn't it be rather fun to have masses of toothpaste worms all over the place?'

'No it wouldn't. It reminds me of an incident in Paris when

I was very young. I went into a gallery that was showing abstract paintings that were made entirely by squeezing the paint from the tubes directly onto the canvas. I couldn't resist putting out my hand and stroking one of the worms and to my horror a chunk of paint came away on my finger. And then the artist came up and started talking to me and I had to conceal the paint and leave the gallery discreetly.'

'And no-one noticed?'

'No... I got away with it. But the seat of my pants got smeared badly.'

'So I take it you don't want to see Mr Toothpaste?' Hazel said when she had finished laughing.

'No way!'

'By the way, there is a bit of good news. Herr Gropius has been in contact again and his client has agreed on a good price for the Rum Tugger.'

'Good Heavens − I thought that was gone for good.' Inwardly he shuddered and felt queasy. Why would an anonymous buyer from Eastern Europe want to spend a fortune on a pile of dog turds on a black box? Just why?

He rang Louisa. She sounded very happy. They discussed arrangements for her house and whether she would be able to move before the baby came at the end of August. Then she said, 'By the way − there's a new guy in my life... like. He's ever so nice... Very gentle and... he seems devoted, like.'

'Oh, I'm just so glad to hear that. Will he take care of you?'

'Yep... He seems to want to. He's got a big old house in the country and not enough money but we've got plans.'

'Like what'

'Can't tell you at the mo. It's under wraps like.'

'Louisa dear, I have to explain just one thing. Sometimes unscrupulous men get hold of ladies who own a house and then sue them for half the property when it things bust up.'

'Oh… but he's not going to.'

'No… of course not. But as a precaution I've set up a trust for you. The trust will own the house and you'll be paying a nominal rent. You can sell the house and move any time you want, but your partner won't be able to get half the value of it if things go wrong.'

'Nah…' ees not like that Mark.'

'Dear… I really hope he won't. I just want to see you happy. What you deserve. What I'm doing's just a precaution. Am I going to see you soon? Before I go away in August?'

They arranged to meet for lunch in a few days time. Mark put the phone down and sighed. He wanted her to be happy and cared for – he could not bear the thought that someone might exploit her – she was so innocent.

The meeting with the Men in Grey took place as usual in the eighth floor offices of a merchant bank. The light was clear and cool, but everything, including the large house-plants, seemed to radiate a paler shade of grey.

The group examined the report and the future programme with a minute attention to detail. This was odd because they had already received it. Then Max Finkelstein started to speak.

'Income is good. The exhibitions are all going very well.'

'Yes I'm very pleased.'

'You had an accident – a bump on the head?'

'Yes, fortunately I didn't crack my skull. I've had several x-rays and I'm all right now.'

'You sure?' Max tapped a gold propelling pencil on the blotting pad opposite him.

'Yes of course.' There was an undertone in this exchange that sounded as if it was not entirely due to compassion.

'And your wife has left you?'

'Yes... I don't know why you are asking me all these questions.'

'Ah... well, you see there are some things that we need to make clear to you. We thought everything was going very well and now we are not so sure.'

'The galleries are both doing very well. I don't know what the problem is.'

'Ah... you see, the funds that we have to invest come from other interests and these other interests have an interest in seeing that their interests are secure.'

'Interesting.'

'I don't think you quite understand. Business these days is controlled in the last resort by two or three of the greater powers. We are controlled by our backers – we are not as free as you would think. If they back out, we have to withdraw.'

'But why would they want to?'

'You are altering the focus of your gallery. That is not so good. We have to preserve the interests.'

Mark interrupted, 'What interests? Can you tell me just what these interests are?'

'Multinationals, agri-chemicals, medicinal drugs, petrol, tobacco – you know all these things. Well, not all of them are touched by your new programme. There are just a couple of shows we would like you to reconsider. We cannot have anything which tempts the public away from the status quo – anything that, in other words looks the least bit, "wobbly" or "organic" as it were.'

'Which shows in particular?'

'This thing – "Country Idyll" with the motorised bunnies.' He tapped again.

'But that's ridiculous. It's got almost nothing to do with the country and organic farming. It's all a fake – a sort of satirical pastoral, if you like.'

'You don't understand. You are one of the leaders of

fashion and taste. People follow you. If you start them off in the direction of fresh air, there's no knowing where they will go. You are just giving them a start.'

'With motorised bunnies?'

'That's right. It's only a step away from anti-GM protests. We can't have that.'

'And the other?' But he knew only too well.

'This thing with Angel Theatres.'

'But that's got nothing to do with organic farming.'

'We know. But it sounds a bit too close to religion and spiritual life.'

'What have you got against religion?'

'It discourages consumerism and it makes people think too much. When they start thinking, they get into alternatives. That's not good for us. Religion is only all right when it is in season and that season is Christmas. People have to stay dazed and confused.'

'But what about what Jason Crowpick's doing at the moment. He seems to be into religion in his new show.'

'Ah, that is fine because; it fits with the formula; the three "Cs".'

'What on earth are those?'

'Oh, Cruelty, Crudity and Crud. Very good artist Crowpick is. Helps the pharmaceutical companies no end. We never have problems with him.'

'I see,' Mark said. 'You have given me something to think about. Are you saying that if I go ahead with these two shows, you will withdraw your backing? Because I just have a feeling that the public is getting a little fed up with cruelty and crud. They might appreciate a new direction in the gallery.'

'We have been thinking and consulting with one or two people and we have an idea for you. If you cancel the thing about angels this would be something that might fit with a new direction.'

Granville Barker now spoke. 'You might be quite right that people now want something a little more positive. So here we have it. A show called "Smiles" with lots of smiling faces, culminating in an enormous plastic inflatable mouth with a wonderful grin.'

Cogs were turning in the back of Mark's mind.

'And lots of shiny white teeth? It wouldn't have anything to do with toothpaste by any chance?'

Max said, 'Funny you should mention it. We've had an offer we really don't want to refuse from a manufacturer of toothpaste.'

Mark wondered how much they had been paid and whether it was cash or in kind – a week's shooting on a Scottish grouse moor, days fishing on the Tweed, or a holiday in Antibes.

'Well, thank you for telling me all this. You've given me the information I've wanted.'

They took their leave with little forced smiles and damp flabby handshakes. Mark was reminded of the underside of a eel he had seen in an aquarium. Sharp little teeth facing backwards in a small white mouth.

He went back to the gallery in a dark mood. The scales had finally fallen from his eyes. There was no way that he could alter the direction of his ship – the forces opposing him were too powerful. He had never had it spelt out for him clearly like this, but he realised that there was a level on which he had known it all along. He had deceived himself and there was only one solution. He had to get out.

It was an enormous step. The gallery, the girls, the boys, Hazel, the friendlies, the installation teams all had to go. Curiously enough, it was a relief to face up to the truth at last. And he was in the fortunate position of not being financially insecure. He had enough capital for the rest of his life if he lived a little more frugally. He had wanted for some time to move from the Canonbury house which he hated. He was beginning to feel that he wanted the country – somewhere with a garden, a place where the children could romp about and climb trees and throw sticks in a river. More and more he knew that he was wearing a pair of shoes that no longer fitted.

He asked Hazel to set up a meeting of the directors just as soon as possible.

CHAPTER 43

Tea With Roses

He went home and settled down to write his letter of resignation. He felt he couldn't write it in the gallery.

The phone rang. He picked it up. It was Lucy.

'Lucy! How nice to hear you – how are you?'

'I've been thinking about you and wondering how you are,' she said.

'Just decided to resign from the gallery.'

'Good heavens – that's a bold and brave step. Congratulations! I was just wondering whether you might like to have another visit here.'

'Lucy, how did you know? I'd love it. Going away quite soon though – can I come before I go?'

'Yes, of course – you can come this weekend.'

He went back to his resignation letter. Suki kept jumping onto his lap which was comforting, but she was unable to advise him on the wording. Eventually he hammered out something to his satisfaction. He would make copies of the letter for each of the five directors and hand to them at the meeting.

It is with regret that I have decided to resign from my position as director of this gallery.

I have loved working here and am attached to the team who also work here. What we have been doing has been enjoyable, varied and a tremendous scope for creative ingenuity. Time spent here has not been wasted and I believe that our work has some value.

However I am no longer able to subscribe to the pretence that what we are doing has any connection with fine art. Art should elevate the spirit and give the onlooker an increased awareness, even if this is very slight, of the positive values of life.

I also feel our belief that what we are doing has to do with progress and innovation is a fake. We are being financially supported by institutions interested primarily in maintaining the status quo as well as making money. The real purpose, far from doing something to help the general public is to distract it from the growing concerns for the way we are treating all life on this planet. We talk about change but we are trying to keep things the same. I cannot continue with this fraud.

I will do everything possible to ensure that there is a smooth handover to my successor and will follow your decision as to the timing of the public announcement.

May I suggest that you consider my personal assistant Hazel Beresford as a candidate. She has a lot of experience and is an extremely competent administrator as well as possessing a sound creative intelligence. (I have not mentioned this to her and have no idea whether she would be agreeable.)

Finally, I would like to thank you for the privilege of having worked here. As I have already said, it has been enjoyable.

It was a long, hot and tedious drive to Somerset. There were many holdups for road works but eventually he arrived at the flower bedecked cottage.

Lucy was in the garden wearing a pair of striped dungarees, with a very battered straw hat shielding her eyes from the sun. She was dead-heading roses into a basket. 'I'm so glad you've arrived,' she said putting away her secateurs, 'I was longing for a cup of tea but I'd promised myself I'd wait for you!'

She took him inside and made tea which they had in the garden under the clematis and wisteria. There were home-made scones and a superbly light sponge cake filled with raspberry jam.

'This is almost too much.' Mark said, 'Can one have too much perfection?'

'Well... I think we have cause for celebration. You've taken a very big step. I have to congratulate you. Was it hard handing in your resignation?'

'No... not in the least. The directors are a different bunch from the men in grey who are the backers and a bit sinister. The directors are fatter and jollier and very urbane. I've put in a plug for my dear Hazel to succeed, but they have to think about that.'

'And you don't feel too bad about leaving the team?'

Mark sighed, 'Oddly enough, no. Perhaps it hasn't really sunk in yet, but a part of me has known that this has to happen for a long time – and now it has... there's a huge sense of relief.'

'Another scone?' said Lucy.

He took one. 'They're delicious.'

'So what are you going to do now?'

'Well... there are going to be a lot of changes. I want to sell the house – it's too large for me and too full of old associations. I might buy a smaller one, or even a flat just large enough for me and the children. And I also want a house in the country. Something with a garden.'

'In Somerset?' Lucy asked, innocently.

He smiled, 'No... nearer to London. But I'd like to be near hills. I'm going to look at a farmhouse on the Welsh border, I rather like the sound of. Not too far from Somerset. Perhaps you'll come and stay with me?'

'And what about your lady... Jane?'

He sighed. 'There's been some progress on that front. But not enough. Problem is she doesn't trust me.'

'But why doesn't she trust you?'

He told her about Millicent and Louisa.

Lucy said, 'Jane has her reasons then.'

'Yes… but I've changed. Things are so different now.'

'Have some cake?' Lucy started cutting it.

He took some, 'Wonderful… I've never had anything so light!'

'My mother showed me the secret!'

They enjoyed the cake for a minute in silence and then Lucy spoke.

'It's not an easy matter when someone doesn't trust you. And Jane has her reasons. Some of them from your past and some from hers – she talked to me a little when I visited her gallery. There's not anything you can do by giving her arguments, because the more you speak the more resistance the other person will put up. All you can do is to show her. And that is actually what you're doing.'

'But I don't seem to be winning.'

'No.'

Mark sighed, 'Haven't you anything you can tell me that would help?'

'Dear Mark, I have to say that I'm not a prophet. I don't know what the future holds. You've shaken yourself free from something that has gripped you and this means that in future you will choose your actions in such a way that they'll bring greater happiness – to you and the people around you. Two things are on your side – time and the ability to bring happiness. If you use them wisely – which you will, then your life is going to be much better. But no-one knows exactly how, or whether things will work out for you and Jane or not.'

'I wish I knew. I spend so much of my time thinking about her and longing for her.'

'I know. What you have to do is not to argue but to give her great pleasure. And not worry about what happens next.

It could be that she's not the woman you really want – another case of mistaken identity. If it doesn't work out, then you've nothing to lose. Do you see?' She poured him out another cup of tea. 'By the way have you told her?'

'No… you see when we met at the National Gallery, that was before my resignation, she seemed rather delicate – it was clear that she didn't want to see me again before the holidays and we came to the tacit conclusion that we would wait until September.'

'That sounds like a good idea. She will appreciate your sensitivity and consideration. You just have to wait and see how things turn out.'

Mark sipped his tea thoughtfully and said nothing.

Lucy felt that they had exhausted the subject of Jane and started talking about something else.

During the weekend they spent a lot of time in the garden – he even helped her with the weeding. She told him all about her life and her time in India and even regaled him with her photos.

He returned to London feeling, as usual, much the better for the benefit of her company, although rather saddened by her uncertain prediction for the future of his obsession.

CHAPTER 44

To The Hills

For Jane, the month of August slipped by, painlessly at worst, delightfully at best. It was a relief to be out of London.

The visit to Ireland was peaceful and restful. It rained a lot but with the sort of gentle rain that's Ireland's speciality – a rain which never hides the sun for too long, and a sun that never quite forgets the rain. Her cousins were not too interested in her life and she welcomed this, spending a lot of time in the library or the garden, when it was not raining and just reading books.

Croatia was a marked contrast – dazzling light and strong colours in a sea in which turquoise flirted with emerald. They were on an island near Split and spent the time, when not sketching, with swimming in the clear blue-green water in the little rocky coves, cycling, boat trips or just sitting in the sun. Although Croatia was not so gastronomically exquisite as Italy or Greece, it was enough to have terraced restaurants with grape-hung pergolas overlooking the sea and beautiful Italianate buildings. Everywhere there were large rosemary hedges and the smell hung on the evening air.

On their last evening, they were sitting watching the sunset and feeling a little reluctant to return home. By mutual consent they had avoided all mention of boyfriends but Freddie was well aware of who was occupying her thoughts.

She sighed. 'Dear Freddie – I feel so blessed. This is one of the nicest things you've done for me.'

He smiled. 'Thank you... I've enjoyed it too, you know.'

She nodded and fell silent.

'You don't have to be a great detective to know who you're thinking about,' he said.

'It's just that I'm dreading telling him.'

'Telling him what?'

'Telling him I'm not going to see him again.'

'But... I thought you liked him?'

'More than that I think. I just can't bear the thought of being dumped yet again. I've thought it all through now I've had some time and it just seems so reasonable and sensible to end things before they get out of hand, as it were.'

Freddie leaned over and touched her arm. 'Look Jane... I know about what happened. But that doesn't mean it's going to happen again. Why can't you just let go of the past and just enjoy what he can give you.'

'I can't. That's all.' She picked a sprig of rosemary and started rolling it in her hand. 'It's sad because I think he has changed and he's done good things for me. Did I tell you I met him in the National Gallery?'

'No... but that's a sign of a big change – surely?'

'Yes...' She was silent for a moment. 'But my mind's made up now. It'll be better this way.'

Freddie knew better than to try to argue the point.

'Let's drink to our friends in London and the success of your new-look gallery!'

'And to Freddie... and Robbie!'

London in August is hot, full of exhaust fumes, dusty and frayed. But September brings a revival – a breath of fresh air – the promise of Autumn and the return of energy. It was Jane's favourite month.

She did not ring Mark straight away. There were things to

do in the gallery – glitches to sort out and bills to pay, as well as work to be done on the new season's programme.

Every day she told herself she would ring him and every day, somehow she forgot.

When the phone rang in the gallery, she picked it up in trepidation fearing that it was him. But it was Edwin, 'I have news for you.' He was so excited his hesitation seemed to have gone, 'Louisa's had her baby! It's a lovely nine pound boy and I'm hoping to adopt him. We're going to get married in about a month's time when she's had time to recover. I held back about proposing but then I couldn't any longer. We're just so happy together... Oh Jane! I just have to thank you for introducing us!'

Jane congratulated him and then asked about the baby and their plans. 'We're going to convert the stables and make the coach house into a Teddy Bear Museum. The big house needs some repairs but the worst is over and my agent thinks he can let it to a school.'

She noticed that his speech impediment was better. She said 'I'm just so glad that things have turned out so well for you. Please give Louisa a big hug for me. It's lovely news.'

As soon as she put the phone down it rang again. This time it was Mark.

'I hope I'm not bothering you...' he began.

She started to tremble all over. 'Look Mark... I've had some time to think now and I have to tell you something. I just can't go on with it.'

'Yes.' He sounded quite calm. 'I've thought a lot about it too, and been thinking about how you must be feeling. If you don't trust me, there's nothing I can say... except that as life goes on, you begin to see different levels of reality. I've reached a new one – a level where telling the truth matters and deception only reaps a constricting reward.'

Jane sighed heavily. 'It's not just that… it's the whole art set-up. It's corrupt and you know it.'

He sounded as though his anger had risen a little. 'Yes. I know this. Perhaps… you'd be surprised to learn I've just resigned from the gallery.'

'You've WHAT?'

'I've just resigned from the gallery. It's a top secret at the moment – they don't want to announce it until they've found my replacement, so please, please don't tell anyone.'

'Good Heaven! You've blown my mind!' Suddenly she felt tears running down her cheeks. 'Well done… well done.' She began to feel a sensation of hope, of light at the end of the tunnel. 'You did that for me?'

'Yes and no. You started me on a track – but I had to do it for myself.' He was silent for a minute, then he said, 'Might I just be allowed to take you out to dinner – it's so much easier if we can talk face to face?'

'OK…' she was now sobbing profusely.

'There's quite a bit to do at the moment… tying up loose ends and writing reports. I'm working every night. But I've a window on Saturday evening. Going away later on, so it'll be an early supper and I won't be drinking alcohol.'

They arranged to meet at a small restaurant a few streets away from her home.

He arrived before her and watched with delight as she came in. She looked sparkling in emerald green, her hair glossy and her eyes shining.

They embraced and sat down opposite each other. It didn't need to be said, but it was said all the same, that they were so glad to see each other.

'But was it hard telling them?' Jane asked.

'No… not in the least and they took it very well. But we

haven't told all the staff yet. Only Hazel.'

'But... what finally made you do it?'

'Do you remember I told you I had a plan to steer things quietly and gently onto a more optimistic and positive front?'

'Yes... I think so – something about angels. And moving bunny rabbits.'

'Well – I worked hard on the plans but the backers vetoed them. It was nasty but quite revealing. I don't believe in conspiracy theories but there is a general malaise in the air – too many large corporations have too much invested in resisting change. Real change – in the direction of what we are doing to the planet and ourselves... and how we can alter it. Quite funny the way it came out. So then I knew absolutely that my time was up.'

'I see.'

The waiter came and took their orders. They ordered trout with almonds with green peas, followed by fruit compote. He asked for a bottle of elderflower champagne.

'It's good stuff this – I have to drive later on tonight and I've stopped believing my driving improves with a bit of drink.'

'But are you happy with what you've done? Or are you just bravely covering up? You seemed to get great enjoyment out of your job.'

'It's like this. It's something I've known for a long time but was hiding from myself. Haunted me in various ways, like a Romanian song I was obsessed with. But I didn't really understand. The trouble was that I was under the illusion that I was in control when actually I was being controlled by puppet masters. So it's really a huge relief to have got out of it. I've escaped from something nasty. And once I realised, it was all easy.'

'That's funny,' Jane said. 'It reminds me of a line I read in a not very good novel 'It's easy to get out of a labyrinth. The difficult bit is realising that you are in one.'

He laughed, 'Yes I've read that too. It seemed meaningless at the time.'

The waiter came with the elderflower champagne and poured it out for them. He took a sip, 'Ah... this must be a specially good vintage.'

Jane agreed, 'But I find it's even nicer with a bit of the real thing in it!'

'You may have a point there!'

'Anyway... where is it that you have to drive off to in the middle of the night?'

'Oh... I've just bought a farmhouse on the Welsh border near Hay-on-Wye. I'm making big changes at the moment. I'm putting the Canonbury house on the market and looking for something smaller just for me and the children when we have to be in London. But I really want them to be with me in the country. They're in a huge place with Millicent's new husband but I suspect it's all a bit prim and constrained. So I've just taken possession of the farmhouse – it's just habitable at the moment but it needs a lot of tender love and care.'

'But why do you have to go off in the middle of the night to see it?'

'I don't have to actually, but I happen to enjoy night driving especially in summer. You get much less traffic and my car just hums along at a good speed. It's a lovely farmhouse – stone built, long and low with an archway into a courtyard at the back and lots of old barns and a duck pond. It's got beams and open fireplaces and a lovely staircase. It just has a certain feeling about it – I can't really explain. I just fell in love with it at first sight.' He paused while the waiter brought their food.

Jane thought about what he was describing while she tackled her trout. 'It sounds lovely. I'd love to see it.'

He looked at her intently. 'Well…' He paused for a signif-icant moment. 'Why don't you come with me?'

'What?'

Jane sat in a stunned silence.

'Look,' he said as he dealt with his trout, 'I'm only going for two nights. The place is minimally furnished – I've bought a comfortable bed, but the rest of the stuff just came with the house.'

She opened her mouth to say 'I'd love to but I can't', but something got in the way. She was frantically searching for reasons why she couldn't, but there didn't seem to be any. She had nothing on that Sunday and the gallery was closed on Monday. Before she really knew what she was doing she found herself saying. 'Ok… but… I haven't anything with me.'

A smile of wild delight swept across his face. 'We could pick up some things for you from your place. You won't need more that a toothbrush, some jeans and a sweater.'

And so in the dying light of the day the great pale green car surged quietly along the M40. They were silent now having said everything that needed to be said over dinner.

Mark was happy, knowing that he had what he wanted. Jane was more nervous, doing her best to silence those voices still rising up from inside asking if she knew what she was doing and whether it was wise to go away with him on an impulse.

The car glided along under the full moon and Jane began to understand why he enjoyed driving at night. He turned on the hi-fi and they listened to a sequence of old songs – Beatles and Bob Dylan.

They turned off onto a succession of increasingly minor roads until they reached one that was particularly narrow. The moon lit up the small drifts of mist that rose up from the ground and lay across their path like strips of white fur or gauze. Amongst them, rabbits played, blissfully unaware of any other road users. The car slowed to a crawl.

A hand gently landed on her lap and she let it lie. Then Jane softly placed hers over it. In that moment she knew. In that moment she finally let go of the future and the past. They both knew that what they had together and what they were about to enjoy was a happiness that more than compensated for any possible pain in the future.

The car turned in through a gateway onto a dilapidated driveway, scrunched on the gravel and came to a halt. In the moonlight Jane could see a long, low, silver-grey building framed by dark trees – its shape accentuated by dark blue shadows.

'We've arrived,' he said as he opened the car door.

They got out and stood together – taking in the scene.

Then Jane put her arms round him.

'I love you,' she said.

The End

Acknowledgements

No book is the product of one person. As an artist used to working on my own, I have enjoyed working with the three people who have helped in the production of this one.

Duncan Wherrett right from the start has given me support in many areas including proof reading, publication advice and modelling for the cover drawing.

Sally Orson Jones, my editor, is responsible for reshaping and making the whole thing readable. She was tactful and supportive, took it all to bits and advised me how to reconstruct it. I cannot thank her enough.

Finally my dear daughter Vicky who not only did the cover from a drawing I did, but also the whole layout of the book. She has given me the magic of seeing a rough manuscript transformed into book format, working with her usual perfectionism to produce something that fits with her dictum – "a good book design is never noticed - only a bad one."

And I'm grateful to Maharishi Mahesh Yogi for just about everything else.

Printed in Great Britain
by Amazon